The Sea was Calm

Jorge Majfud

Humanus

San Diego-Acapulco

The Sea Was Calm
Copyrights
© 2025 by Jorge Majfud
© HUMANUS
© Rebelde Editors 2021
ISBN: 978-1-956760-43-9
cuauhtemoceditorial@gmail.com

Yes, I would like to repeat the usual, that what matters is the future, that everything moves toward tomorrow. But the only truth is that our ultimate future is the past. That is where we are headed, inexorably. Until the light goes out, that mysterious light.

THOSE DAYS

About the Principal Characters of This Story

Listed in alphabetical order; all have at least one
marked day.

Alejandro Spinelli. Though he spent his entire childhood in
Buenos Aires, he moved to Montevideo when his father married
Enrique Sosa's mother. With Negra Laurie, he had a son named
Dieguito.

Almeida y Laprida. Known as "Don Xico." He achieved the
rank of lieutenant in 1974. He retired with the rank of major.
He first visited Dr. Santiago Zabala's office on March 15, 2011.
On Friday, April 6, 2012, the same doctor performed coronary
bypass surgery on him.

Carlos II and Willian. Merchants in the thread and button
trade. They met at the restaurant El Águila in 1944. In 2013,
regular patrons of the bar El Asturiano confirmed their existence, as well as that of President Pepe Mujica.

Enrique Sosa. Known as "Quique" or "El Torito," his mother
was the prostitute Liliana, known as Laira. His father married
Alejandro Spinelli's mother.

Ernest Hatuey Hernández: Iraq War veteran. He served in two
deployments and returned to the United States on March 21,
2007. In 2011, he moved to San Francisco, and later to Hawaii.

Jordi Caballero. Born in Barcelona in 1933. The son of Republican parents, he emigrated to Uruguay in 1956, where he
eventually founded several businesses, including the bookstore
El Escorial, later renamed *i Margall*, and the most successful tech
company *Metassoft*. On March 16, 1985, he adopted Lucía.

Juaquín Fuentes. Biological grandfather of Santiago Zabala
and father of María Ocampo. He was dismissed from his position at the state electric company in 1978, four years after his

daughter disappeared and one year after the death of his wife, María Fuentes. Upon his death in December 1986, he left behind an incomplete investigation into the disappearance of his daughter and grandson.

Lucía Caballero. Likely born on March 14, 1983, in Montevideo. On the night of March 16, she was found by Jordi Caballero, who would effectively become her adoptive father from that moment. From a young age, she managed the used bookstore *i Margall.*

María Arbiza. Adoptive mother of Santiago Zabala.

María Fuentes and *José Ocampo.* Biological parents of Santiago Zabala Arbiza. Medical students, they secluded themselves in a field in Rivera, where they were detained by the army in 1974.

Miguel Polzin. Childhood friend of Santiago Zabala. On February 15, 2001, he fled to New York and returned to Buenos Aires nearly ten years later. In Manhattan, he met the Russian Glinka.

Pedro Zabala. Adoptive father of Santiago Zabala. In 1980, a household accident left him in a coma, from which he awoke in 1987. He passed away in 1991.

Santiago Zabala Arbiza. Likely born on September 23, 1971, in Paso de los Toros, Uruguay. His official birth certificate does not differ much in the date but does in the place of birth: September 19, 1971, in Colón, Argentina. He was adopted by the Zabala Arbiza family in 1974. In 2004, he began his postgraduate studies at Emory University in the United States, from which he returned at the beginning of 2010. He met Lucía Caballero on either the 9th or 16th of January the following year.

US TO SINK GHOST SHIP
DRIFTED BY JAPANESE TSUNAMI

The US Coast Guard plans to use explosives to sink a ship drifting at sea since it was swept away by last year's tsunami in Japan.

The shrimp boat, which has no lights or crew, was floating Thursday morning about 313 kilometers (195 miles) south of Sitka in the Gulf of Alaska, moving at about 1.6 kph (1 mph).

The ship contains more than 7,500 liters (2,000 gallons) of diesel, and authorities fear it could interfere with the paths of other vessels, as it travels through shipping lanes. A Coast Guard boat is heading toward the ship with plans to use explosives to sink it. If left adrift, the ship would eventually run aground somewhere, said Coast Guard spokesman, Petty Officer Charley Hengen.

The National Oceanic and Atmospheric Administration, as well as the Environmental Protection Agency, studied the issue and decided it was safest to sink the vessel and let the fuel evaporate in the water.

The Coast Guard has warned other ships to avoid the area.

The ship, called Ryou-Un Maru, is between 45 and 60 meters long. It has been drifting from Hokkaido, Japan, where it was swept away by the tsunami following the magnitude 9.0 earthquake that struck Japan in March 2011. Around five million tons of debris were thrown into the ocean by the tsunami.

La Voz of Arizona, April 4, 2012

FOR SOME REASON, HE FLED. For some reason, he was pursued by that idea that sometimes took the form of a sea monster and rose up at sunset. For some reason, he always sailed in the opposite direction of the sun, contrary to the natural path that had been traced on his heart thousands of years earlier, that is, from East to West.

For some reason, he had to devote all his days to moving in a direction he didn't want to go. That was fleeing. That clearly meant that a crime had driven him away from where he belonged. But what crime? He couldn't remember clearly. All he had were memories of the ship and some particular days, like those afternoons he had spent sitting on the stern, imprisoned by disbelief and the realism that had led him to think the sea was infinite, and that there was no such thing as the bottom of the sea rising above the surface beyond the horizon.

The rest was as implausible as the absence of the sea, like that man who lay asleep in his own blood, wounded somewhere, just like one of the small beasts he occasionally managed to pull from the sea for sustenance, but similar to himself. It could have just been part of his dreams. The man could have been himself, escaped from the mirror in the main room, and taken on the fate of the fish that accompanied the ship. It could have been, just a monstrous fantasy that for some reason had repeated itself over a long time. Until he managed to convince himself it had never been real and, little by little, he forgot about the incident.

But the worst kind of forgetfulness is a betrayal or just a distraction of memory. He was left with the worst. He was left with guilt, uncertainty, and the endless struggle to keep the ship afloat and from veering off its path toward the East.

Ernest Hatuey Hernández

Fallujah, March 16, 2006

The story of Ernest Hatuey Hernández begins with his death in Iraq. This first sentence is not a poetic figure. In our time, we are all a little bit like zombies, soulless bodies, but in the case of soldier Hernández, there's no doubt. More or less, what follows is the description of that day as written in his war diary, dated March 31 of the same year. The first pages are written in English, and the last in Spanish or Spanglish. Why did he write in a paper notebook and not in some electronic medium? Did he think he was in a Vietnam movie? Had he discovered something the rest of us zombies don't know?

As I was saying, what follows is a somewhat more organized translation of that chaos, of that very human order:

On a street covered in asphalt and dust that blurs everything, at the hour when the day divides itself between afternoon and evening and the smells of the villages in Iraq become as intense as the grain and spice shops of the Arabs in Manhattan, the convoy entered the ancient city without changing its pace. Through the small window of unit 16, Ernest watched the first flat-roofed houses without lights inside pass by. He saw the same people as always, walking like gray, silent shadows, as if they were trying to exist as little as possible, just enough to return to their homes, or as if they didn't know any other way to live. He had grown accustomed to the houses and the streets, always faintly outlined, as if they were a sketch unfinished, without clear borders, without precise colors, without anything sharp that would make that city a city and those people concrete men and women instead of characters from old children's stories.

Between 17:00 and 17:15, an explosion lifted the unit in front into the air. As the procedure dictated for such occasions, the units ahead that hadn't been affected didn't stop. The one in front of Hatuey slowed down to steer around the wrecked unit while a soldier opened fire on the locals who hadn't yet recovered from the blast.

In the usual vertigo, heightened by the deafening boom, Ernest leaned out of the hatch and saw a man trying to lift a child. Somehow, he didn't know how, he had seen that man and that child an instant before the explosion. They had been walking hand in hand. They were dressed similarly, without colors, in loose shirts and pants, white, gray, or simply dirty. At some point, for some reason, the child started running as if he had seen the Devil himself. He was barefoot. A few seconds later, the explosion occurred, and almost immediately, the gunfire from the unit ahead of them.

Two comrades from Arizona died, though he never found out who they were. Nor did he learn the name of the child who had fallen in front of his unit. But he remembered the cries in Arabic from someone calling out to him. He remembered the child's scream and, above all, he remembered, like an eternal curse, the silence that had followed that raw expression of pain or fear. He also remembered his father's desperate cries: *Johef,* or *Yohef,* or *Youssef.* It was a scream like a vomit, as if in one of those names he was vomiting up his entire life in that Godforsaken land. The vomit stretched into the *e*, into the last *e* that dragged out in a snarl that then choked into the *f*. *Yousseeef*. He didn't know why, but this vowel had become something important in his life. Why did the vomit choke in that *e* that sometimes turned into an endless *i*? Why had those details stuck with him when there were more important things in the war? The man who screamed must have been the father. Because only a father"he dared to think"can scream in a way that cuts to the bone. Maybe he was screaming for the convoy to stop, he managed to recognize once, completely drunk in a bar on Ocean Front Street in Jacksonville Beach. Maybe he was screaming for the soldiers to stop clearing the area before continuing the march, he refrained from saying that afternoon, but he acknowledged it in an email he sent to his cousin Eduardo in San Francisco, just as he was leaving Hawaii on the tuna boat that would finally take him to Japan.

He also acknowledged, in that same email, that when he heard the first scream, he almost stopped the Abrams. It would have been against regulations, which is why the unit continued on its planned route.

"If it were up to feelings," one of the comrades who had noticed the first signs of Ernest's illness told him, "no army would have ever won a single war in all of history. Sad things happen out there, *brother*."

But the best reasons to forget didn't matter. Ernest couldn't shake that scream, the *e*, and the man trying to lift something shapeless. As if that had been the only casualty in the entire war.

"The only *casualty*," he repeated twice in that same Ocean Front restaurant, as if he were trying to grasp the meaning of such simple words.

"What does *casualty* even mean?" the Argentinian asked him.

"I don't know," Ernest replied. *"Casualty* is *casualty."*

"It must be 'baja'."

Hatuey's face showed disappointment. A dead hero couldn't be a "casualty."

"Isn't there another word for *casualty*?"

"Ask your folks," said Santiago. "But a *casualty* is a *baja*, it's someone, usually a soldier, that an army loses in a war."

The child had been left behind, sprawled over a pool of blood. His father insisted on lifting him up, but for some reason, he couldn't figure out how. Hatuey cursed him for it. Over and over, he had seen him in his dreams trying to lift that bundle tangled in a white or gray tunic while his comrades cleared the area, which meant while they fired, riddling a handful of men who were still standing or had managed to get back up.

Ernest Hatuey was going to stop the M1 Abrams. He could have done it, even though it was against regulations. He could have done it, and he didn't. He also couldn't tell if the child had died in the explosion or under the Abrams' tracks. And even though he had handled the situation correctly according to the rules and the standard, even though he had seen many people die before and after that afternoon, that afternoon wasn't like any other"and only God and the Devil know why.

Santiago Zabala Arbiza

Emory University. Friday, November 20, 2009

For as long as he could remember, Santiago had been searching for something that moved powerfully in a deep part of his past, something silent like a giant turtle gliding through the bottom of a calm lake. He knew what it was soon after turning 41.

Memory doesn't reside in the heart, but the heart must be something like the gateway, he thought as he sank the scalpel into the cold chest of a drunk driver. The young man had met his end a few days earlier on the 403, the interstate that runs from Atlanta to Chattanooga. He was in a hurry and didn't know where he was going, he thought.

He carefully cut the aorta. An aorta like any other. Like that of any animal without complex worries. As if a human being and their body were two different things, he thought. The dead man was a young guy no older than thirty. Given the recent absence of a foot and the brutal scars on his abdomen, he must have been a veteran of Iraq or Afghanistan.

Like crazy Hatuey, he thought, stopping his hand for an instant, imperceptible to the professors surrounding him, but long enough to revive a long story he had never lived.

Hatuey had his feet and hands intact, and although he had taken to alcohol and fights, he had survived. Better said, he had been reborn, though the man who had died that afternoon on March 16, 2006, on a dusty street in Fallujah had never fully died, and so he could never completely be reborn when he returned.

On the same Friday night, while helping the Colombian from *family housing* revive the fire in a grill at the park, he admitted he was excited to go back. He had his dissertation defense in April, the graduation ceremony in May, a few days on the beaches of Florida, and then return to the murky waters of the Río de la Plata. That's where his real life was, he had said. He was tired of so much perfection, he had joked. At the university, everything worked so well that they had to import problems from elsewhere, the Colombian had confirmed, a specialist in Chomsky's generative grammar who couldn't convince himself of the benefits of returning to Bogotá.

Don Jordi Caballero

Montevideo, April 6, 2012

Don Jordi Caballero was going to solve the mystery of his life on Saturday, April 7, 2012. Maybe he would have preferred not to, but the most important things are neither calculated nor foreseen. It's not that they happen whimsically or chaotically, but certainly, in those cases, human understanding always arrives late—when mistakes become evident, when what seemed important finally reveals itself as an insignificant occupation or a distraction with tragic consequences.

When he caught the metallic smell that always reminded him of his vacations in the countryside, hunting all kinds of small animals for fun, animals that tested their skills to escape by flying, running, or crawling, he imagined Marina calling José Ignacio. He could see the body of the gun but couldn't quite make out the terrifying hole that smelled like vacations and death. He could easily guess the sequence of events. First things first. Marina, José Ignacio, Carmen, the secretary with her impeccable pens and keyboard, and poor Erminda, nearly invisible, unable to empty the trash bins or run the vacuum. Then the others: someone who would find Lucía's number, and Lucía, taking a taxi at the corner of 18th and Rio Branco. At another moment, Lucía embraced by Santiago. Who knows why he imagined the young doctor might show some tenderness toward Lucía.

For a moment, he hesitated. His pupils dilated in the darkness until he saw a luminous rectangle that looked like a door.

He returned to the reality of the office and, once again, to the most recent memory of his best employees.

"Next week," he had told José Ignacio, delaying for no reason the much-awaited promotion. He didn't know why he had done it. Months ago, he had decided on the promotion. He knew the boy was worth his weight in gold, and he knew Marina waited day by day, month after month, with unconfessed anticipation for the boss's decision. The boss.

Maybe it was a game. He thought that by nature he was somewhat sadistic, but his sadism wasn't pointless—it was rather didactic. Don Jordi was a practical man who, at every step, needed to show his employees that all good things came at a high cost. He wasn't just the boss. He was like a father to many of them. A misunderstood father, like all fathers. Everyone complained about his refusals and his arbitrary orders, but every night they went to sleep knowing someone was looking out for them and their children. Deep down, as some said, he wasn't so bad. He was fair, added he himself and a few who admired him in secret or flattered him in public. He was terribly fair if you considered that the world was a garbage dump, don Jordi would say, and it wasn't in his hands to change it but only to manage it as best as possible in the absence of better alternatives.

He thought he heard the double knock of a door knocker. But the building was empty at this hour, and there were no knockers on the modern glass doors. Without getting up, he turned in his chair and looked toward the door that led to the hallway. The bulletproof glass multiplied the silence and the indecipherable reflections, as if at that moment spaces were mixing like a deck of cards.

"Who is it?" asked a frightened voice.

It was his mother's voice, drowned in a crowd of footsteps that accumulated at the entrance of the door.

"He's not here, I tell you…" insisted the voice.

That voice was still there. It wasn't a hallucination or a product of his imagination. It was his mother's voice, still murmuring, in a corner of 1939. More precisely, on the evening of February 9, 1939, in Barcelona, the same day Juan Negrín crossed the border, a few hours after his father managed to start the Ford A, and just minutes before the Falangist boots entered his room.

Much later, he heard his mother, completely defeated, like any woman of her standing at that time, speaking in codes and whispers with another woman draped in black, that the cross and rosary his mother had sent from A Coruña, and which, through some dark intuition, she herself had hung in Jordi's room days before, had saved the family, or rather, what was left of the family, from an even greater misfortune.

Though he couldn't hear that last part; he only remembered it.

MARKED DAY. The first death

Uruguay, January 1998

When he saw him for the last time in Barcelona, that cold afternoon of 1939, his father was thirty-five. Jordi Caballero knew the exact date one summer day, almost sixty years later, lying on a beach on Uruguay's Costa de Oro, reading a tiny article from *Selecciones* in the *Reader's Digest* that spoke about the preludes and premonitions of World War II. A little less than a page was dedicated to the Spanish Civil War. "To resist is to win." But England had betrayed the Republic by making a pact with the Falangists to ensure that Menorca didn't fall into Italian hands. On February 9, the *Reader*, President Negrín had crossed the border into France. It was then that he remembered his father's words. "At this moment, Negrín must be crossing the border."

He didn't remember the voice. He only remembered that the revelation was something important and probably dramatic. His mother, leaning on the kitchen table, had rested her forehead in one hand and remained like that, without saying a word. Jordi played on the floor or pretended to play with an empty matchbox—*fósforos*, as they called them in Uruguay"that had become a newspaper delivery truck, just like his father's. What could all that mean to his mom? *Resist, border, Negrín…* To Jordi, that name sounded like the name of a gnome, a character from fairy tales with some attribute or a dark, ominous destiny. *Negrín, the paladin, Negrín, the leaper…*

Sixty years later, Jordi had lowered the magazine and placed it on his chest while looking at the flat horizon of the sea with astonished eyes. "*At this moment, Negrín must be crossing the border,*" he repeated several times. The last time, out loud.

Lucía, who was fifteen at the time, asked:

"What did you say, Dad?"

"Nothing, sweetheart," was the response.

"What do you mean, nothing? Who's Negrín?"

"A client who owes me money. Better to forget about it."

"That's what I'm saying, Dad. Sometimes losing a deal is a gain for your health."

"That's right, sweetheart. Better to forget."

In that dumb magazine, Don Jordi thought, was the most important date of his life. But other questions remained. How could a worker, rather poor like his father, have known about the secret movements of the president of the Republic of Spain, even if it was a dying republic?

"*The poet died far from home…*" he murmured.

"*…The dust of a neighboring country covers him,*" Lucía continued. "I love Serrat… *As he walked away, they saw him cry, wanderer, there is no path, the path is made by walking…* Hey, Dad, did you know the lyrics are about Antonio Machado?"

"Yes, of course. I'm not as educated as you, but I'm still Spanish."

"*Spain, white shirt of my hope...*"

Post-traumatic stress disorder

Jacksonville, August 2008

The case of Ernest Hatuey might be the most predictable. Anyone could have imagined it would end badly, but not how. His grandfather from Puerto Rico always remembered that his father used to say that worse than living a bad life was finding a bad death. One had to know how to die; a bad death negated the meaning of any past joy. It was like laughing without knowing you're on your way to the firing squad. Or the gallows, because the firing squad had gained its prestige in Spain, his grandfather had said. But hanged or drowning in shit, as they did in the war, was no good death, no matter how you looked at it, his father had commented, and little Hatuey, who had been listening without permission, had asked: "Is there a good way to die?" Despite his mother's protests, his father had concluded his reasoning: "I don't know; I don't know if there are good ways to die... but I do know there are bad ones..."

A few months after his return, doctors diagnosed Ernest Hatuey with PTSD, that is, *post-traumatic stress disorder*. As they explained to him, no one yet knew why the same experiences have different effects on different people and, even, on the same person. But at least all the fury against the strangers who had stayed behind and the indifference toward his wife and his parents now had a name, and, likely, the doctors had some idea of how to alleviate a problem that had become chronic due to not having been treated in time, according to them.

So, little by little, he discovered that on that day, March 16, 2006, he had died in the explosion or shortly after, and his corpse had lain on a dusty street in Fallujah, in the hands of an unknown father, as unknown as the one Ernest himself found upon his return in Atlanta, on a fall afternoon in 2007.

MARKED DAY. Lucía walked lost

Montevideo, March 16, 1983

José Ignacio was like a son, Don Jordi thought, returning to the darkness of his office. A good employee. A decent young man who would soon forget the boss who helped him find his way at the start of his career. And who could blame him?

Immediately, he thought of Lucía.Lucía would remember him forever, just as he remembered his mother and father, although he wasn't entirely sure how. He had found her one night walking alone through La Aguada, on March 16, 1985. That night, a Saturday, he had attended the wedding of a client friend at the church in El Prado out of obligation. He couldn't remember the man's name or face. When the ceremony ended and the guests were ready to head to the reception hall, someone on the entrance steps remarked that the moon looked like a scar in the sky. Don Jordi looked up, smiled, and began to feel ill. It struck him as an unnecessary, cheesy poetic flourish to say that it was a waning moon. There's always someone at weddings who wants to draw attention to themselves, he thought. But there was something about that corniness that made him feel worse than was reasonable, as if something had suddenly given him indigestion. He leaned against one of the pillars supporting a dozen virgins, who in turn held up rows of small stone angels forming a Gothic or Arabic arch. He looked at the arch and the endlessly multiplying angels and swayed. Someone steadied him while joking, "Don Jordi, did you get a head start on the drinks?" A woman asked if he was feeling okay. Yes, he replied. But he quickly changed his mind and headed home to Pocitos. It was God's will, he told himself. If the cheesy poet hadn't pointed out the waning moon, if he had compared it to a smile instead of a scar, if he hadn't felt so ill that he skipped the best partof the wedding, he never would have returned at just the right time to find that innocent little girl walking alone down a deserted street, scared and shivering from the cold. Her father, apparently an alcoholic, had abandoned her on the corner of Rondeau and Colombia, and Don Jordi, by chance or divine providence, saw that lost girl running from no one, as if shadows were chasing her. The girl never, ever, remembered that night. Nor did she ever remember her father, even though she was nearly three years old. No one could explain how the Child Welfare Institute had granted Don Jordi custody without ever putting him on a waiting list. It was said that Don Jordi had bought off the director, the minister, and the devil himself, because he never lost a case and was capable of giving up his fortune just to outmaneuver his rivals. It was said that none of his own successes brought him as much happiness as the failures of others.

He was crazy about that child, which is why he never told her she was adopted. A common mistake in those days, but one that cost him Lucía's fury and rejection when she turned sixteen and discovered the truth. Lucía was at her worst back then, needing a mother to guide her through her discoveries as a young woman, and in some way she threw it back in Don Jordi's face. In a fit of rage, Lucía went to live alone in a boarding house in Parque Rodóuntil Don Jordi bought her the apartment on Bulevar España. But she refused it for a year, until two guys from the boarding house tried to assault her after a night of smoking pot and drinking beer. She smashed a bottle over one of their heads, landing herself in the police station until her father came to rescue her.

Lucía Cordero de Caballero

Montevideo, February 24, 1962

A letter from his sister Clarita, dated January 22, 1962 in Madrid, informed him that their mother had passed away on the 16th of that month.

Clarita had married a regime official, named Alberto with a last name Jordi couldn't recall, and from then on her letters became less frequent until the last one, which she wrote more out of obligation than feeling, and to avoid telling the maid she wasn't home every time her brother called from America. As was the rule, Clarita had adopted her husband's convictions

—namely, Francoism—shortly before their marriage. Just like in their grandmothers' time, thought Jordi, when women would convert to their husband's religion, in the rare case that back then there were still heretics who belonged to a different religion or none at all.

During that time and for many years after, Jordi had wavered between the suspicions of his Republican father and the unconditional defense of General Franco, as if from afar a country were synonymous with its government. He had vehemently faced the criticisms of Emilio Frugoni's followers and conceived the idea of founding a newspaper after reading the Marxist slander in the weekly publication *Marcha*. His accent, the blurry but persistent memory of his homeland, the nickname "gallego," left him with little room to maneuver.

Perhaps Clarita would have had a better image of her exiled brother if she'd known about some of these debates in America that earned young Jordi the labels of *fascist* or *falangist* at the tables of Café Sorocabana, a nest of poets and pseudo-intellectuals enamored with French culture. And so much was he accused of being a Falangist that for a time he even believed it himself. Until he found a middle ground for his ideological and personal conflicts by declaring, and making himself believe, that he didn't care about politics but about money, that one was just words when it wasn't death and imprisonment, and the other was only progress or, at the very least, well-being.

This confusion had arisen much earlier, with his mother Lucía, who since the disappearance of her husband had devoted herself to instructing her children, especially the eldest, to repeat condemnations against the Republicans, the Reds, the savage atheists who had wanted to destroy Spain. It took Jordi a long time, in fact his entire life, to understand something of the pain of that woman who had had to curse all her beliefs, her youthful superstitions about women's suffrage, about the education of peasant children, about the nonexistence of hell or about a hell made by men here on earth, and had had to instruct her own children on the virtues of her father's murderers, to avoid losing them too, like a Moorish or Jewish woman in the times of Ferdinand and Isabella. Like a witch in any age of barbarity.

Apparently, Lucía had died under strange circumstances. She hadn't been kidnapped by the regime, because the regime would never do that. She hadn't died of grief because, apparently, according to Clarita, she had everything. Apparently, she had decided to seclude herself in the little apartment that Clarita's husband had commissioned to be built at the back of their property, with the money from the house in Bonavista. It had been her decision. In the last two years, she had secluded herself in her tiny apartment and only went out on Fridays and Saturdays to an unknown destination.

Until one day they found her motionless, lying in her bed surrounded by old magazines, rings, and gloves that had once been white and which, had she thrown them in the trash in time, her story would have been different, ended Clarita's letter.

Jordi folded the letter three times, as was the custom in those days. His sister's words, somewhere between sad and indifferent, were scattered randomly across eight rectangles that only saw the light one more time, on an extremely desolate and hot afternoon in January 2010.

He had seen his mother for the last time on the afternoon of Saturday, October 3, 1959, at the port of Barcelona. "I'll be here next summer, old lady," he said to her, but she only gave a small smile. Jordi knew that sad expression of those who don't believe or have stopped believing. His lips would forever remember that soft cheek of an older woman, the lavender perfume she had never abandoned and which was perhaps a kind of secret code, a final complicity with the thirties, with his father. He watched her from afar until she became a small rosy flame in the light of the sunset and then a motionless little shadow that resisted leaving the dockside or tried to seize every last minute of what fate had left her of her son.

More and more things came between them. Jordi moved into the summer while she entered the long days of winter. She never tired of asking about his life in Uruguay, and he didn't dare ask about his father. The future was the great distraction for both of them.

He called her on the phone every two months, then twice a year. Each time, he went to ask about his father, but the pact of secrecy that they had somehow established between them, who knows when, always appeared like a wall of ice, transparent but unbreakable. Once, Lucía preempted any questions by saying that well, there were many things to talk about over tea one day, face to face, not from thousands of miles away and through a plastic tube.

"Let it be coffee, my beautiful girl," he wanted to confirm, with that need people have to trivialize something in their life when they suspect it's of great importance.

Lucía paused. Jordi imagined her pressing her lips with two fingers, because that was one of her most common gestures when she was thinking about something and then fell silent.

Despite this promise (or because of it), Jordi kept postponing the next summer in Spain. Perhaps it was true that business had become increasingly complicated as it grew. By then, more books and magazines were being sold than ever in Montevideo and Buenos Aires, which had forced him to open his own printing press first and later to import and distribute *offset* printers. A distraction at that time would have been disastrous, the end of all his efforts since 1953.

He called her on the phone on December 24, 1961. That was the last time he had spoken to her. She didn't seem sad. She didn't seem ill. But all those sweet trivialities that had always been there, deep down, meant the same tragedy, as if every human act carried the seed of the Great Truth hidden within it: each of those words, Jordi remembered, had been the last he would hear from his mother's lips while he laughed and she did too.

On December 31, he couldn't reach her. The lines were busy, or he wasn't in the right mood to insist more than four or five times.

One Sunday in January, he almost called her. He picked up the receiver and, for some reason, it slipped from his hands as if it were made of lead.

By the end of February, the number 54, Lucía's age, began to haunt him, just as 39 had for a long time. The cars that stopped in front of him had license plates ending in 54. The lottery numbers he bought always ended in 54, but the connection never came, except for a very modest sum for a close approximation, almost a refund. 254 was the number of the house he rented every summer in Punta del Este, though he swore he had discovered the numbering when he first inserted the key into the door. When he turned 54, his employees at the young *Metasoft* gave him, for the first and last time, a surprise welcome at the company, with a red and yellow cake and the number displayed like a tombstone. Jordi thanked them and ordered them never to do it again. The numbers 54 and 39 kept repeating in the most unexpected circumstances until early 2001.

In the winter of 1988, while reading the newspaper, for almost two seconds (probably no more than that, as is often the case with important things), Don Jordi suspected that he had spent his youth trying to make his mother love and admire him as she had perhaps loved and admired his father, the disappeared man. Like his father, he had followed the most indirect path of disappearance, and just as fate had willed that she had to speak ill of her husband in front of her own children and against her own convictions, the only thing the Uruguayan newspapers could say about the successful Spanish businessman was about his greed and his sympathies for the despicable Franco regime.

There were too many Spaniards in Uruguay, he told himself.

Paraguayan woman didn't need so much light

Montevideo, 1999

Lucía accepted the boulevard España apartment but didn't abandon the *i Margall* bookstore. She had stubbornly resolved to save the old business on Tristán Narvaja Street, her second home since she was a child, and especially because it was managed by Raquel, the Paraguayan maid who had managed to convince Don Jordi that she was capable of running a small business.

"Yes, of course you can run your own business," said Jordi, pensive yet concerned. "But a bookstore?"

"Yes, a bookstore," Lucía answered for Raquel. "Why not? Does the greengrocer on the corner know anything about botany? He just needs to know the name of each vegetable and little else."

Don Jordi had let himself be convinced. In truth, he had been pleasantly surprised by the idea from the start, but his style prevented him from admitting it. He thought that later, if things went wrong, he could lend a hand.

"Well... why not?" he joked. "Do the priests who've spent centuries advising newlywed couples know anything about sex and married life?"

Poor Raquel, Don Jordi thought in the darkness of his office, was happy in her final years among so many books, all of them strange. Raquel couldn't answer any of the questions from those thick-glassed crazies, but she was so happy there and had put so much enthusiasm into it that the dinosaur, as he called it, had lasted longer than expected, thanks to the affection of that nearly illiterate woman.

Lucía loved Raquel like a mother, and as soon as she left Elbio Fernández High School, she went straight to the bookstore to rescue the poor woman from so many *nerds*—who over time had also learned to love that wide smile that revealed "the sweetest Castilian beneath the happiest eyes," as one of those literary characters had said—to explain why Faulkner and Tennessee Williams belonged in the contemporary authors' section, more precisely in the room dedicated to *The Deep South*, even though both were North Americans. And she made an inhuman effort to explain why *Love and Pedagogy* belonged in "non-fiction," and why *Blindness* was categorized as a "novel."

Lucía would stay late into the night with Raquel, telling her what the books said, drinking tea, and listening to Raquel's stories about her life in Paraguay, in a neighborhood on the outskirts of Coronel Oviedo, a city like Durazno but covered in a red dust that even invaded the streets of the town center. Sweet Raquel, with her Guaraní accent and her unique gestures, would tell her about her childhood so far away, with wood-burning stoves and no TV or electric lights at night. But Raquel didn't remember any of that with sadness, only nostalgia: she missed her grandfather's stories and her uncles' lies in the dim glow of a night without a lantern due to the lack of kerosene.

"Now everyone's glued to their computers," Raquel would say.

"And you know what?," one of her admiring nerds would chime in from behind the counter, "technology addiction causes depression. We live in a world that's too full of excitement, an overstimulated and understimulated world; and when we lack stimulation, excitement takes over. When we don't have a lot of artificial stimulation, we get depressed."

"I'm leaving," Don Jordi would say. "These folks are already talking complicated."

"As a result, the kids today are tired," Raquel complained, "tired from doing nothing. Many of them have no idea what real sacrifice is, what it's like to work like beasts, and yet they're tireeeeed. When I was five and would tell my mother I was 'bored,' she'd make me clean my room. Then I'd have to go out into the field to help my older siblings plant potatoes, pick fruit, milk cows. There was no heating, no air conditioning—we worked hard… and we were happy. Those are the best memories of my life, a life of poor children, sacrificing and happy."

"What have we done wrong in this consumerist, obsessed, depressed, and sick culture?" Lucía would ask, and Raquel would shrug.

Then Lucía would beg her to describe over and over again what those nights without electricity were like and would ask her to turn off the lights to experience it, and to tell her everything again, but Raquel would say no, that it wasn't the same anymore. Instead, she'd tell new stories, some that might not have been true, but even she didn't know. Lucía would ask her to tell her about her first time, and Raquel, a little embarrassed, would share her fears, those silly fears that girls as young as her had to face: she confessed when she had her first period and thought she was going to die because no one had explained to her that the blood wasn't a wound or that menstruation wasn't an illness. No one had explained; quite the opposite.

Lucía was drawn to the books, the company, and Raquel's wonder, who was in her final days, suffering and hiding that cursed uterine cancer that could have been cured with a timely test.

The Galician Suárez

Montevideo, June 28, 1973

One Thursday, the day after the coup d'état in Uruguay, old Suárez, the Galician man who would bring coffee from the corner bar every morning, said to him:

"How do you expect me to be, Don Caballero? You already know. Good news for some and terribly bad for others. That's how it goes when there's no democracy or when too many people hate it. I asked the doorman how long he thought the military would stay in power, and he told me to start saying goodbye to Wilson and Zelmar. That they're done for. I asked if he was happy, and he asked if I was a communist, you know? When someone asks you if you're a fascist or a communist, things are really messed up. No way, I told him, I was just a Spanish Republican. I told him that I *was*, just in case. And he told me to start looking for another country because this one wasn't going to work out for me either. To the Congo, he said, to the Congo. So today, the coffee was on me... They gave me the coffee, they gave it to me. Do you know what that means...? No, no... you're talking to me like a Uruguayan. It's the same in Argentina. Here they say 'they gave me coffee' to mean someone scolded you, treated you like trash, like that crazy doorman treated me. The thing is, you came here very young, Don Caballero. Back in Spain, the Francoists would sing... (old Suárez shaped his mouth into an *O* and looked up at the ceiling searching his memory):

> ...*they say you're leaving, you're leaving*
> *and you never quite go*
> *to see that blonde they say*
> *you've got in Valladolid...*
> *I'll give you,*
> *I'll give you something,*
> *I'll give you, lovely girl,*
> *something only I know: coffee!"*

Old Suárez, with his yesterday's beard and his gray eyebrows drooping over his eyes, looked at Don Jordi as if he didn't understand why he didn't understand.

"Well, you heard it," he said. "I'll give you something, something only I know, *coffee!*"

He looked at him again as if the office had suddenly darkened.

"The thing is," he said, sounding disappointed, "you're much younger than me, and I don't know if I'm doing the right thing by telling you this, but when I was a young man, I worked making tiles, those same gray tiles with nine little gray squares on top, the ones you see everywhere in the neighborhoods here. And well, I had to be a Republican, and when we heard someone singing that coffee song from outside the factory, a chill ran through us because we knew that 'coffee' was their way of saying 'Comrades, Long Live the Spanish Falange'... And look at you, Don Caballero, that's how life goes—I had to cross the whole ocean, like you, and I started as a waiter at the Lugano bar, so I've been bringing and carrying coffee for more than thirty years now. And to top it all off, on the day after the worst day this country has ever seen, they give me coffee... and it feels like there's no turning back. At my age, no Congo, not even in my dreams, can save me now."

Old Suárez hunched over as he turned toward the office door, and Don Jordi remembered the silence of his mother across the Atlantic.

"Don't get like that, Pepe," said Don Jordi. "None of this is your business... Why should you worry?"

The Zabala-Arbiza Hologram

Saturday, December 15, 2010

Santiago also managed to unravel one of the central mysteries of his life. Of course, these moments are rather rare. Usually, people take most of their secrets to the grave. Not because they want to, but because things can't be any other way when we're stumbling through the dark streets of a troglodyte city as if we knew where we were going.

The beginning of this revelation for Santiago, once again, like everything, almost always, happened in the most unexpected way—at a welcome party in an exclusive restaurant on the rambla.

Celebrating events and exaggerating the accomplishments of some of their members was an Arbiza family tradition. Santiago's graduation in the United States and his return to the country warranted a party with relatives and friends in a room at El Congo. Santiago joked about the Rio de la Plata irony and the custom of calling *cantegrils* the shantytowns of Montevideo and *Congo* one of the fanciest restaurants in Punta Gorda.

"I don't know what's worse," observed Rosario, "the Rio de la Plata sarcasm or the Peruvian euphemism. In Lima they call the slums 'young towns.'"

"Well," said María, "at least they resolved it in an elegant and optimistic way. I'm fed up with the chronic sadness on this side of the continent."

Of all the gifts he received, the strangest was Cristina's. A hologram of Jesus so well-crafted that it seemed to step out of the frame. For a moment, he thought it was the best of all the gifts. He hugged the old woman and promised he'd put it in his office.

But after a while, as Santiago opened Paulina's package, Alejandro Spinelli noticed that from where he was standing, the angel had turned into a demon, a mix of Batman, *Terminator*, or a galactic demon.

"Batman's not a demon," Lidia interjected.

Well, it was something between Batman and a demon, most of them agreed. It wasn't clear. You had to put yourself in Alejandro's place. From the chair facing away from the beach, you could see a dark figure with a somewhat terrifying expression in its eyes. Anyway, whatever it was, from that angle it wasn't the Jesus you could see head-on, with the window light shining from the side.

Cristina's face changed. Her expression was indecipherable, Santiago thought. First, she started apologizing for not having noticed the second image. She wanted to return it at all costs, but he protected the gift, telling her that it was God's will, that maybe it was a sign about the struggle between good and evil, and that she herself had once told him it was bad luck to return a Christmas gift. He didn't want Cristina to feel bad; Grandma was suffering from advanced diabetes that worsened with any strong emotion. She'd joke that she'd been dying for twenty years, but she'd learned to keep the Devil at bay.

Elena said the seller should have shown her the painting up close, and Cristina confirmed that she hadn't even tilted it a little to allow Alejandro to see the demon he claimed was there.

"I bought it just yesterday in Buenos Aires," said Cristina, "but if you give it to me, I'll return it first thing in the morning."

"You shouldn't get like that, Grandma," said Santiago. "After all, you've always taught me that the devil exists too, right? He's part of the reality behind all things, and in my profession, I'll have to battle that son of a…"

Santiago realized he was starting to talk to her as if she were a child. Maybe she wasn't so old as to not notice it.

By the time Quique asked who the cuckold's mother was, Cristina had already taken her spot. She sat down, looked at the painting resting against the wall, tilted her head several times trying to spot the demon, but saw nothing. Or she said she saw nothing besides the serene face of Jesus.

Soon, the guests split into two groups: one that affirmed or confirmed the possibility of the ambiguous image, so common in holograms, as a possibility, an artist's heresy, perhaps, but a real possibility nonetheless. The other group denied the second image. As the night went on, two more groups emerged. One defended the anonymous artist; maybe he just wanted to emphasize the struggle between good and evil, between the divine and the demonic. Denying the devil's existence was attributing all the world's evil to God or, worse, suggesting that no immoral act had punishment—that is, meaning. Another group, which didn't want to admit it, began to think that Alejandro and the others who had seen the demon instead of Jesus had something grave to confess or something fatal to change in their lives. Each saw in the hologram their own interior, much like we see our obsessions, our fears, and our own hallucinations—that is, our past and our future—in the damp stains on a wall. Or in our dreams.

Santiago remembered that the night before the welcome party, he'd dreamt of a beetle crawling down the trunk of a tree. The beetle descended along the coarse folds of a massive oak in Tennessee. For hours, or minutes that felt like hours, he watched the beetle, unable to do anything else: he learned the movement of its slow legs, the shine of its dark wings, every detail of the oak's bark. When he woke up, he kept thinking about the beetle that was still crawling down the trunk, now very close to the roots. Then he thought the dream symbolized his return to the country and the dark roots were his childhood. That was the easiest interpretation, a product of his psychoanalytic readings. But the truth, he thought then as he watched Carmen sitting in Alejandro's chair, was that the beetle didn't represent anything: it was what he felt returning to his country, to his deepest fears. The fear of return *was* the beetle crawling slow and dry toward the dark roots that with the slowness of years were penetrating the earth, just as roots delve into the soil to draw life from death.

Most likely, he had concluded, the beetle was just the result of indigestion he'd caught at Hartsfield-Jackson in Atlanta. Overcome by anxiety, he had eaten *cheesecake* without restraint, downed one coffee after another while reading every newspaper in the waiting areas and the lonely seats of American Airlines.

"Let's take it step by step," insisted Quique, Alejandro's half-brother. "Why are we assuming the first image was Jesus?"

"Because of the beard, the long hair, the serene gaze, the outstretched arms," said Claudia, and Cristina agreed.

"Claudia, never argue with Quique. You'll waste your time," warned María.

"With the beard, long hair, serene gaze, and outstretched arms, it could be Che Guevara," said Quique.

"Typical Argentine irony."

"I'm Uruguayan. Are you going to claim ownership of irony too?"

"Don't be ridiculous, Quique," complained Don Xico. "Clearly, that's not Che. Believe me when I say it…"

Don Xico was about to mention Quique's blindness, but he stopped himself in time. His daughter had schooled him in the art of prudence, as he often said at the retirees' club. Quickly, he added:

"Leftists like you are capable of claiming things even you yourselves don't believe, because, in fact, you don't believe in anything."

"No, it's not Che, because his eyes are blue." "It's Jesus," insisted Carmen.

"And when was this photo of Jesus taken? Who was the Korda of the time? Since when is Jesus blond? Right, what goodness could a mulatto inspire…"

Santiago hesitated. For a moment, he considered secretly disposing of the hologram, feigning a loss or a theft, but he quickly realized it was impossible: he couldn't throw away a Christmas gift, a gift from Cristina, and certainly not an image of Jesus. It would be a mortal offense.

Quique had gotten his way, making things even more complicated:

"To say the image in the back is a demon is as arbitrary as saying the other one is Jesus. It could be an angel, one of those countless celestial beings with unknown names. As if that weren't enough, to say that one of the images, the supposed demon, is *the one in the back* is also arbitrary, since from Alejandro's position, the only image visible is the demon. So, which one is in the back and which one is in the front? What can objectively be said about the painting is that the dark image is not the first thing one sees when looking straight ahead, and therefore the dark image is in the back, like everything that seems dark and unpleasant, like the truth itself. How many truths are exposed to the light of day? If they were, there would be no need for philosophers or scientists. Ergo, we confuse desire with reality. Or worse: in this case, we confuse *fear* with reality."

"I don't care if Jesus was white or black..." said Santiago. He was about to continue but didn't know how. The others waited for two or three seconds, which, under the circumstances, felt like an hour of silence. Once again, Santiago sensed that his thing was the mysteries of the body, the reasons behind blood-flows, the logic of the heart that resembled more a Ford engine than a Flaubert novel; he cared little for the immeasurable mysteries of the human soul, as he once said, paraphrasing an Argentine writer, to a literature student at Emory. On the contrary, the fewer mysteries, the less ignorant a man was, and the lower his chances of being unhappy.

The Second Death of Jordi Caballero

Punta del Este, February 1968
His father died again when Jordi turned thirty-five. He was that age when he saw him for the last time in Barcelona, that Thursday, February 9, 1939.

Until then, he could look in the mirror and see his father's face, the gaze anxious for a sudden hope or weary from a new failure. All his intimacies had been his father's as well. Every time his eyes wandered to the behind of a woman passing by the window of a bar where he read the newspaper next to a steaming coffee, it was his father's gesture in 1930s Barcelona or 1920s Madrid. At least that's what he believed. He believed that one more or less repeats the dreams and frustrations of their ancestors in different settings. Then, he would close his eyes and see the grandfather he never met, Grandfather Caballero (his name was Jordi, just like him, just like his father, because of that old-fashioned people's habit of not being content with passing down only the surname to their children, haunted or harassed by a futile longing for eternity) climbing a rocky path beside the mountain, shielding himself from the snow, dragging a cart with a skinny mule, trying to start an old Ford in Oviedo with his son watching anxiously from inside the broken-down car. And he saw his father discovering the world in Madrid, at a lonely little table in the corner of a workers' bar, with an old pen, and it was himself in the bar at Canelones and Ciudadela with a cell phone in hand.

He couldn't imagine in detail any of those other people who came before his grandfather, who miraculously saved their lives so that, unintentionally, he, Jordi (Jordi the third, Jordi the fourth), could be there looking at the small Renoir painting. But ultimately, all those were details that don't change what really matters in the human experience: love, jealousy, the pain of injustice and moral violence, insult, the threat from a stranger or an unhinged neighbor, the death of a grandfather, an uncle, the guilt for having done the right thing or for having made an irreparable mistake. All of that is reality. Or rather, the profound reality of reality. The rest is just settings. As if in every era, in every generation, in every century, the same play was staged. Romeo and Juliet in Verona. Romeo and Juliet in Paris during the Second World War. Romeo and Juliet in John Lennon's New York or in Tinelli's Buenos Aires. Romeo and Juliet walking the dusty streets of a village in China. Romeo and Juliet dying on the border of Gaza.

Until Don Jordi turned thirty-five, all those images of that distant, understanding, and sometimes absent father had gradually taken shape. His father's mustache disguising imperfect teeth. His kind words embracing the boy that Don Jordi once was, much like Don Jordi's own words when he tried to comfort and, above all, protect with advice his little girl with her thin arms—not so much to ease her fears and frustrations but to spare her from the future pains he imagined Lucía would face.

What he lacked, however (Don Jordi told himself, resorting to those secretive forms of self-flagellation that a person plagued by a hidden sense of guilt always finds), was all the idealism of his father. That political idealism, republican by circumstance, which for so long he had dismissed with disdain and only when approaching thirty-five could he partially feel, when in a fit of romantic madness he gifted a small plot of land in San José to the family that had been hired to care for the fruit trees. Every now and then, he would visit, and the couple's five children would come out to greet him as if he were the founding father of a micro-republic. The father, whom the neighbors called "El

Negro Silva," had hung a sign at the entrance that read: "Caballero's Farm."

Again, he got involved in an unnecessary fraud, back in the seventies, in the middle of the dictatorship. He had managed to evade thirty percent of his taxes that year. A move that wasn't worthy of Don Jordi, he told himself, not because it was dishonest, if there's anything dishonest about evading taxes, but because of the clumsiness of the scheme. Someone noticed and reported him. For a few weeks, he felt the vertigo of being pursued. He could have aligned himself with one side or another—with some group of exiled dissidents, with the artists in Libertad prison who painted abstract doves and weeping butterflies, or with one of those sects or lodges that the military occasionally created to feel important. He could have attempted something more elegant than a crude evasion, he thought when the storm passed, which cost him a considerable sum to avoid jail and keep his name out of the papers. At least it would have been more honorable.

But he lacked some of the elements that had made his father, he thought. He lacked courage. He lacked that stupid idealism that had made and unmade his father and his mother. At least that's what he wanted to believe, since the possibility that his father had actually been much more like him than he could imagine terrified him. He didn't want to taint certain memories. It would have been like demolishing the central pillars of his existence. Perhaps he chose not to know the full truth. Or maybe he wasn't wise enough to understand that even heroes defecate and, at times, partake in the market of human misery.

But when he turned thirty-five, he realized he could no longer keep discovering his father in his own fears, in his joys, in his obsessions, in his tics, in his unjustified sadnesses, in one drink too many. From then on, he had to walk alone. When he reached the age his father had been when he disappeared, when he died or was murdered, he knew that everything new he could feel and experience in this life had been foreign to that other Jordi Caballero: the depressions of the forties; the less frequent erections; the worries of raising a teenager; the occasional arrogance of pragmatism; the absolute lack of fear when speaking in public; the inability to be moved by the scent of lavender or by the sight of the naked sea; the increasing scarcity of beautiful women who deigned to look him in the eye; the growing hatred of the younger generations who couldn't find a way to reach where he was perched, like a dictator usurping a public and private space for an excessively prolonged time; the suspicion that people were beginning to view his death with growing indifference; the awareness of being on a ship that was moving away from the shore, away from the world of the young who were beginning to take over the cities and rewrite their own histories and those of their elders.

He knew that none of these inner landscapes had been part of his father's world, cut short so young. All of that was now his world, and he had to discover it alone. Starting from that thirty-fifth year, he had to begin living alone. His father had died a second time, and yet he knew that even this wasn't a definitive death.

Without frivolity, there is no party, he thought

Saturday, December 15, 2010

"Come on, Santi, tell me about how at Emory University you took a course with the great Frans de Waal," Quique, as if rescuing him from the tangle he'd gotten himself into, which showed that despite all his sarcastic bitterness, he still had that noble sense of kindness". So, what's this about the monkeys? Is it true they have politicians like we do?

"What do you doubt, dear?" said Negra Laurie. "Don't we have orangutans in parliament? The fact that monkeys have politicians isn't a sign of their evolution but of our regression to those primitive states…"

"And Chomsky? Did you take any classes with Chomsky?"

"No, how could I? MIT is up north. Plus, cardiology has nothing to do with linguistics or politics. Though I've heard some rather negative opinions about him…"

"Like what…?"

"Well, several…" said Santiago. "Now I recall a TV commentator who once said that while Chomsky was a genius in linguistics, he was rather stupid in politics…"

"I see," said Quique. "I heard something similar about Einstein. 'A genius in physics but stupid in politics.' Maybe because he was a socialist living in the United States. The more one ignores the history of that country, the more surprised they are to discover dissidents and socialists over there. Historical amnesia lets them label such people as unpatriotic or something like that. As *idiots*, in a word, as is the case with our Eduardo Galeano here. Of course, everyone has the right to be wrong, even geniuses. But the idea that Noam Chomsky was a genius in linguistics and stupid in politics implies he was a semi-idiot. Now, calling a genius a semi-idiot can only be said by a complete idiot, someone who is consistently and coherently stupid."

"Quique gets away with these outbursts because he's blind," someone whispered into Mayor Laprida's ear.

The Pi i Margall Bookstore

Fall 2009

After Raquel's death, Don Jordi said enough was enough and decided to sell the obsolete business. Consequently, he faced all the fury and determination of Lucía, who persisted in a battle lost from the start. It's true that Don Jordi also held a special affection for that old house full of used books, the famous i Margall *Bookstore*, which for a few days was called *El Escorial*, until someone remarked that it made sense for a palace of kings and parasites cloistered in their own holiness to bear such a name, but not a palace of books that had nothing to do with a repository of scum. Along with the *London Paris store* and the *El maestro cubano cookies*, it had marked an era in a still prosperous Uruguay. The bookstore had been the first business he owned since arriving from Spain, one that had catapulted him in the 1950s into the circle of the country's most successful entrepreneurs. At its peak, he had five branches with nearly forty employees, not counting the literary geniuses who worked for free, or almost for free, writing reviews for the papers in exchange for books Don Jordi sent them every week.

But his practical spirit outweighed his nostalgia. Though not more than Lucía's unyielding resistance.

"Lucía, my dear," Don Jordi would say, "the bookstore barely turns a profit. You can hardly cover your needs keeping that dinosaur alive. Soon there won't be readers selling old books, and even fewer who'll want to buy them. I'm not sure there'll be readers at all. Even new bookstores are dying. It's a different time, my dear. You have to adapt or reality will run you over."

Old Jordi, a hawk for business, had quickly grasped the new digital age, and, much to the confusion of many, it was his young daughter who was the romantic, if not the fool, stubbornly insisting on saving—or rather losing herself in—a world that was fading away. If it hadn't disappeared already.

He thought about that Santiago fellow, the young doctor from the American Hospital who, with all his academic naivety, his scientific mindset or whatever they called it, had tried to deceive her. And Don Jordi almost sent one of his trusted employees to scare him a little, if he hadn't realized in time that the good doctor wasn't so bad after all. At least not dirty enough to deceive Lucía. Because Lucía was stubborn, hard-headed, like her father, her adoptive father, but not stupid.

The Return

Atlanta, March 21, 2007

For the remainder of his deployment in Iraq, Ernest Hatuey fulfilled his duties within the expected objectives and forms. In war, it's impossible to notice that something is wrong, so in the following months, he worked with discipline, waiting for the definitive return. Finally, on Wednesday, March 21, 2007, he arrived at Hartsfield-Jackson Airport in Atlanta.

When he took the metro that would take him from Terminal B to T, he tried to think about Claudia, about his parents. He wanted to feel the same anxiety as his comrades.

Next stop, concourse C... C as in Charlie...

He knew they were waiting for him. The old man, emotional but inexpressive; the old woman crying; and Claudia, the delicate butterfly who had escaped the paramilitaries in Colombia almost ten years ago, nervous, as always, thin and unable to control so much anxiety, because for her the world hung by a thread, and every detail of every event was a terrible threat.

He wished he could feel nervous, but he couldn't. There were no strong emotions in his stomach, no tears like the ones he had imagined so many nights, lying in the bunk at the outpost unable to sleep, a cigarette occasionally lighting up the ceiling, like in Vietnam movies, recounting details about his mother and his dog, listening with little interest to the details about the mothers and dogs of his comrades, listening *Paint it Black* by The Rolling Stones to disguise reality. Every time he recounted something about his nearly forgotten life in San Juan, he traveled to the Caribbean and smelled the guavas, saw the flowers from his grandmother that surrounded the water well and climbed the back wall, which he imagined as the last bastion of the fortress hiding a beautiful young woman kidnapped by pirates, never realizing that pirates didn't own castles but ships, their own and others'. And the coquí, of course, the coquí multiplied by a thousand in the carless nights. Co-quí, co-quí... When Aunt Eulogia was dying in Orlando, her daughter played a recording of these little frogs in her hospital room. Two nurses had entered upon hearing the strange noise and took a while to understand that it was a recording, that the recording was of little frogs, and that the little frogs made the patient feel better. But Aunt Eulogia needed nothing more than silence and the coquís. She had smiled and, before dying, thanked her daughter for taking her back to Puerto Rico.

"Hatuey, besides being a strange name, has a very creative memory," said Jesús, the Dominican ballplayer who slept in the bunk below.

"Don't be ignorant," Hatuey replied" *"don't you know who Hatuey was?"*

He let himself be carried up one of the escalators. Then another. Two women ran exhaustedly to catch their flight.

"I know," Carlos had answered from the darkness: *"It's a Cuban malt brand. A Chilean friend of mine loved drinking malt, and the only place he could find it was at a Cuban restaurant in West Palm Beach, full of Cuban girls though born in America. My friend, who liked Che Guevara more than the Miami mafia, would go there*

to eat Cuban empanadas, because the Yankees had no idea what malt was. The worst part was that he ended up falling in love with one of those girls and I think they even got married."

"I don't want to know what the story turned into after that."

"Now that I remember, it had an Indian on the label. The malt."

"And the cigars, and the Cohibas and all that. But the truth is, it's a Taíno Indian, the first rebel of America."

Next stop, concourse T... T as in tango...

But all that had been before Fallujah. Before Fallujah, the horrors of war were just that; they were the horrors of war that happened every day to someone who was still alive.

Without realizing it, he suddenly found himself walking in a measured pace in a line that meandered through the airport. *I see a red door and I want it painted black.* A blonde woman with a little flag in one hand guided the line of soldiers and paraded them through the different waiting rooms so the heroes could receive the welcome they deserved. *No colors anymore I want them to turn black.* A crowd of unfamiliar faces, some disfigured as was customary, was there to cheer them. He barely saw two or three men and a woman reading the newspaper or drinking coffee, with an indifference that seemed deliberate to Hatuey. He didn't even feel hatred or anger toward those ungrateful people. He almost understood them. He almost wished one of them would stand up and say something, maybe an insult, but something that would put an end to that hero's agony. He could see on their faces all the patriotic passion that he, Ernest Hatuey, had lost in the war. *I see the girls walk by dressed in their summer clothes...* He held no grudge against the country he represented.

55

His resentment came from elsewhere, but the noise of the applause didn't allow him to understand even minimally where that resentment came from, the one that led him to despise that fat woman whose face was red from clapping so much, or that old man shouting *"welcome, welcome!"*

From all these signs, he knew he was sick or something wasn't right. A doctor would explain to him years later that there is a soldier syndrome that transferred all his frustrations and traumatic experiences to the authorities who had sent him to war, and that this could be cured by forgiving and enabling a dialogue with those who had made the decision that ultimately ended up affecting the life of the renegade soldier. But Hatuey discovered, to his great surprise, that the comrades in his same situation were many, at least far more than any of them could acknowledge.

As he walked silently, dragging those sand-colored boots from the East across the shiny floor—boots he was supposed to treasure as the greatest trophy of his life—Ernest kept waiting for the emotion to well up in his eyes while he went through the welcome ceremony. All his comrades had been anxious since they sighted the shores of the United States until the very last minute.

When the ordeal of the welcome parade ended, they all fell into the arms of their parents and their wives. Some even had young children. He felt envy for those small children, running like crazy to throw themselves into the arms of their father, who had been absent in a mysterious land, in an ungrateful distant country that had devoured many of those suffering heroes. And thanks to them, their children were now free.

Ernest Hatuey tried to do the same. When he saw his parents and Claudia with tear-streaked faces, he extended his arms and smiled, though his eyes didn't join in. He couldn't feel moved. Much less cry or squeeze a tear from those eyes dried out by the desert sand. Dried out, he thought, as if they were dead. He tried to feign emotion, but he couldn't.

There they were, his wife and his parents, and there he was, doing what he was supposed to do: hugging them, telling them he was happy to be back. But all he could think about was getting home and lying down. It was as if a great exhaustion, after days of walking, had inexplicably taken over him.

At home, he found his dog Glory, the dog he had missed so much. There she was, nervous, jumping as high as her paws would allow. Ernest Hatuey knelt down and hugged her, trying to avoid the desperate licks of that little beast who hadn't understood a thing.

MARKED DAY. The doctor and the major

Saturday the 15th, 23:55
The meeting at El Congo ended at midnight. Santiago lamented not having enough time to talk with Alejandro. Since his return from the United States, he had done nothing but reproach him for the lack of opportunities to sit down for half an hour and chat in a bar in the Old City.

Now, every time he approached Alejandro's table (always looking like an eternal teenager, thin, with long hair like in the seventies and skeptical like in the sixties), he seemed distracted, as if something was seriously bothering him. Alejandro was like a brother to him. They had struggled through university together, exam after exam, and Santiago didn't know what worried him more: that his friend would fail an exam or fall so far behind that it would no longer be possible to keep studying together.

That night, Alejandro had a face of death, Santiago thought. He was going to ask him what was wrong, if he wasn't happy about his return, but incredibly, he never found the right moment. That's what happens when people gather in a festive mood, and even the most serious get swept up in the inner carnival.

Five years ago, Alejandro had bet him that Santiago would stay up north, because there they had the resources for a brilliant mind like his. But Santiago returned. When he found out, the skinny guy wrote to him with the excitement of a kid. However, now he didn't show as much enthusiasm, despite the effort he made to smile every time Santiago approached the table where he was sitting with half a dozen other university classmates, improvising obscene jokes, remembering humiliations like fainting in front of a poorly opened or closed corpse.

Santiago headed toward the skinny guy, who was already leaving with his wife, Negra Blair, but his grandmother intercepted him to introduce him to a gray-haired man they called Don Xico, pronounced with a Portuguese accent, like Major

Almeida and Laprida, an old friend of his father. The major extended a bony hand and told him he would have liked to be his first patient in Montevideo, but since he was as strong as an oak, it would be a waste of time for both of them. The major smiled, his breath smelling of alcohol and his eyes glassy.

"Pleased to meet you," said the major.

"Likewise," Santiago replied.

As often happens, neither Santiago nor the major knew that in that moment, their lives had converged on a single path, like two passengers who at the last minute decide to board the Titanic and smile with their tickets in hand.

The Future of Lucía

Montevideo, January 16, 2011

The little doctor was on the far side of thirty, almost forty, but Lucía was older than him in many ways. Once, at the bookstore, he heard her telling a customer who hesitated or pretended to hesitate, that *Loving Everyone* was a masterfully written novel because it was so easy to read that it could be finished in one sitting at the beach. The poor guy never noticed Lucía's irony. Not even Jordi would have noticed it if he weren't her father. So he didn't mind the idea of the guy hanging around her, after he had him investigated, the second or third time he happened to see him at the bookstore, reading books upside down.

Don Jordi wanted to see Lucía on some solid, credible path, even if it was marriage, even if it went against all the feminist speeches she had defended with passion and not without rhetorical skill. Parents become understandably conservative, he thought once. When one is young, one might not have as much experience or wisdom, but one is sincere. Later, one has no choice but to be responsible and compromise with the monsters of the moment. Even the most Republican ends up becoming monarchist and repeating stories of princes and princesses just to avoid seeing the younger ones suffer the consequences of useless rebellion.

More than a few confirmed that, deep down, Don Jordi hated the male gender and that, in some unimaginable way, the Spanish Republicans had transmitted to him both feminism and a permanent frustration that didn't waver even in his moments of greatest triumph. Not a few saw, of course, a glaring contradiction or, perhaps, a rigid consistency with his own principles: one defines oneself by what one does, he said, because one hates what one is.

He was tired, tired of many things, and something made him sense that he needed to start fixing the most important ones. And nothing was more important to him than Lucía.

As always, Don Jordi had a kind heart that turned practical, terribly blind, and effective when things didn't go the way he thought they should. Lucía was wandering aimless, he said, and despite all her intelligence and her tough-woman appearance, she was the perfect candidate to spend the rest of her life suffering frustrations and mistreatment in exchange for a miserable job or some unpayable debt.

Those Faces at the Bottom of the Well

Sunday, December 16, 2010

Santiago dropped Paulina off at her house. She gave him a long, wet kiss, looked into his eyes, gave him her best smile, and told him to call her as soon as he got to the apartment.

But shortly after driving away, he parked under a streetlamp on Avenida Brasil and Bulevar España. He took out the hologram and placed it under the orange light. He had a pebble in his shoe, and all that double cream food hadn't sat well with him. He looked at the hologram, turning it several times. Maybe it was the light, he thought. Maybe that was it. It had to be. He kept moving the image, but the angel's face only appeared when he wasn't looking at it directly.

Suddenly, straining to scrutinize that face that slipped away in the shadows, he realized what troubled him most. Out of the five long years at Emory, the first two had been marked by a deep nostalgia that didn't fade even on party nights, which weren't few among the graduate students. Not even the beers in the dark shadows of the *Family Housing* trees on Saturday nights, nor the gatherings at *Steve B's Pizza* with the Uruguayans and Argentines from the university could lessen that personal little catastrophe. But considering the change and the distances, he had taken it as something predictable. He listened to tangos and Argentine folk music and let himself drift into memories of the South. Family, his friends from the medical school in Montevideo, nights of mate and coffee studying for exams, the

Prado, some weekend walking along the rambla, imagining more interesting days.

Luckily, he had forgotten or was no longer haunted by the gaze of the first cadaver he had to cut open, a woman who had reached her forties, a prostitute who had committed suicide when she discovered one of her clients was her son. At least that was the rumor among the students who always knew what a good professional shouldn't know.

From this dangerous exercise of remembering and forgetting everything he had left behind, he moved on to his adolescence, to the younger days in Buenos Aires, Villa Devoto, Avenida Lincoln and Gualeguaychú, Recoleta, the Once neighborhood at dusk, La Boca, walks through San Telmo in December and Mar del Plata in the summer. Mostly pleasant memories, except for the years at the nuns' school in Liniers. That period had impenetrable forgetfulness but also surprisingly vivid images, like the abandoned house on Andrés Vallejos Street. With other kids, he would sneak around the side of the gate to spy on the French mansion, peeking through the cracks of the boarded-up windows at the fallen or poorly hung paintings, the armchairs no one would ever sit in again, the dirt and dust that always triumphed over any care, and above all, that smell of dampness and abandonment that made his skin crawl because he knew it was the smell of ghosts.

Miguel Polzin, Alejandro Espinelli, and he, Santiago, had built a bond of affection beyond the obligations and solidarity imposed by the rigor and boredom of high school. Those years are unforgettable. He managed to see the Russian, Miguel, on a trip to New York. He had changed, or he was the same but with some traits amplified and others diminished. He had less hair on a forehead that threatened to extend to the back of his neck and less patience than he had had in school. He would get anxious over anything and change the subject. When he talked about the economy of Europe and the United States, he got agitated like a reporter for Bloomberg or the Wall Street Journal. When Santiago asked him about his father and other personal matters, his tone shifted, and his voice became slower and quieter, as if he didn't want to talk about personal things, or as if he talked about the economy to avoid talking about what he had left behind in Buenos Aires.

From the nuns' school, he barely remembered the stone walls, the tall stained-glass windows he would stare at obsessively as if searching for an escape, the thick skirts of the nuns who took care of him, the gentle hand of one of them, Sister Tamara, who was the only one who comforted him when he started crying and nothing could stop him, not even the ear-pulling of the Mother Superior.

Another hint of that second dark face trying to surface was his fondness for old photographs. Shortly before leaving Buenos Aires, he scanned the disordered collection of his mother, mostly black-and-white photos, that his grandmother kept in a shoebox. At the time, as is normal and predictable, that little obsession of taking the family's memory with him seemed more like a consequence of affection than an ancient obsession that never fully defined itself.

At Emory, whenever he could, he spent hours scrutinizing each of those mysterious images. There was something in all those faces staring at him from a white and deep past that was slowly disappearing, like a consciousness giving way to sleep after a long day. There was something that seemed to appear in that hologram but slipped away just as he thought he knew what it was. The Arbizas, the Zavalas, the Costas, the Hertzogs, and the Rossis. The Costas were the darkest, the Rossis and the Hertzogs the blondest. They were all more or less blond like him, but none fit the shape of his face, none shared his thick eyebrows or his gaze, which wasn't particularly distinctive but was, as with everyone, the secret key we use and no one knows: one can recognize the gaze of a relative even in a photo, Ramiro, the Honduran from Emory, had told him, and Alexandra had confirmed it with stories from her travels through Calabria.

Santiago knew that over time, children tend to resemble their parents more and more. In his case, the opposite was happening. As he grew into adulthood, his features, the way he walked, and the way he pressed his lips were increasingly diverging from those that identified the older generation. His way of thinking, and probably his emotions as well, but this was much harder to notice.

Only at thirty-six, in Emory, Santiago felt what everyone feels at some point: the inevitable need to know more about his parents. But when he tried to dig into those mysterious lives that preceded him, with their particular stories similar to his own, with the same fantasies, hopes, and fears, with similar quirks, with comparable abilities and similar madness, he began to uncover a void opening up like an abyss beneath his feet. At some point, he started to feel what someone feels who has left on a trip and realizes they've forgotten something very important and doesn't know what it is; something that will prevent them from continuing the journey or destroy the home they've left behind; something that could put someone's life in danger, like forgetting a child playing at the edge of a pool or in a crowded market.

If there is an afterlife...

Buenos Aires, March 1962

At the Hotel Rivadavia, Don Jordi Caballero stayed until two in the morning staring out the window. That window, that air, those indecipherable noises were the same ones he saw every night in his room in Barcelona.

The same moon. The same sky. A similar nostalgia.

He didn't know if God was beyond that moon. The only thing he wanted, he thought, was for his mother to be with his father.

The only thing he could ask for. The only thing he wanted.

Miguel had told him

Sunday, December 16, 2010

At that exact moment, he thought of those elders he loved the most and looked at his face in the car's mirror: his face, his difficulty gaining weight, his still abundant hair contrasted with the most notable characteristics of his parents and grandparents. Considering the documents he had, like the birth certificate he had to obtain when applying for the Emory scholarship, it was an unfounded idea, but for a while the idea had grown without him being able to do anything about it, like the crying fits that used to overtake him as a child and enrage the Mother Superior: he was not the natural child of his parents and, as often happened in the past, his parents had chosen to hide the truth from him. That ancient custom made no sense, it was an absurd practice, he thought, since the only thing that can hurt an adopted child is the lie. On the other hand, if this story were true, then the birth certificate that had once innocently rested in his hands would have been falsified. Which increased the absurdity of the hypothesis but didn't decrease his anxiety; the monster in the hologram disappeared with the light but didn't disappear from the picture.

Was this the ghost that haunted him? he wondered as he looked out the window to breathe fresh air. After all, he could solve the mystery with a DNA test. Or was the beast something else, still struggling in his dreams—the naked woman, the runaway horse—that monster that from time to time tried to emerge from its slumber, stretching limbs trapped under the cold weight of the earth, turning into explosions of his character every time something frustrated him, shortly before sinking into a pathological sadness he confused with nostalgia for his country?

His mother insisted that all his fears and insecurities stemmed from the accident his father had suffered when he was nine. His father had been in a coma from March 23, 1980, until the fall of 1987. During that time, Santiago had gone from despair to near indifference. When his father woke up, Santiago had already been expelled from school for marijuana use, but he managed to pull himself together again and even stay on the right path despite his father's unexpected death three years later.

Someone (he didn't remember who, perhaps his grandmother) had said that Santiaguito's life had been a roller coaster. Santiago had heard it by chance, but not by chance had he never forgotten it.

Like a genetic illness (programmed from the day his parents' blind orgasm decided his fate in this world) that awakens at a certain moment in a man's adult life, Santiago sensed the imminence of collapse after a long slumber that had allowed him to become a successful professional and an almost happy man.

For a while, his phone conversations with his mother became subtle inquisitions. Nothing, not a hint, not a single hesitation from María justified his suspicions. But Santiago couldn't move past this stage until the final exams and his dissertation absorbed him relentlessly. Now, freed from those responsible distractions, the same ghost returned—like the hidden hologram image behind the bearded angel, like the beetle crawling down the rough trunk of a tree in search of the earth's entrails.

One afternoon during an argument with friends in San Telmo, Miguel had told him that he, Santiago, wasn't even his parents' child. What did that mean? Over time, he realized that even Miguel didn't know exactly what he had meant. But Santiago, for some reason, with the same persistence with which he had dismissed it, had never forgotten it, unlike so many other inconsequential days from his life.

The Spirits of the Well

Jacksonville, Friday, July 31, 2009

He practically had no memory of the first days after Fallujah. He had said "practically" succumbing to the tyranny of language that almost always thinks for us, Ernest Hatuey thought, because the truth was he had no recollection at all of the first seven or ten days after the explosion. Years later, Dr. Reinoso had told him that everything that had happened to him in those seven days was still somewhere in his memory, buried deep in a well, like a Mayan cenote, but it hadn't disappeared. In the same way, things that fall into a stagnant well of water can't be seen, but they remain there, in some corner of those dreaded depths.

Ernest Hatuey had been struck by the image Dr. Reinoso had used, because he had never spoken to him about any well before. He had the conviction and the purpose that his healing consisted of safeguarding a part of himself, of protecting at least the last corner of his individuality from the scrutiny of professionals who saw everything, knew everything, and ordered everything into formulas that later resulted in wars and perfect bombs and living dead like him. The latter was barely an intuition, an attitude of caution and resistance. A dark but very strong intuition. Maybe because he was still a human being or maybe because he hadn't yet recovered from post-traumatic stress, he thought.

The dream he had never told Dr. Reinoso, he had confessed it to two drunken strangers, two Hispanics he had met hours before playing soccer on Jacksonville Beach and with whom he had gone up to Joe's Crab Shack to have lobster with crab sauce. Apparently, neither of them gave the dream much importance. But he did.

It was a persistent dream about a water well in the backyard of his grandparents' old house in Puerto Rico. At least it had become persistent after his return to the United States in 2007. The dream, or its persistence, had managed to rescue that part of his existence that had disappeared for almost all of his youth, even though his grandparents had died shortly before he enlisted in the army soon after September 11, 2001. He had been pained by the news of his grandmother's death first, in August of that year, and his grandfather's a few months later, but not enough to cry like his mother, who took the first flight to San Juan the same night her mother died and didn't return until her father had fulfilled his absurd purpose of not delaying his reunion with his wife.

"Must be something bad," said the Mexican.

Who knows how that conversation at Joe's Crab Shack had started. Ernest Hatuey hated talking about personal matters, but the language of his grandparents, unknown to the couple of old fat men devouring a huge lobster at the table next to him, and his lack of familiarity with those two travelers who would soon disappear from his life, provoked that kind of miracle.

One of them, the Argentine, had studied cardiology in Georgia and seemed more interested in esotericism and communication with ghosts than in something as monotonous as "the dummy," as he referred to the heart in the deep South. Maybe that's where the topic of dreams had come from.

"What's so bad about dreaming of a water well?" the Argentine had asked with a different tone. The Argentine easily shifted from seriousness to sarcasm. Ernest Hatuey had thought this was a form of personal protection, like the impulses of violence he himself felt when he wanted to protect something he didn't quite know what it was and couldn't control himself.

"I don't know. Dreaming isn't bad in itself," answered the Mexican. "A well, neither. But if it's something that repeats, it can't be good. All doctors say that something repetitive is something bad, an obsession, a compulsion, who knows... Like someone always saying 'good morning' to every person, two or three times. Or like repeating the same tic every two minutes, something that serves no purpose or reason, something you do without any need."

Above the drunken Argentine's head, Ernest couldn't stop staring at the enormous shark's mouth hanging from the ceiling, which seemed to be pointing straight at the table where the three Spanish speakers were sitting. Behind and higher than the shark, almost touching the ceiling, floated a life-sized boat carrying a skull, and beyond that, small windows where the horizon of the sea was visible at two in the afternoon.

"Someone with a tic does it out of necessity too..."

"No, what necessity. I once knew a guy who played *tic-tac-toe* all the time with an imaginary opponent, right on his own chest, except when he found a wooden surface. Why wood?

Who knows, maybe it was that thing about knocking on wood for good luck. So if you do something repetitive, it's because you're crazy."

"Don't be dumb," the Argentine had said. "Doctors, instructors, pastors, senators, and all the jokers you can think of say what's convenient for them. If you were sick every time you repeated the same things, then having sex and working would be two chronic illnesses. At least more than half the jobs I know should be declared epidemics. Haven't you ever wondered why some poor devil has to interrupt his best dreams with a shitty alarm every morning, just to wake up and go do the same thing for a pittance that barely pays for his beer? At best, you see, because the rest you've got to leave to the doctors who'll someday poorly cure you from all that bad life you have to lead to save money for that day."

We had joy, we had fun, we had seasons in the Sun.

"And you're not a doctor?"

But the wine and the song,
like the seasons, all have gone...

"Yes, but that doesn't mean I can't tell the truth from time to time..."

The three laughed. Ernest pretended to laugh. He had noticed that the skull on the boat was tilted toward them, with a perpetual grin that wasn't tragic but also wasn't funny. He

71

perfectly remembered the secret hatred he had felt for Dr. Reinoso when he used the image of the well to refer to those seven days after Fallujah. At that moment, he wanted to grab the small statue of the African woman, half-naked and thin as a knife, and slit the doctor's throat down to his chest. Dr. Reinoso must have noticed. After all, he was a psychiatrist, Ernest thought, and he must have known something about all that. Ernest Hatuey was sure the doctor kept a gun in the right drawer of his desk because, during the tensest moments, he never strayed far from it. Ernest went there to confess, to say everything he knew and everything he didn't know, believing that Dr. Reinoso would know what to do with all that garbage fished out of the stagnant well water. He was willing to trust him with everything. Or rather, almost everything. There was something he had to keep for himself, if he still wanted to remain a man after healing, an individual with some freedom to decide something.

"Something, but not everything," Ernest thought, with infinite hatred. "Not everything," he repeated.

"'Not everything' what?" asked Santiago.

Goodbye my friend, it's hard to die,

"Nothing…" said Ernest, and took another long sip of beer. At Joe's, they had gotten dramatic, sweetly dramatic, Hatuey thought for a fraction of a second, while in the background he heard *Seasons In The Sun*.

when all the birds are singing in the sky,
Now that the spring is in the air,

pretty girls are everywhere
when you see them I'll be there.

MARKED DAY. The day Polzin left it all behind

Buenos Aires, February 15, 2001

On a Thursday of infernal heat, Miguel Polzin left Buenos Aires on American Airlines Flight 900 at 9:45 PM. That day began the long process of just over ten years that would lead him to discover himself one August evening in 2011, facing the Hudson, on a bench at the promenade of *South Cove Park*, although a predictable but not inevitable decision of his prevented any revelation from affecting his convictions and interests, which basically boiled down to professional success and money as the way to visualize it.

The decision to leave everything behind bore Miguel's signature. He didn't say goodbye to anyone. He didn't prepare anyone to replace him at the company. Perhaps the opposite. A few hours before taking a taxi to Ezeiza Airport, during a rare visit to La Boca, he calmly threw his two cell phones into the Riachuelo (for a long time he would remember the pleasure he felt in this irreversible act) and dropped his resignation letter into a red mailbox on Avenida Hipólito Yrigoyen, below the raised word "Marshall" and above some graffiti that read *She's already forgotten you, dumbass.*

Those who knew him understood that he had left for good. When a man like Miguel breaks something, his colleagues said, he breaks it without leaving room for repairs. "Any rectification or turning back offends them," said Sonia, the human relations expert, "and since they don't know how to express their emotions as well as they express their ideas, they need to break an ancient Chinese vase to make clear the high value of such an object."

They all imagined him somber and determined, though not enraged. Ernesto Iturria, the projects director, guessed that at some point Miguel must have considered the architects and the investors, must have imagined them running around desperately in the futile task of finding a replacement, and must have smiled. Paula, the boss's secretary, who had discreetly suffered his indifference, was more precise and convincing: the engineer had ruined his career and his life over an ungrateful love. She didn't mention a name, but in the office, they all knew who she was referring to.

Beatrice didn't find out until, alarmed by the impossibility of reaching him by phone, she went looking for him at his apartment on Corrientes Street and a neighbor gave her the news. The engineer had left on a trip with two suitcases that suggested he would be away for some time.

She called Santiago Zabala in Montevideo. Miguel wasn't there. Santiago tried to calm her down.

"Miguel's like that. On the least expected day, he'll say something that makes no sense, and then even he doesn't know why he said it," Santiago said, shortly before regretting it.

He immediately tried to fix things:

"But I know him well, and I know he's a good guy… and he's changing…"

"I don't want to think about what he was like before," she said, and hung up.

Beatrice wrote him only once, but he didn't respond.

Santiago imagined (or rather, remembered) Beatrice's anguished face. Her black eyes and her cheeks white as paper. He saw her again, hiding that silence that characterized her, and saw her beautiful face, like something out of a fairy tale, he once thought, sometimes hidden beneath a mass of reddish, abundant hair that time would dramatically thin, as a result of her nerves, as an old Palermo doctor had concluded, a doctor whom Beatrice's parents had lost faith in years before consulting him for the last time.

Then he remembered the time when, between beers in San Telmo and the tensions that the mutual admiration for Beatrice had caused between the two friends (tensions that were only expressed through the insurmountable differences they had about the virtues or curses of Carlos Menem's government), Miguel had accused him of being capricious and suggested that Santiago wasn't even an only child but adopted.

Miguel hadn't recanted after the anger had passed. He had recanted almost immediately, which revealed the seriousness of the accusation, Santiago would say much later.

Santiago returns to Montevideo to stay

Thursday, November 11, 2010

When he arrived at Carrasco Airport, Santiago couldn't even imagine that his academic exile in the United States had been, in fact, an indispensable part of answering the question Miguel had once posed. As always, one is impressed or moved by everything obvious, while what really matters, what can radically change a person's or a country's life, presents itself in seemingly insignificant, unnoticed details. Sometimes, Santiago had said, one thinks they're making frivolous, inconsequential decisions, when in reality they're deciding the difference between a long-awaited future and a hellish one.

Upon arriving, he was surprised by the new airport building. The country had forgotten the crisis and was trying to reflect its recent economic prosperity in a small but ultramodern airport, with nothing to envy from the giants of the United States and Japan.

As soon as he took a taxi and began driving rapidly into the chaos of Montevideo, he thought that maybe the country hadn't changed that much in recent years. The lines on the streets still appeared somewhat blurry or faded; drivers honked unnecessarily and cursed to themselves or shouted some obscenity out the window before speeding away. He had seen this same behavior in Naples and Rome and had commented on it to some friends at Emory, as if it were a *spectacle* more typical of Buenos Aires.

As the week went on, he confirmed the resilience of traditions. The differences between the rich and the poor remained distinctly Latin American, although, measured in monetary terms, the rich were now much richer and the poor slightly less poor. After a hundred years of conservative governments, a long democracy, and a few dictatorships, Uruguayans were living the debated utopia of a government formed by former guerrillas.

The victory of a Tupamaro president in the latest elections had left him indifferent. Since childhood, he had learned to disdain the danger of overly elaborate ideas about society and had discovered on his own that utopias are not killed;they commit suicide. And an electoral triumph was the worst thing that could happen to those madmen of the sixties who had stopped imagining a perfect world and begun trying to figure out how to avert catastrophe.

Interestingly, what had most embittered Santiago during his entire stay in the United States had been the news about the 2009 plebiscite, when the people ratified, with a majority of abstentions, the old law that protected and left unpunished the murderers of the past military dictatorship. He had secretly grown bitter because he never had the courage to admit to his friends and family that he retained an inexplicable hatred for those years of which he had almost no memory. So he didn't add anything more when Paulina wrote to him from Montevideo commenting on the news and congratulating the Uruguayan people for the wisdom of maintaining the peace and democracy that had been so hard to regain, despite the romantic stupidity of electing as president an old guerrilla who lived in a cave planting flowers.

He was fortunate to enter the American Hospital, though no one was surprised. The most important medical institutions (the British, the Italian, and the Spanish) had vied for him, but the American Hospital offered the best pay and certain conditions to carry out the projects he had in mind since long before earning his Ph.D. at Emory University. Paulina was hopeful about the reunion. That sort of academic exile had matured the young doctor, they said.

His mother, his grandmother had said, must also be proud for reasons she would never reveal. With her first husband, thirty-six years earlier, she had rescued Santiago from a dysfunctional family in northern Uruguay, marked by a rural culture of domestic violence and, likely, the abuse perpetrated by his father, which, it was said, had left Santiago with aggressive and wholly inappropriate behavior, along with a predisposition to asthma that he never fully recovered from. From the age of four, he had exhibited behavior that went beyond the typical tantrums children his age have. When he entered kindergarten, he still had violent outbursts, and in school, there was a period when he would touch his female classmates' buttocks, which caused an uproar among his teachers and led to his expulsion for misconduct. His adoptive parents transferred him to a Catholic boarding school, and the psychologist confirmed the suspicions about the bad habits of his biological parents, which was why they had lost custody. By the age of ten, he was a normal and hardworking child. He had miraculously overcome his asthma attacks, and from then on, he stood out for always being the best student in class and for never involving himself in politics, not even in the eighties, when Argentina regained democracy, nor in the nineties, when he entered university in Uruguay.

The Well of Baghdad

March 9, 2006

It might not be a coincidence, but a well was, precisely, the first of the memories he had managed to salvage from those days of blindness and deafness that followed Fallujah. Ernest Hatuey saw himself in the narrow depth of the well and tried to distinguish something of his facial features. He had always been struck by the well in the courtyard of his grandfather's house in Puerto Rico. A very old woman, whose name and face he could no longer remember, had told him that if he stared too long at the image he saw at the bottom, his soul would remain down there. Then he would have to wander many paths in this world until something reminded him where his soul had been left. Perhaps the old woman had said it to prevent Hatuey from leaning over the well where, according to Aunt Claudia, his grandfather's brother had died, maybe by accident.

But now Ernest had nothing to fear. "*The* army *will make me stronger, Dad,*" murmured the boy in the advertisement, sitting at a table with his worried father. "*That's the plan.*" Then his mother would come out of the kitchen and smile from the *background*. Now that Ernest was stronger, now that he was a soldier in the *Army*, the most powerful army in the world, he could lean over as long as he wanted to see if he could find his soul down there or, at least, some lost memory. "*…you'll have to wander many paths in this world until you discover where you left your soul*," the old woman from San Juan had said. What he saw most clearly was the soldier's helmet and the black glasses. For sparse moments, he could make out the blurred outline of his face. But there was *something*, perhaps in his nervous movements, that told him that it was him. As time passed, he realized that that something was his lost soul, trapped in the bowels of that cursed land, and that, perhaps, with luck, it could follow him around the world, peering out whenever he leaned over a water well.

Someone approached him and said:

"*Nothing there…*"

Ernest tried once more to recognize the face staring at him from the depths, but once again was interrupted.

"*Nothing there, sir…*"

In a fury, he struck the man's face with his forearm. The man flew back and crashed into the dusty ground. Ernest had lunged to hit him with the carbine, but a woman stood in his way, screaming. The woman threw herself over the boy, who couldn't have been more than thirteen years old, and that's why he had dared to get so close to tell him that there was nothing hidden there.

Ernest stopped. He saw the boy's nose bleeding profusely and walked away.

Polzin Returns in Secret to Buenos Aires

Buenos Aires, January 3, 2011

Almost ten years later, Miguel returned in secret and wandered the streets he had frequented in happier days, as he had tried to say to himself in a failed act of irony one afternoon, walking along Santa Fe Avenue toward Darregueira. At the book and magazine stands, he caught that scent that must have come from the paper in fresh ink and let himself be carried away by the sentimentality that had taken him so much effort to overcome. He thought about a book by Ernesto Sábato that he had bought for her on a sunny afternoon like this one, which she had treasured like a sacred book. Then, he smelled her sex and her demands to talk. He didn't know about what, but she always needed to talk.

One morning, he saw the open windows on the fifth floor facing Las Heras Park, the place he had rented with Beatrice for a year. "The best year of my life," he remembered admitting once. And Beatrice, with her lips slightly parted in a smile, her eyes closed, and her breasts relaxed, had asked him why he said "the best year" and not "the happiest year." Miguel didn't understand. Apparently, neither did Beatrice. He couldn't explain the difference. So, why make the distinction?

Strangely, he remembered the scent of the perfume she wore but not its name or the apartment number. Strangely, because a man like Miguel always remembers numbers better, except for anniversaries. Scents and anniversaries are women's things.

By then, Beatrice had become an obsession. He thought about her whenever he wasn't with her.

In the morning, he visited several perfume shops in the *mall* at Alto Palermo. In one of them, he found Beatrice's perfume. *Opium* by Yves Saint Laurent. He had finally remembered the brand. He bought a bottle and tucked it into one of the pockets of his suitcase.

In the afternoon, he went to Palermo. He had gotten Beatrice's address thanks to the indiscretion of an old acquaintance who had worked as the secretary at the law firm where Beatrice had been employed until 2006.

She hadn't moved. He saw her step out of a silver Peugeot with a blond-haired child who was demanding something. He estimated the child to be about four or five years old. The boy had resisted walking, and she had stopped to say something to him without letting go of his hand. She hadn't gained weight, but he couldn't quite see the passage of time on her face. The boy had furrowed his brow with contained anger but soon decided to keep walking.

"At home, you have another just like it," she had said.

"It's not the same," the boy had replied, still resisting walking.

Miguel didn't reveal himself. He only tried to recall those insignificant words exchanged between the boy and his mother. Beatrice still balanced gracefully on her high heels, but she had cut her hair. Her voice was the same, though more impatient now. When they were lovers and the future hadn't yet begun, she used to speak very softly, very gently, like her moist lips and her tiny feet.

The city was different (or so Santiago thought)

Montevideo, January 2011

As with everyone, the journey toward self-discovery was confusing and filled with false leads: some events were celebrated or remembered by family and friends as if they were significant (a graduation, a wedding, the return home), while other events, which might have shaped the destiny of many people, appeared as trivial circumstances or had simply been forgotten, whether out of ignorance or convenience.

As if it were the rediscovery of a long-yearned-for terrain finally reclaimed, as if he suspected that not everything was as it should be, Santiago spent Saturdays exploring the Costa de Oro area and Sundays taking shorter walks through different neighborhoods of Montevideo. At first, some afternoons of anonymous strolls through familiar streets had left him with that sense of freedom one feels when breathing fresh air, when winter gives way to spring or summer yields to autumn's first cool breezes. That feeling of freedom before the unreality of the new or a foreign past, before being caught up in routine or the obligations of the present.

Less known, except through police reports, the outskirts and older parts of the city center remained as part of the collective unconscious, repressed, Santiago thought, while the luxurious and pristine apartments along the coast presented the city's best face to the world and its own residents.

Though everyone claimed otherwise, the streets felt emptier to him after six years. "It's because your eyes got used to the bustle of the Americans," someone told him at the party. But no. Americans don't know what it means to walk through a city unless it's Manhattan or San Francisco. It wasn't that. It was something else. Or was it exactly that—the solitude of private space that had finally reached the third world?

The streets were emptier, especially at night. "Well, if that's the case, good. Fewer opportunities for criminals..." someone else replied at the same Arbizas' party, probably the woman with the feathered hat who took every opportunity to complain about the rabble that had taken over governments across the continent, while repeating almost like a tic, "I'm very democratic *but*..." which was like saying, "I'm not racist *but*..." As Lorenzo, an Argentine student of Italian linguistics at Emory, had said one night over beers, everything before the *but* is just lip service. "Vulgar," his wife had complained, as if to make it clear they'd never used that sexual resource. "Vulgar, yes," Lorenzo had grumbled, "every now and then people stop using inappropriate words. Nowadays, no one says *filthy negro*, or *Negro stuff*, they don't even say *Negro*, which is a total victory for Yankee moralizing in our southern countries, where being called *Negro* could be a sign of friendship. Still, now no one says *Negro* in the Río de la Plata. Not because there are fewer racists, but because racists have become more sophisticated," Lorenzo had said.

Crime had increased anyway, Santiago thought, despite the country's recent economic prosperity and the fewer people on the streets. There was something more in those empty streets—something more, or rather, something less, that he saw in the faces of those women and girls leaving the shops of a *mall* in Atlanta, laden with bags, their gazes absent, offended because Santiago had watched them invading their famous "personal space" or checking messages on their phones while dodging other human bodies fresh from a Chinese massage session. It was that, that "something less" that was everywhere, among the rich and among the poor, almost equally.

There were no more book browsers in the bookstores on 18 de Julio at eleven at night, buyers who occasionally shared an interest in a new dress and the moon between the buildings or the branches of a tree. Cheesy, maybe, but more human than this... The plazas too seemed to have suffered a devastating plague.

That was it. At that hour, everyone must have been stuck in their virtual bubbles, exposing themselves as righteous exhibitionists and spying on others' egos, repeating like a blocked computer always the same, always the same, always the same, always the same, always the same, always the same, always the same, same, same, same, same, same, same, same, same, same, same, sa-sa- sa-sa- sa-sa- sa-sa- sa-sa- a- a- a- a- a- a-

Maybe that was it. Or it was him who hadn't quite fit into this world that was now everywhere, like a plague, like one of those García Márquez stories where the inhabitants of a town are infected with insomnia. Like masturbatory zombies who amuse themselves and live consuming human flesh. Like him too to some extent when he returned from his walks in public solitude to the private solitude of his apartment on Avenida Brasil, and the first thing he did was turn on the computer and Facebook, like an alcoholic who hates alcohol but can't stop consuming it. Indirect communication is more comfortable than face-to-face communication, he thought, because it's less profound. In face-to-face communication, there's more commitment; you can't press a button and make the other person disappear when you no longer want to talk to them. In virtual communication, assuming there is communication, the other is another product of consumption: when I no longer want to talk to him or her, I press *disconnect* and the other disappears. It's not even a crime because the disappeared one was never really alive. It's the magic button. We can disconnect from everything, from everything except that world of connections between zombies.

Miguel's father was waiting for him

Buenos Aires, January 4, 2011

When Miguel visited his father in Once the following Tuesday at six in the evening, neither of them brought up the topic of Beatrice. Or almost.

They did talk about Santiago and poor Alejandro. Why poor?, Miguel had asked. The old man didn't know exactly. Maybe because he had been the least favored by luck among the three friends. Did he still remember his friends?, Miguel had asked. Of course, the old man was always keeping an eye on his son's friendships. Miguel didn't know that, he had never stopped to think about those things, but a father never sleeps soundly if he doesn't know something about his son's friends, said the old man, adjusting the mate straw, as if searching there for the words he was missing.

"You should get yourself a woman," said the old man, "get married, have kids. Are the Yankee girls very ugly?"

"Dad…"

"They say they're bland, but not ugly. From what you see in the movies, they're not ugly. They must be those damn bitches, but that's something you can live with. It doesn't fix itself, but you can live with it."

"What's with all this, Dad?"

"I'm just thinking you should settle down already, get married. Only then would you have an idea of what I'm talking about. You're missing out on a whole part of life…"

"Don't think I'm going to do all that just to understand you," said Miguel, smiling as he finished the mate his father had offered him.

"Didn't you know?"

"What?"

"About Santiago."

"No."

Well, the old man knew that Santiago had returned from the United States. He had earned a doctorate (yes, he already knew that, Santiago had written to him once by email) and as soon as he had settled in Montevideo, he had called him.

"Seriously?"

"Yes. He remembered this old man, that rascal. He called me one day while I was making dinner. I stopped peeling a couple of garlic cloves and said, 'Holy shit, you remembered Miguel's old man!' He must have known it would make me happy. After all, a doctor must know something about other people's pain… So it gave me a tremendous joy when he showed me he still remembered this old man, that damn sly fox…"

The guy, Santiago, was still that same noble skinny kid, the father had said. Well, he didn't know if he was still skinny, but he sounded like the same noble skinny kid he always was.

Miguel had twisted his mouth skeptically.

"I'll have to call him at some point," he said.

"And poor Beatrice… she got married, did you know?" said the old man.

"Why poor?"

"I don't know, son. It's just that you left like that, without saying anything…"

When the old man was about to ask him the reasons for his disappearance, Miguel redirected the conversation. He told him he had been in Moscow.

"In Moscow?"

"Yes."

"In Moscow…" repeated the old man, raising his eyebrows, which by then had grown considerably and now covered his eyes.

Over the years, his face had faded. The lines that once defined it had become blurry, imprecise, almost expressionless. The old man (Miguel thought in a split second, noticing the

recent absence of a premolar in his jaw) was increasingly incapable of crying or laughing. Had age wiped out entire months
and years, joys and sorrows, deaths, marriages, and births that
no one, not even he, would ever recognize again? He would
never know. Of that he was sure.

Those traits that had set them apart so distinctly, father from
son, had faded. Over the years, his father had come to resemble
his grandfather more, and Miguel himself had grown more like
his father.

"Yes, in Russia..." Miguel said, noticing the blank expression in his father's eyes. It was partly due to cataracts, but at his
age, eye surgery probably wasn't advisable. In that moment, Miguel realized he couldn't know what was really going on behind
that apparent indifference. His father's eyes had grown smaller,
and his nose bigger. The wrinkled forehead reminded him that
soon (a year? three years?), he would stand before that same face
he loved so much, lifeless, bidding farewell in a funeral home,
remembering their modest strolls through Colonia del Sacra-
mento, smiling behind a cup of chocolate ice cream during
summers free of school and college.

But he was still there, though threatened by a near future.
So Miguel reached out and brushed his hand over his father's
forehead, as if smoothing the hair falling over his eyes.

"You're holding up well, huh," Miguel said.

"I do what I can."

They had always shared certain peculiarities, family traits.
His father struggled just as much as he did when it came to
broaching certain topics. It was easier for them to discuss

politics or soccer than to talk about his brothers, whom he hadn't visited since 1976, or the cataracts that had dulled his vision. Maybe that's why he had specialized in more complex and entirely impersonal debates.

"When did you go?" he finally asked.

"About a year ago, more or less."

"You didn't tell me," his father said.

The comment was unnecessary. Like everything else, Miguel thought.

"I brought you a cap that belonged to a soldier from World War II. I bought it at a street market, though it's probably fake, like everything in Russia these days. Even capitalism there is counterfeit. Their practices for getting rich resemble Sicily more than Wall Street."

The old man shook his head. He was about to ask about the difference between Sicily and Wall Street but immediately realized it was pointless. They'd end up in another argument.

"That's nice. But you should've written to me sooner," he said. "I know places I would've liked you to visit, since I never could."

Another unnecessary remark. The old man knew Miguel wasn't one to share or announce his plans.

"What did you think of it?"

"Nothing. I didn't feel anything. To me, they were like strangers."

The faces and a few names had reminded him of his uncles, Anastasia's daughters, Grandfather Mikhail. Noses made for the cold, drooping eyelids, but above all the way they looked, a mix of sadness and joy, as if they had just woken from a nap they never actually took.

"Of course," his father remarked. "We stopped belonging to that culture a long time ago. We're strangers. We're gauchos who drink mate in a city where trees are scarce and snow never bothers us. No one would ever know your grandparents were Russian if it weren't for the surname. You've never had anything to do with Russians. You didn't even learn a single word in Russian."

"I learned a few last year. Just enough to get by."

"Like any tourist."

"Yeah. You didn't learn Russian either."

"A few inevitable words. Some very amusing insults. You already know why."

He had told him many times, as many as necessary to suspect that it wasn't true or perhaps only a minor truth that served to hide something more serious. His grandfather had made sure his children were Argentine or anything else—but not Russian. He never spoke to them in that language. For his wife, Grandma Clara, and for his children, Cyrillic was just an incomprehensible web of symbols. Incomprehensible and useless.

"*Inconvenient*. That's the word," corrected Miguel.

"Yes, yes, of course. It was also inconvenient…"

Still, his grandfather could never speak Spanish without a foreign accent. And he couldn't help getting angry when the neighborhood kids yelled "Russian" at him. "How old are you, kid?" Grandfather Mikhail would ask. "Eight," the boy would answer. "Then I'm more Argentine than you. I've been living in this country for ten years."

His father's smile at the end of the anecdote was always the same too.

DAY MARKED. Lucía, Lucía

Librería i Margall, summer of 2011

One hot morning (he never knew exactly if it was Sunday the 9th or the 16th of January), he met Lucía, at first just a girl who worked at her father's book stall at the Tristán Narvaja fair. As was customary, after showing interest in an original edition of *Hallucinations et Délire* by Henri Ey, the young woman had given him the family business card. That coincidence, which was not really one, that discovery, like everything capable of changing a person's life, was experienced by Santiago with the insignificance of the other things that were part of his new routine.

The established shop was located near Arenal Grande Street, in an early 20th-century house. It was probably the result of merging two neighboring houses, which would explain the peculiar labyrinth, the structure, and the illogical layout of the spaces. The disorder of old books and the lack of light in some rooms suggested a world that was about to disappear or had managed to survive, moving from the center of a great civilization to the darkest and quietest margins, dragging along decades and centuries of books with yellowing pages, often abused by the notes of the most passionate readers, as if they were the remains of the tombs of powerful pharaohs that might never be discovered. Some rooms had skylights with dirty stained glass. Thanks to the transparency that those traditional glass pyramids, characteristic of the old modernity of Montevideo's roofs, had lost, the old books had been protected from the sun for decades without preventing generations of *nerds* and young romantics from the habit of stealing hours of reading hidden among the shelves, until they were finally seduced by one or two volumes and gave in to the temptation of trading a fantastic story for the possibility of having dinner for the rest of the week. The carelessness of the readers, the lack of staff at the bookstore, or simply the disinterest in order had accumulated an irreversible chaos (like the entropy of the Universe, he thought), making it nearly impossible at that point to find a title without relying on chance.

His eyes and nose were accustomed to the perfection of North American university libraries, so he could now rediscover that world in a way he wouldn't have been able to before exile. That reality of Lucía was his unreality, a sort of journey to the past, to a dreamlike past he had never lived before and now experienced as a mysterious memory, like a persistent *déjà vu*.

At the *i Margall* bookstore, there must have been, according to a comparative estimate with the *main library* at Emory, about a hundred thousand books, including magazines, a vinyl record section, and another of documents consisting of several shelves of personal letters and postcards from people who, evidently, were no longer around to defend themselves from that invasion of privacy, now turned into archaeological artifacts and stripped of any individual rights.

Santiago went several times and several times explored books at random, experiencing that sensation of being in a labyrinth where countless treasures were hidden, protected from any ruthless and immediate electronic search engine. Most of those books had been forever closed to the eyes of any reader. In one corner, tightly packed and with its spine almost illegible, was *La nausée*, the real one, in a second edition by Gallimard, riddled with marginal notes, underlinings by people who by then would surely be dead, people so distant who were interested in such things, Santiago thought with almost a sense of nostalgia, as if suddenly the last decade, filled with emails and web pages, had turned into fifty, into a hundred years of arrogance.

At the *i Margall* bookstore, he bought dozens of books, as if he were saving them from a collapse, a fire, a flood, or some other inevitable catastrophe that was bound to afflict an exceptional world that refused to disappear.

One afternoon, the inevitable happened. While she was working the register near the entrance, Lucía challenged him to sleep with her without touching her. Santiago blinked. Lucía had noticed the way he looked at her, and without any preamble, she told him he wasn't the first to try to seduce her between the book on *Le Cordon Bleu* and the *Hogar* magazines.

"I'm not trying to seduce you," Santiago said. "I was just admiring you."

"For a woman, it's the same thing," she replied, putting two items into a plastic bag.

For a moment, Santiago thought he was searching for new problems for his new life. That's what happens when you don't have real problems; you invent them, he thought, walking to his car. He still retained that problem-seeking instinct that had marked his childhood, he thought once again, when in the afternoon he saw Paulina approaching down the street by the hospital.

The Pig of Baghdad

April 2006

They had stopped in front of an isolated house on the outskirts of the capital. Six soldiers got out to inspect, and he stayed behind covering the side facing the Tigris.

He heard the familiar sequence: two knocks on the door, the creak of an old door, a murmur, the sound of boots fading inside.

Not far from there, a bend in the river formed a kind of dark lagoon. On one edge, with its legs half-buried in the mud, a wild boar was contemplating its own reflection. He thought of all the animals that, for thousands, millions of years, had leaned over their own images throughout their lives to recover the spirit of each one who, during the days of intense heat, fled to the cool depths of the earth and only returned to their bodies after quenching their thirst at the dangerous mirrors of water.

But the boar didn't drink from that water. It only seemed to be watching something moving somewhere beneath the surface.

Ernest Hatuey approached, and the boar remained motionless. So he had to throw a stone at it, which hit the beast square on the forehead, causing it to let out a sharp cry and run off.

The lie or the mysteries of truth, Santiago told himself

Montevideo, March 2011

He thought about Lucía, about Paulina. From her days in the convent school, she had learned not to cheat on exams and refused to collaborate with her classmates who asked for her help to break these early rules of high school. Some didn't even cheat out of necessity but to defy the teachers or simply to prove themselves or show off to others, like someone taking a risky extreme turn in a gymnastic jump or rounding a curve at an unsafe speed. Once, he himself had discovered how to write formulas with an invisible acid and how to make them visible later in the exam by passing a marker filled with a chemical reagent over them. His classmates used his invention in a physics exam to avoid memorizing all those formulas by Newton, Ohm, Biot-Savart, and Ampère. All except Santiago, who almost reported the fraud to the principal, if it hadn't been for Tony, his best friend at the time, who convinced him to forget about it with the dubious argument that betraying friendship was worse than the abstract, useless, and servile fidelity to the truth. He never forgot it.

Now Santiago acted like a child, like that child who in the early years of boarding school amused himself by lying to the nuns or tearing up notebooks and curtains when one of them caught him. And like someone slowly slipping into sleep, or into the addiction of alcohol or a powerful drug, he thought he had everything under control: all he had to do was resolve to end it, to stop going to the *i Margall* bookstore and actually do it. So he persisted in stretching the lie that led him from Paulina to Lucía and from Lucía to Paulina, not out of necessity, he thought, but as a dark challenge, like that of his high school classmates who cheated as if it were a game of Russian roulette.

But Lucía began to uncover it through sheer intuition. At first, she didn't care. She didn't care about fidelity, she once told Inés at a bar on 18 and Minas, but she couldn't stand lies. She had her own story, too. It didn't weigh on her"it was simply her story, she said, not his.

"If you don't want to tell it, it can't be anything pleasant," Santiago probed once in the same bar, after they ran into each other by chance in Plaza de Los 33.

"Don't come at me with bourgeois morality," Lucía shot back. She had short nails but a touch of lipstick on her lips.

"I get it, the boy wore a beret with a little star and kept the sparse beard boys have at that age."

"You men with macho complexes think women only acquire ideas through their uterus, don't you?"

Santiago fell into silence that he hoped came off as respectful. But then he continued in the same tone as Lucía, without the joking manner that usually shielded him from irreversible judgments.

"Am I right, yes or no?"

"Let me tell you, my dear, with me you're wasting your time. I'm not a virgin, not in body nor in soul, and I don't want you confusing me with some delicate little doll of that kind. If I don't want to talk about how I started having sex, it's simply because I don't want to. I reserve that right, and I don't overthink it. The ones who obsess over their secrets are the ones who are really sick. That's why they go to psychologists."

"Have you never been to one?"

"Yes, when I was a kid. That's why I hate them."

"Doctors too?"

"No. I have more faith in doctors. Once in a while, they'll kill you without you even noticing, because they do it with style, but at least doctors are like engineers." They're not scientists, but they're not exorcists either. My doctor doesn't demand that I have faith in him to cure me. What's more, when a psychologist proves their professional incompetence, the only thing they can think of is to resort to dogma and blame the patient for their lack of faith, which they elegantly call resistance or denial. Besides, why would I lie to you? I'm happy with all my secrets. In fact, I love my secrets. The person who wouldn't like them at all is my future husband—assuming I ever end up with one and that, to make matters worse, he's some well-to-do gentleman from Pocitos or one of those insufferable snobs from

Carrasco who talk like they have a hot potato in their mouth, because dressing expensively isn't enough to mark their distance from others, as if the little sing-song in their speech couldn't be put on and taken off like a blouse or a tie. They don't understand that a genius can pretend to be an idiot, but an idiot can't pretend to be a genius. Some idiots, at least, have the sense to pretend to be other idiots, which is always within their capabilities…

"Well, the truth is, you're narrowing your options. There probably aren't many candidates out there who'd be willing to accept that, whether they're bourgeois or revolutionaries."

"Candidates… Marriage isn't an obligation, either. I still think I'll be a happy single mother. I'll get some sperm from a hospital, or something like that."

"Isn't it easier to just ask a boyfriend for the favor?"

"Come on, Santi," she laughed, calling him that without permission. "I'm surprised to hear you say that, being a nurse. Anonymous donation is always better."

"Well, with anonymous genes, you never know what kind of kid you're going to end up with."

"Are you telling me a woman knows what kind of crazy old man she's getting into bed with? At least with an anonymous donation, you avoid all that nonsense of regretful fathers showing up when the kid's already grown and educated… It's always better not to know when you really don't want to know. Now, when you want to know but don't dare to look, that's a whole different thing. Then you've got a problem."

Santiago felt overwhelmed; he had never been good at argu-ing, which is why he had dedicated himself to medicine. Lucía, on the other hand, was the living product of her father's bookstore, especially the section on French existentialists, mixed, like the others, with works by Charles Bukowski, Ernest Hemingway, and issues of *Gente*.

"Someone has to tell you. You're not special. At least not to me. You're someone pretending to be a poor guy, a humble nurse, while secretly believing you're not." What interests you is seducing me and ending up taking me to bed shortly after telling me you don't want to take me to bed. It's a trophy that men need to win from time to time. They're not interested in the trophy; it's not love or desire for a woman but self-love. Look, I'm not for sale, nor do I play hard to get. I'm hard – hard to be used as a sexual object while believing in romantic love, but I wouldn't be surprised if we end up in bed one of these days. That won't prove I'm easy but that you're just like all the others, even if you pretend to be different.

Lucía was something different, Santiago thought. The more she spoke, the more he wanted to kiss her lips.

"Before, everything was standard," Lucía had said, though he couldn't remember if it was that same time they were at the bar. "Cars, clothes, the news with which the newspapers and television bombarded us. The individual was part of the mass, they didn't exist. Now it seems the only thing that exists is the individual. *Me* on Facebook, *me* in the way I read the news. Companies of all kinds know our habits and interests based on what we usually do, read, and search for online, in eBooks. So newspapers, books, search engines, and everything around us show us the world as we're supposedly interested in it, as we supposedly are. What you read and consume seems different from what I read when I open a digital page, when I open a digital book. Now everything is personalized. The truth is, I don't want a world customized to my measure, which I doubt is really my measure. I'd like a world that helps me be free, that is, a world free of myself to be explored as it is. A world that challenges me and manages to give me something I don't have.

Lucía was as beautiful as an angel. She was full of secrets, but none of them were like the hologram monster. Lucía could handle any ghost. Lucía owned her own monsters. Lucía, Lucía…

MARKED DAY. Grandfather Polzin's letters

Buenos Aires, January 2011

Miguel's grandfather couldn't help getting angry in Russian either. He cursed in Russian, insulted in Russian. Miguel would never know if he also reserved his true tongue for when he made love or for asking for help or forgiveness when he froze to death in his car one night, stranded on the side of Route 51 on his way to the ranch in Bahía Blanca. In the back seat, they found a coat that could have saved him, but inexplicably, the old man hadn't used it.

Again, Miguel reproached his father for the grandfather not having had the intelligence or the slightest interest in leaving him the greatest asset he could have now, that language so few speak in Argentina. Since living in the United States, he had understood the economic importance of culture and, above all, of a language like Russian. This inexplicable ignorance had kept him below other bilingual employees at the company who were often sent abroad.

"It was different before," the old man said. "We were poor workers in a time when not knowing a language like Russian was more important than speaking it. The old man didn't want his children to be persecuted or discriminated against for it."

This explanation had never convinced him. Now he simply didn't even consider it a good excuse. Another truth that crumbled on its own, like the Berlin Wall, without need and without the desire to blow on it a little to see if it held. He remembered his childhood, always admiring everything Grandfather Mijail represented, like an impeccable patriarch. A practical man, more intelligent than reasonable, capable of solving everyone else's problems and with a clear idea of how to save Argentina from the progressive decline that had set in after the war.

But over time, Grandfather Mijail had shrunk. While listening to his father repeat the same explanations, the grandfather had already been reduced to the handful of dust that was his body in an urn at Chacarita Cemetery.

Grandfather had denied him the best inheritance he could have left him: a piece of the heart of Russia. The reason why his visit to Russia was like that of any stupid tourist, looking for photographs on a cardboard stage. His insensitivity to the language, the food, and the history of Russia had turned into resentment against the grandfather.

Like every brilliant grandfather, Grandfather Mijail had made a fortune from nothing and had died rather poor and in debt, rummaging through the ruins of a glorious past that barely survived by the force of anecdotes. The grandfather had left them nothing, aside from a handful of memories that his father kept in the safe. A useless but curious watch, coins with promises of unfulfilled value, keys, keychains, pieces of some unrecognizable artifact. And a cardboard box with letters written in Russian.

Miguel had never forgotten those letters but had also never taken an interest in them. That day, he realized he had almost lost the only chance to uncover his grandfather's secrets. The most important things, Santiago used to say in school, are almost always irreversible and are decided in an instant right before our eyes, without us even noticing them. Almost always, it's our own fault, like when we invest everything in stocks that are on the rise but on the verge of collapsing. Even when we read the cause of the future collapse in the headline of the *Wall Street Journal*—China's inflation, a French CEO caught in the act attempting rape—we fail to recognize them as a future cause, and sometimes we even take joy in someone else's misfortune, unaware it's our own ruin, thought Miguel.

Wasting no time, he asked his father for the letters, promising to return them soon. His father handed them over, telling him they were his, with the only condition that he take care of them as he had done for fifty years.

Lucía had been born in the wrong time, he thought

Montevideo, March 15, 2011

The Monday after meeting Lucía at the bar on 18 and Misiones, he parked his car in the clinic's garage and headed to his office. As he pressed the metallic button with the orange light of the elevator, he remembered that the last time he had been there exactly at 7:55 in the morning. As the shiny stainless-steel door opened, he glanced at his watch: 7:52. He wondered if over the days and years he would perfect that punctuality or, on the contrary, at some point in his life and career, he would enter a process of disarray. Disarray, for lack of a better word.

Once in his office, he looked down through the window. Several people were walking hurriedly, dodging others, with their right hands pressed to their ears.

Then he remembered, albeit vaguely, Lucía's words at the bar on 18 de Julio. He wasn't entirely sure what she had said, but looking at the other young people passing by, Lucía had quipped about humanity, with that authority, he thought, that book-maniacs or prophets who are always warning humanity of some catastrophe possess. But then it struck him that she might have had a point, though he couldn't quite recall it.

"When I see all those people walking with wires in their ears," Lucía had said, "holding a tiny device in their hands that contains their existence, I think about the surprise humanity will get when it realizes the error it's living in, more alienated than ever, believing itself at the peak of progress like never before. They are bodies walking next to each other, avoiding and protecting themselves from each other with their phones, which they pull out whenever they sense someone is watching them or might ask them a question. And then I look back at all those people, mostly young and proud of their lives (proud because they have no clue about other ways of living), and a shiver runs through my body. It's the realization of an irrefutable possibility: perhaps humanity will never realize its mistake and will forever perpetuate that arrogant illusion of being at the pinnacle of history, deepening more and more, every year, every century, its condition as a vegetative species."

He glanced at his agenda and read: *Laprida*.

MARKED DAY. The major seemed healthy

Montevideo, March 15, 2011

For that Monday, they had referred to his office a 69-year-old patient with the last name Almeida and Laprida. That was one of those moments in life, one of those decisive instants Santiago often spoke about. Much later, he would keep this page from the cheap *Hallucinations et Délire* by Henri Ey, this page from the *made in China* calendar that had innocently or not been waiting on his desk that day. Early in the morning, Luisita, the cleaner, had entered his office and had wiped a cloth under the calendar. She had picked it up with one hand, and neither she nor he had the slightest suspicion that perhaps that had been *a marked day*.

The man entered with a freshly restored smile and walked up to shake his hand with a familiarity that surprised him.

"Don't you remember me?" asked the new patient.

"To be honest…" Santiago tried to recall.

"We met at the welcome party, in El Congo."

"Yes, the colonel…"

"Laprida. And to be honest with you (what need would I have to lie at my age?), I'm not a colonel, I never made it that far nor could I have. But I did make it to major. The thing is, people call *colonel* any distinguished soldier, you see? And since it doesn't bother me, I let it…"

"Of course, Colonel Laprida," Santiago confirmed, reading the header of the medical report while pretending to remember. "Please excuse my poor memory for faces. My friends from university get furious when I walk past one of them and don't recognize them. I think I've lost more than one friendship over that flaw."

"That's serious."

"A chronic distraction and perhaps some natural incapacity, I suppose."

"The second reason is enough," said the major. "But don't worry. I've also lost a few friends, though I'm very good with faces. Or rather, I used to be. Over the years and without practice, memory declines. Luckily."

"You have a sense of humor."

"I'm serious. I was an expert marksman and had a great ability to remember the names and aliases of my soldiers. What use are those skills to me now? If someone tries to rob me, I hand over the money. A year ago, I was walking peacefully along Constituyente when a kid who couldn't have been fifteen showed me a knife and took the few pesos I had on me. I'm not going to walk around with a gun on my belt, and even if I had one, I might shoot and complicate my life even more. So, what's the point of being an expert marksman, other than bragging a bit at the shooting range where anyone can do more or less the same? And that memory for names? I can't stand crowded places anymore. Sometimes I go to the gun club because there are just a few of us crazy cats, but I can't stand environments where large gatherings happen, like stadiums, assemblies, carnivals, you can imagine. I immediately feel like I'm running out of air. Ten people is already a crowd for me these days. Knowing multiplication tables or Asian capitals has no value anymore. It's all here, in a little gadget in your pocket. Besides, having an elephant's memory is not only useless but also unhealthy. You, being a doctor, must know this better than I do, though my daughter, who is almost a doctor, doesn't agree when I tell her that the insane laugh like crazy because they don't remember anything. The less they remember, the more they laugh. It's even enviable to see them so happy. Imagine if you remembered all the garbage you've come across in your life. What would you be, doctor? Memory would be a garbage dump. You have to clean it out from time to time; you have to forget. They say there are tribes in Africa that practice the delicate art of forgetting as a form of healing. From a young age, we're taught to remember, to have a good memory, but no one has ever taught us how to forget. There's a subject called History, but none called Amnesia, which would be the anesthesia or the relief of the soul."

"Originally, anesthesia was used as entertainment. Anesthesia caused laughter, and both alleviated pain."

"See? That's what I mean. It seems we always have to resort to chemicals to learn how to live, because our culture teaches us to die, to drown in a sea of useless memories. We're more backward than the Africans. No family, no school teaches how to forget, and that's why no one knows how to do it. We don't know, and we don't have the skills. People kill themselves because they can't bear a memory, and they laugh when they've dissolved their sorrows in alcohol, because they don't know any other way. We always say, 'remember this or that,' and we know how to make the attempt, at least. But if they tell us, 'forget about that,' we all know it's just a formality. 'Forget about that' doesn't mean you're actually going to forget but that you're going to try not to think about it so much or, at least, that you won't talk about it as much. And that's how you get sick, not because you've forgotten something but because you remember sad things. That's why there's so much cancer these days. Don't you think, doctor, that there are more diseases now than before?"

"In some areas. There's also more people now than before," said Santiago, discreetly glancing at the wall clock.

"I stay young in spirit, always optimistic, thanks to my memory, which, if it's not bad, is at least very selective."

"What should I call you, then?"

"For you, Xico. Some neighbors call me Colonel, but don Xico for my closest friends. Consider me one of them. I knew your father."

The name of the son

St. Augustine, Monday, May 10, 2010

Ernest separated from his wife in April 2009. He realized he had lost the Daytona Beach house when the divorce proceedings were in their final stages. He didn't refuse the last signature, which reminded him of the one he had, for some unknown reason, stamped in the guestbook at his father's funeral over ten years earlier. Just his name, written with some difficulty, with the slowness of a kindergartener, which the lawyer observed with the condescension a Princeton professor might show when watching an illiterate laborer trying to explain the theory of relativity. In the first case, the confusion was understandable: his father had taught him the first six letters of his life, *Hatuey*. When Ernest wrote them with such difficulty, he felt immensely happy because his father, almost always absent due to his construction work, would take his tiny hand to help him trace all the letters of the same size. In the second case, at that enormous mahogany and walnut desk in the lawyer's office, he didn't know why that signature had come out so childish, or why that memory of his eighteen years, when he lost his father, had resurfaced. The lawyer must have thought, he imagined, that this strong man with such a heavy hand who could barely write his name was the embodiment of the defeat of machismo before the law of a civilized society.

He didn't refuse; rather, it was a kind of self-immolation, or worse, something far less heroic: a simple act of self-destruction, a stupid suicide, like any other. The outcome of the division was unfair. There wasn't even a division, he said as he left the lawyer's office, but at least there were no children to fight over or debts to anchor him to that life of mistakes.

The dispossession was unfair because, even though an outburst of domestic violence, however isolated, is severely punished by the laws of this country, it was also true that the Daytona house had been bought with his Iraq salary, a salary that both his wife and he himself knew they could hardly earn again for the rest of their lives.

In the car, he rummaged through the glove compartment for a new CD. Or rather, an old CD. He picked one at random, or perhaps he secretly knew what he was putting on.

> *...Now Paul is a real estate novelist*
> *who never had time for a wife*
> *and he's talkin' with Davy,*
> *who's still in the Navy*
> *and probably will be for life...*

The Spanish version wasn't the same. "Play it again, old loser, you make me feel good." Who knows why they translated it that way. Who knows why *Piano Man* and loser are the same thing, Billy.

He discovered why he hated don Gendaro

Montevideo, 2012

He took down the old Colt, and for a moment, he thought of the engineer from the AutoCad division, who had had a child a few days earlier, and he thought that none of his employees had faced hardships in the last ten years, since he decided to restructure the company during the 2002 crisis by laying off thirty percent of the staff, but saving the rest who would have ended up on the streets if the company had gone under.

Almost fondly, he thought about what the newspapers said about him (like that annoying rag *La República*, which claims to be a pluralistic newspaper and the whole country knows it leans to the left) and what his closest friends said privately: don Jordi was a stingy guy; don Jordi was a mediocre character, not even a mediocre man, no, a character. Not entirely bad, but his greed outweighed any setback and any feeling of pity. One of those intellectuals who lecture in Europe or the United States once said, what a coincidence, in the same newspaper *La República*, that it was, precisely, greed that had been the main driver of the success of all his companies and that if any other feeling had nested in the heart of the famous *entrepreneur*, it would surely have sunk all his projects, and with them the mediocre fate of thousands of highly skilled employees. The Carlos Slim, the Donald Trump of Uruguay. Or worse: not even that, since there were many bigger fish than him, true predators, like the Peirano brothers, who took the savings of thousands of humble workers to the Cayman Islands and who barely The Yankees extradited one from Miami, Uruguayan justice couldn't handle the lawyers of this tiger who easily found a loophole in the law, big enough to let him walk free. As usual. But don Jordi almost always played, from the start, within the generous limits of the law. Like the ever-patriotic Carlos Slim during the Mexican crises of '82 and '94, like other tigers and sharks during the Brazilian crisis of '98, the Argentine crisis of 2002, the American crisis of 2008, the European crisis of 2010, and all the social and economic crises past and future, the vultures had multiplied their fortunes by buying all kinds of assets, real and virtual, at fire-sale prices. And don Jordi wasn't going to be the idiot who, being a vulture and not lacking some capital, would let so many opportunities slip by to take almost everything during the 2002 crisis. After all, if it hadn't been for him, many more would have ended up on the streets, and many other children of those same unfortunates would now be part of the legions of young street kids who burn their brains with cheap drugs and low-quality reggaeton.

At least, don Jordi didn't send his dollars to some tiny Caribbean island. No, sir, the much-criticized don Jordi invested almost all the remaining capital he had in properties and small national businesses. Like don Slim. True, he took almost all of them, but at least the small businesses kept running, and their workers kept their little proletarian lives, their wage slavery, as the bitter Ernesto called it, who never missed an opportunity to drink the best Rioja wine with him while criticizing him from head to toe and he, don Jordi, took pleasure in at least letting himself be criticized by someone who didn't hate him. Because a true Marxist doesn't hate "he thought, with a smile, while deciphering the lines of a fake Picasso floating in the darkness against a wall;" a true Marxist, like Ernesto, only understands reality. This drove don Jordi to despair, though he couldn't quite understand it. It wasn't that Ernesto was wrong, but rather that his truths were useless. He, Ernesto, understood reality better, but only capitalist pigs like don Jordi knew what to do with it. Which is an irony for a disciple of Marx, he thought, who "as that Lucía from the nineties used to say, entertained in one of the corners of the bookstore" became famous for saying that modern philosophers should not only understand reality but act upon it. And it turned out the opposite "don Jordi had replied to his daughter" just like psychoanalysts who were much better at understanding the madness of others than curing it.

True, he had taken advantage of every crisis, including the collapse of the Tablita in '82, but anyone in his place would have done the same. It was almost an obligation. Because a man can be forgiven anything except stupidity. Anyone, rich or poor, he thought, can tolerate being called stingy, lazy, ambitious, distracted, a son of a bitch, insensitive, but never an idiot. Anything but mediocre, a failure. So he took almost everything he could, thanks to the Great Crisis of 2002.

In a way, don Jordi had managed to spread his one passion, money, through personal enthusiasm and the often-fabricated example of the heroic origins of *Metasoft*, to a legion of new believers, which is why "he thought, every time he ate, drank, or had sex excessively" one day his death would be widely and uselessly commented on in the newspapers and social media, but it wouldn't bring down the enduring technological and financial empire he had managed to build from nothing.

Age hadn't been an obstacle to becoming a leader in new technologies but, on the contrary, a stimulus. He boasted of his ability to reinvent himself and adapt to every new situation, to rise from the ashes and the worst crises with his youthful appearance, his dyed hair, a perfect smile that had cost him almost a quarter of the shares of a mattress factory, and all his experience in the service of the future rather than wasted on nostalgias of the past.

In short, he couldn't be surprised by the insults. When one has achieved something in life, he said, the chances of some poor devil calling you stupid, ignorant, mediocre, even if you've won the Nobel Prize in physics or built a business empire from scratch, increase exponentially. When you start to read and hear those things, you can rest assured that you've reached a higher level. Because no one is shouting anything bad about the village lunatic. Deep down, all those poor devils who can't have a life of their own and dedicate themselves to pursuing and defaming others are just that: they're the village lunatics who, thanks to some small merit, aren't recognized as such.

But it was also true that, in some way, he had repeatedly failed in the vulgar attempt to be loved by others. As compensation, he had achieved admiration and fear from others, like an ancient god, though in just the right measure. But not affection, much less love from anyone.

Perhaps for this very reason, he was as proud of himself as he was filled with self-loathing. Over time, he had developed his own psychological theory, despite his intellectual limitations: every individual who loves themselves for what they do, hates themselves for what they are. It wasn't a theory. More of a feeling that had accumulated through experience and that he couldn't articulate in a satisfying way beyond that simple definition.

He had also discovered why he hated don Gendaro so much, a businessman who had gone bankrupt several times but, like an Emilio Reus, had managed to rebuild all his businesses under different names and who knows with what resources. He, on the other hand, had been quite successful in all his ventures. He had never gone bankrupt and had hardly ever relied on the help of any friendly politicians. But he also hadn't been able to demonstrate, as don Gendaro had, how a true champion of business rises from their worst and dumbest investments. Maybe that's why don Gendaro was an old man doted on by the newspaper *El País*, by *El Observador* because he served as an example and a consolation to the countless army of anonymous failures who would never make a front-page headline like he did, just a small number followed by a percentage symbol. He hated don Gendaro much more than the intellectual leftists and other minor annoyances from the newspaper *La República* or the weekly *Brecha*.

A flash of light in the dimness showed him why. He hated him because he was so much like himself; or he hated him for something, for a quirk they both shared. But after hating him for so long and with so many new arguments, he continued to hate him, though in a different way, in a more rational way that allowed him to offload all his flaws onto someone else and save the best of his own ego for himself.

Pedro Zabala

Montevideo, March 15, 2011

"Wow," said Santiago, looking up at the major. "I would've started with that."

"Why do you think I'm here?" asked the major. "Doctor Genaro gave me three options: Doctor Lucas, Doctor... what was the other doctor's name? Gonorrhea... it comes to me. See my memory?"

"Aguerrebere?"

"Yes, that's the one."

"Excellent cardiologist."

"And you."

"So, were you friends with my father?"

"I wouldn't say we were thick as thieves, because I saw him once or twice a year and we never lost that kind of respect that distinguishes true friends from two acquaintances who appreciate each other. If someone can't call a black man black or a fat man fat, then they're not a real friend. And I wasn't that close. I had retired and was looking to start a new business and didn't really know what, just when don Ramón showed up in his classic black jacket. He always dressed impeccably, in a tie, even in summer. He had several businesses on this side of the pond and was looking for someone to handle security for the Marsella hotels. There were two in Montevideo and one in Punta del Este. The last one closed a year before don Pedro passed away... Well, what can I tell you about your father's businesses."

"Don't think I knew much about my father's businesses. I grew up a bit on the sidelines of all that and didn't have much time or interest in developing his business skills."

"Well, don Pedro was somewhat hermetic. But you have to understand that this tendency to speak little, aside from being natural to his character, always discreet, is also a characteristic of executives. Do you know anyone worth their salt who talks nonstop? A barking dog doesn't bite, and a man who goes around announcing everything he's going to do ends up doing nothing."

"Hermetic, that's the word. Like fathers from the old days," said Santiago.

"Exactly, but he was also a man with a broad, open mind, in the true sense of the word, not to justify a lack of principles as young people often do today, but to accept reality as it is. He knew well that his only son wouldn't follow in his footsteps... Well, the concrete fact is that I told him I didn't want to stay connected to the world of weapons. I had hoped he would offer me something else, maybe something in Buenos Aires. He said, no, not Buenos Aires, you don't know what that's like; it's calmer here, for this and that reason. In the end, he offered to sell me the hotel I still own in the Ciudad Vieja, though I no longer manage it. I also thought about my daughter Clarita, who was then a five or six-year-old girl. When you're the father of a child, everything seems dangerous, and you feel responsible for everything. I thought that if Clarita didn't study and become a lawyer, notary, or one of those easier careers, at least she'd have a family business to continue. Anything rather than depending on a husband, I thought. You don't raise daughters with so much care only for some long-haired vagabond to sweep them away. Don Pedro offered me attractive financing, saying he wanted to scale back a bit, that he was too diversified, and I dove in headfirst. So I went from managing the security of his hotels to hosting him in my own. We had a lot in common. Before crossing the pond, he'd call me and say, 'Don Xico, I'll be there on Tuesday...' And I'd take care of everything. Sometimes we'd spend hours talking in the hotel lobby. A top-notch guy, your old man. He loved the promenade. I was really sad when he left, especially because I found out late, about a year late, when one day I called his house asking if don Zabala would need my services that year or if he'd decided to change hotels and why... Your grandmother answered. Anyway..."

Don Xico bowed his head and scratched behind his ear. Then he smiled. Santiago began to notice that it wasn't a smile but a tic, or a programmed gesture, something as artificial as his white teeth.

"After that, I lost contact until not long ago when Cristina called to reserve three rooms. With so many hotels in Montevideo..."

"Grandma is a very sensitive woman. Everything, every place holds a special meaning for her."

"Could be, though she's never been to the hotel before."

"I'm talking about my father."

"Yes, it must be because of that…"

The older man reached behind his ear again and continued, as if the conversation had worn him out:

"I also thought my daughter would follow in the hotel business, but she became a doctor instead. She's graduating as a pediatrician next year. It's a pride for me, can you imagine? I'm one of those old-school fathers who appreciated a son in the military or with a university degree. Look now; becoming a doctor is almost seen as a shame. Just when I left the hotel business, being a maid is becoming a prestigious profession. My generation got screwed in several ways. But oh well…

The older man kept himself in shape. He had no dark circles under his eyes and didn't wear glasses. Thick gray hair and a physique used to moderate exercise showed a man getting on in years, slightly hunched, nervous but entirely healthy. Except for the coronary blockage.

He thought that few things moved him

Buenos Aires, 2011

For a moment, Miguel didn't know what to do with the rest of the days he had left in Buenos Aires. He carefully went through the phonebook that had survived his resignation ten years earlier. Some numbers had been updated thanks to a few acquaintances who had managed to contact him via email. Alejandro's number had been passed to him by Santiago from Georgia. He called from a payphone on Avenida Regimiento de

Patricios. A recording answered for him: *"Hi, I can't take your call right now. Please leave your message and I'll get back to you as soon as possible. Thank you."* Alejandro rarely answered his calls either, Santiago had warned him. Only once had they managed to talk for a long time, and Miguel had concluded that Alejandro had crossed that line where people feel frustrated and, as a first consequence, cut ties with old acquaintances, as if they didn't know that frustration is one of those states of consciousness that has reached a certain level of maturity. Normally, that happens in your thirties and forties. Then (if you survive, of course) things get a little better. Especially in your fifties and sixties. When you get older, you give up on those foolish things and dedicate yourself to others, Santiago had said. But Miguel hadn't understood a word. Back then, he thought Santiago was lost in that typical web of theories that American doctoral students get tangled in. Then they confuse those conceptual labyrinths with reality, he had thought at the time.

Like any tourist, he went to Caminito and San Telmo. He returned to the spot where he had thrown the phones into the river. He stood there for a while, looking. He tried to recall that moment so important in his life. To a certain extent, he was bothered by such indifference. Maybe the old man was right about something. As one learns to survive and do things right, one unlearns how to live. What did he mean? Miguel had asked him. The old man remembered when he was young and could feel the world while sitting on the docks or walking along 9 de Julio. Back then, even the smells were important. Not anymore, unless you were in the perfume business, the old man quipped.

Before, he had said, he didn't have a penny in his pocket, but he owned everything he stepped on. The city was his. He had more imagination than knowledge of reality. He had even written a tango lyric that no one ever read. But since you can't make a living from that, he had had to learn to solve a few problems. Over the years, when those problems had been solved, by then he had lost the city, he had lost the ability to be a bit of a poet in a bar on Corrientes Street, enjoying a coffee more than a movie, more than the best business deal he had made later in his long life, of which there had been many. No, it's not that he regretted it (he wasn't quite sure how to put it), because thanks to being a responsible father, he, Miguel, had gotten an education and everything he needed to be a decent citizen. But...

Miguel realized he was thirsty and quickened his step toward the corner of Almirante Brown and General Aráoz, where he had seen a kiosk selling ice cream on the sidewalk. He bought a *Paso de los Toros* and continued along Olavarría, Suárez, Bransen... He guessed that all those names were of military men. But there were also some writers and painters. On Pérez Galdós, he put a few dollars in the hat of a bandoneon player, who thanked him with an *Adiós Nonino*. On Manuel Blanes, he bought *El Gráfico*, that coveted sports magazine that Santiago and Alejandro used to fight over until they tore it to pieces. He stopped, exhausted and sweating, on Pi i Margall. After all, there were quite a few writers too. All dead, of course. The street signs were like tombstones. Missing were the dates of birth and death. Instead, the numbers went from one corner to the next. What was missing were women's names, he thought.

That night, he ate alone at *Happening*. He strolled through Plaza de Mayo. He turned down a girl's invitation to continue the conversation in her apartment and later regretted it when he got back to the hotel in Once.

The day before returning to New York, he passed through Palermo. He parked the car not far from Beatrice's apartment. Once again, he confirmed that with age, he had lost the capacity for wonder. When he was young, he could spend long stretches enraptured, gazing at the city skyline, the lights that began to flicker on at dusk. Maybe this is what the old man was talking about. Over time, he had learned to survive, to solve problems. He had become a practical man. Maybe that's why, he thought, few things moved him. Russia had been a bad experience. Now, not even the nostalgia of Buenos Aires had managed to bother him after ten years. Nothing.

He got out of the car, absorbed in this kind of indifference, and didn't notice that Beatrice was watching him. Though she wore dark glasses, she must have recognized him, perhaps not without some doubt. When he realized, he stopped, and she quickened her pace until she entered the building's lobby.

Miguel walked in the opposite direction. He went around the block, pretended to enter a bar, and came back out. When he thought Beatrice would have gone up, he headed back toward the building. The city had suddenly grown dark, and the streetlights hadn't yet come on.

When he finally reached the building's entrance, he saw her, expressionless but with eyes that revealed she had been crying. It wasn't just an impression; Miguel knew those eyes. They had changed somewhat, but they were the same eyes that cried over any little thing and then forced her to wear dark glasses for the rest of the day to hide the puffiness.

Beatrice quickly turned the key and entered without looking back. He remembered those eyes that had told him, "It was my cousin, one of my best friends." And he correcting her: "Good friends don't hug like that." And she: "Grandpa died."

After a moment, Miguel looked for her name on the intercom panel. None of them revealed anything. He tried in vain to remember and associate surnames. He saw two older women enter. One with a cane; both seemed preoccupied with something. A young woman smiled at him the way women do in the United States, but in Buenos Aires it meant something else, and he wasn't in the mood for that. Then three young men with books appeared. They were celebrating a joke with loud laughter.

"Living is dangerous," one of them said.

"Yes," continued the other, "if you live too long, you might die."

The three burst into laughter. Their small faces were almost hidden beneath an abundance of hair. They must have been studying biology or math, Miguel thought, those things that are virtually useless to almost everyone but at that age are the keys to all the truths one needs to know to stay alive and, incidentally, pass the exams administered by the frustrated geniuses of high school who can't make ends meet but convince these greenhorn young men that the formulas they memorize are the key to understanding how the universe works.

One of them rang the bell to some apartment, and someone opened the door with an insult. Miguel saw a man his age, impeccably dressed, with a thick mustache and an expressionless gaze. Those cold blue eyes, Miguel thought, he had seen them before. In fact, he had had the same impression ever since returning to Buenos Aires. Everyone seemed familiar, as if he had seen them all before, as if they were all fathers or sons of some friend, or some close relative. A gaze of blue eyes in Buenos Aires had nothing to do with another gaze of blue eyes in Manhattan. There was something, perhaps a hint of northern Italians mixed with a touch of southern Poles. He wasn't sure. But there was something that made them feel familiar. He thought he could distinguish an Argentine from a Yankee or from a European, even if both were tall and blond. It was like distinguishing the Spanish accent of a porteño from that of a Uruguayan. They were the same, but only someone who had grown up on either shore of the River Plate could tell them apart. A year ago, he had identified an Argentine in Philadelphia by the way he laughed. Then an elderly woman appeared, complaining about her poor eyesight as she struggled to get the key into the lock. But she had laughed at her own nearsightedness. "Blind as a bat," she had said.

Finally, the doorman who had seen him hesitating came out with a stern look and asked if he was looking for someone. Miguel looked at him and thought that the poor guy was paid for that. For that face. Just like the poor Yankees who work as inspectors in airports or in the *driver's license* offices: they get paid to be unpleasant, disgusting to the point of nausea, even though that's not in the contract.

From the beginning, he knew something wasn't right

March 15, 2011

While Santiago polished his diagnosis, Don Xico praised the neatness and space of his office. In his day, the Military Hospital was rather dark, the offices didn't smell of fruity candles, and doctors didn't dress so elegantly.

Santiago barely looked up from the lab results as Don Xico detailed all his preferences for morning exercise; for healthy food and black label whiskey; for a very active sex life without any need for Viagra, though at his age he had already started eating out less frequently; for walks along the Pocitos promenade almost every afternoon, from five to six-thirty. He went on at length about his sadness over the decline of society since the Marxists had taken over the government, this time legally—he didn't question that, because elections are elections and must be respected—but undoubtedly relying on the same old lies...

When Santiago told him that surgery was inevitable, Don Xico was surprised. He opened his eyes and immediately furrowed his brows in question.

"What do you mean I have to have surgery, doctor?"

"There's no other way. Your aorta is blocked and needs to be replaced with one from a pig."

"A pig's aorta?"

"Yes. Why the surprise? Surely you know someone who's had heart surgery."

"Yes, yes. I know several. It's like an epidemic. Now everyone's getting heart surgery. It wasn't like that before."

"Not everyone. And before, people simply died of a heart attack." That's what we're going to avoid with a timely intervention. It will improve your quality of life. You think you're healthy, but you have this problem there, and it's not going away by exercising. You need surgery.

"So that's where this tiredness comes from when I walk... right, doctor?

"No doubt about it. You're someone who has always exercised and lived a healthy life. There's no reason for you to get tired walking along the promenade.

Don Xico said he would think about it, that he needed to discuss it with Carmencita, his wife, and his three children. The risk was very low; hardly anyone dies these days from heart surgery. But there were always cases to fill that five percent of fatalities. Besides, the very idea that they would open his chest from top to bottom to remove his heart, like in some Aztec ritual, terrified him.

The Wild West

San Francisco, December 24, 2010
Ernest Hatuey moved to California with his cousin Eduardo in the fall of 2009. But he didn't last long in the house on Embarcadero Road in Palo Alto. Two months. His cousin Eduardo

ended up evicting him as a result of an argument that went sour. In the end, Ernest Hatuey had lost his boundaries after many months of relative self-control.

It had all started, apparently, with a joke. On the 25th in the afternoon, they had been drinking beer in the backyard with some of Eduardo's friends and Vladimir, a Cuban Ernest had met at a *Chili's* in San Bruno. Ernest shared with Vladimir a love for style motorcycles, which in Vladimir was evident from the shiny embroidery of the unmistakable *H-D* on the back of his black jacket. The bikers who boasted so much about freedom and hated the government that harassed them with taxes and regulations always used the highways and roads built by the damn government. But as is typical of this culture, Eduardo thought, you can only see the object, never the context. That's why the highway, the road, the streets didn't count, they were invisible. Their heroes could only see the motorcycles and those guys with long mustaches defying the damn government that stopped them from exercising all their freedom.

But at least, Eduardo thought, Hatuey had found an accomplice. Although it had never been easy for him to make friends, that was practically the only social skill he had left after the war, or after the *tour* in Iraq, as everyone curiously called it: making friends, not keeping them.

During the barbecue on the afternoon of December 25th, Ernest joked about the unbearable liberalism of Californians, especially the hippies in San Francisco who were still living in the sixties, while on TV one of Bush's daughters delivered an ironic response that drew applause from the audience. Ernest

Hatuey paused for a moment to watch the curious debate that must have been taking place in Texas or Arizona.

"That must be Jenna "said John, trying to stoke the fire". I thought we were rid of the Bushes. But it seems like you can't even have a *barbecue* in peace...

"I heard somewhere that San Francisco is the most anti-military city in the country "Hatuey said". Is that true? Come on, you geniuses from Stanford and Berkeley, tell me if I'm wrong... There must be plenty of you here, how do you say it? "Yes, there's... a lot of research on the topic..."

In Texas or Arizona, people stand up and keep applauding. From the backyard, you could hear the applause and see the screen on a wall of the living room, at times almost entirely filled with Jenna's face, who couldn't hold back a satisfied smile that reminded Eduardo of her father: the mouth carved like a slit, the small eyes, like Barney Rubble's, John thought.

"It could be "someone replied.

"*It could be* "repeated Hatuey". *It could be. No evidence...* What do you think, Vladimir?

"What's Barney Rubble's name in Spanish? "asked John.

"Barney Rubble? "asked Eduardo, surprised" Who's that?

"Man, that famous character from the *cartoons* of *The Flintstones*... The families who slept in separate beds so as not to confuse the children. In the sixties, kids must have thought their real parents were perverts because they slept in the same bed...

"Sorry, am I missing something?

"The character who says *yabba-yabba-dooo*

"*You are smarter than your father* "Bush's daughter's opponent was heard saying". *However, you are also mistaken. Your statements contradict all the recently declassified documents by the very government you...*"

"*The Flintstones...*"

"I don't know..."

"Yes, *The Flintstones*. The patriarch was Fred Flintstone, married to Wilma and..."

"Fred. That must be Fred. And the other one?"

"Barney Rubble."

"That's it. That's Barney. Barney is George Bush."

"You're right. Bush is Barney Rubble! How didn't I notice it before. That little Stone Age man already looked familiar to me."

"*...Please, don't stop there. Besides the dead soldiers, there are many other thousands of disabled, many other thousands of suicides. Not to mention the hundreds of thousands of Iraqis, who are also people, even if they are an irrelevant statistic...*"

"I say I don't know because I don't read," said Vladimir. "I don't have time for those things. I work eight or nine hours at the airport. No, no. Don't ask me, like everyone else, if I'm a pilot or a security guard. No. Even though I was a pediatrician in Cuba, here I do baggage wrapping, that is, I wrap them with security tapes. But I prefer this to that."

"*True, five thousand soldiers died. I don't criticize or despise them. After all, they were kids who weren't even of legal age to drink alcohol. What could those children with men's bodies know? They killed and came back broken, claiming their moral prize, demanding*" *that everyone tell them 'thank you for fighting for our freedom; because freedom isn't free' and all that speech they always repeat so they go risk their lives, with fanatical pride and without thinking too much. I don't blame them for that need. If you're missing a leg and half your face, at least you need to think that all that sacrifice was for something and not for nothing, for a lie that wasn't worth a penny. I criticize and despise all those who spent their weekends in their mansions and sent them to a war based on lies. But everyone knows that human justice will never reach them because they own the guns and the public opinion..."*

"How nice..."

"No, not nice. After three hours of doing this, like this, by hand, you don't want to do it anymore, and all you ask for is for the day to end... But then comes the next one and the next one, and there's always something to solve. Of course, I didn't have the same luck as some others who escaped the Regime much earlier. Nor the luck of many who aren't even citizens and are even pilots. Can you imagine? They're not even American citizens and already they're pilots of a Boeing 777."

"Are you a citizen?"

"Yes. I arrived in 2002 on one of those little rafts you know, a little raft made of inner tubes and park benches, which cost me a fortune, man, considering the salaries over there. But as soon as I set foot here, they welcomed me with open arms. In 2004, they gave me residency."

"Speak lower "said John, who was making a great effort to follow the debate from the grill". You don't need to shout."

"Well, you were really lucky to be born in Cuba "said someone opening a beer can". I came from the Dominican Republic on a scholarship to study at Berkeley, ten years ago, and after graduating, I'm still waiting for someone to think of letting me stay or fuck off."

Bush's daughter's opponent had finished his argument. The boos had stopped but hadn't been replaced by applause. A deep silence fell, a moment when the man with glasses addressed the audience and said:

"Sure, silence. Just silence, that reaction so normal, so predictable, so human in the face of truth."

"That's why I made sure," said Vladimir "and didn't wait for the worms to eat me, and after getting residency, I studied for the test and became an American citizen. I was lucky that a Cuban took my exam, because English and history aren't my thing. That's why I'm very grateful to this country, which saved me from hunger and persecution."

"But it must have something bad, right? "asked Eduardo, putting on a CD of music, as soon as the program in Texas ended. John repeated: *'No applause. Just silence, silence, that predictable reaction to the truth...'*"

"This country? Not just one thing. Many. This country has many bad things. Like all that scum that arrives breaking the law and then spends their time criticizing the country that fed them."

Norberto, the Mexican who had remained silent until then, focused on his avocado tacos, coughed as his only response.

So… bye, bye Miss American Pie
Drove my Chevy to the levee, but the levee was dry…

"Let's see…" said Alejandro, with his Andalusian accent. Eduardo was about to tell him not to get involved, but Alejandro couldn't hold back:

"The country that fed them," he said "also exploits all those millions of poor people who come here to work like beasts. Many had to leave countries filled with violence, devastated by military coups or civil wars that the country that was supposed to feed them supported with such enthusiasm."

We were singing, bye, bye Miss American Pie
Drove my Chevy to the levee, but the levee was dry
Them good ol' boys were drinking whiskey and rye, singing...

"Yeah…, I see. Now you're going to come out with all those conspiracy theories…"

"They're conspiracy theories about conspiratorial practices. When I have time, I'll show you the documents from the CIA itself, from Mr. Kissinger, and from all the other conspirators, honorable leaders of their entourage. I mention it because I know you won't believe the victims, but perhaps you'll believe serious and responsible people."

This'll be the day that I die
This'll be the day that I die

"Alright, alright," said Ernest. "I see we're going to keep going on about imperialism and the criminal war in Iraq, which a few of us went to while defending a handful who stayed here drinking beer."

On a dark desert highway, cool wind in my hair
Warm smell of colitas, rising up through the air

"For now," said Alejandro, "everything they did in Iraq wasn't done in my name or for my safety. And I'm not going to argue that with you because I know perfectly well that you were barely a victim of the same old lies. First, they had to invade Iraq because Saddam Hussein had weapons of mass destruction. Then, when they didn't find a trace of what the Reagan administration itself had supported and promoted in the eighties, it became about promoting democracy and brotherly love... But anyway. As I said, I won't get into that, since I know many soldiers like you who were barely victims of all that madness, victims who logically need to think that that leg and those friends they lost had some meaning, that that little medal had some value and wasn't just lead coated in silver, that all of that wasn't a crime but a heroic act... but victims nonetheless."

Welcome to the Hotel California
Such a lovely place (Such a lovely place)

"I don't consider myself a victim," said Ernest. "It took me years to understand that from my therapist. If I consider myself

133

a victim because of my *post-traumatic stress disorder*, I'll never free myself from the demons…"

Such a lovely face
Plenty of room at the Hotel California

"Yes, that other army of psychiatrists who are basically like aspirin to dull the pain of an amputation. The day victims are able to recognize they were victims and stop consuming so much pseudoscientific propaganda, not only will they find more lasting healing, but the country will also embark less often on mass crimes like those in Hiroshima or Vietnam."

Any time of year (Any time of year)
You can find it here

"Can any of you answer a question for me? "said Vladimir, with an anticipatory smile."

"Sure," replied Alejandro.

"Let's see… what do you have to contribute to this great country to help it move forward?"

"Criticism…"

"Now we're talking, bingo!" said Vladimir.

"I don't see what's so funny," continued Alejandro. "At least a bit of criticism, sir, since self-criticism has been in short supply, and newcomers have confused loyalty to a country with submission to a government and an army. Then they pretend to be the champions of democracy. Of course, criticism. New submissive blood, there's plenty of that. Old and new fanatics waving the flag while others march off to some stupid and criminal war, there's more than enough and it's never lacking. So if I could contribute some of the criticism that this country lacks (which, in some way, surely a different way from yours, I learned to love and admire), then I believe I would be contributing something. At least something true and not prefabricated. At least I'd be responding to the patriotic call of its founding fathers. By the way, I'm a great admirer of people like Francklyn, Paine, and Jefferson. Do you know anything about these people?"

"As I said," said Vladimir, rising from his chair and approaching Ernest in a gesture of farewell, "what I don't understand is why there are people who criticize this country so much and instead of packing their bags and catching the first flight back to the country they came from, they insist on causing trouble here. I've never seen anyone as anti-American as those who criticize and yet stay in their high-paying jobs where they earn more than any of us will in our lifetimes."

"Friend," continued Alejandro, "it seems to me there are things you still haven't understood since leaving the island. For example, that there is nothing more un-American, at least in the original sense of the word, than claiming that to live in the United States or any other country and be an honest citizen, one must keep quiet or dedicate oneself to the apologia of a nation, which in the end is nothing more than blind praise for its governments. As if a nation were a religion or an army. What a popular absurdity! How many bewildered peoples let themselves be kidnapped in such a childish way. It's what those who confuse a nation with its church or political party always aim for. Nothing is more un-American, not for the McCarthyists, but at least for those early generations of enlightened minds who founded a country, rather peculiar, if not utopian. If it were up to that other type of infantile patriotism that the kidnappers invented over time, the American Revolution would have been just another revolt. Like so many others. But believe me, friend, there is nothing more un-American, in the original sense of the word, but above all, nothing more undemocratic, than thinking that democracy is defended by the servility of slaves who keep silent or bootlickers who live singing praises. A strange way to defend democracy and freedom. Allow me, I'm almost done. If democracy has advanced in the last thousand years, make no mistake, it has been thanks to the critics, not the apologists of the *establishment* of the day. But, of course, history doesn't matter. That's why, with impunity, they later come to give us lessons on what it means to be American and, worse, what freedom and democracy mean."

Strumming my pain with his fingers
Singing my life with his words
Killing me softly with his song

Vladimir shook Ernest's hand and, before leaving, said to him:

"I'm really sorry for you, brother. You spilled your blood in Iraq for these traitors. A real waste, kid. Good luck to you. Don't invite me to any more intellectuals' gatherings, or I'll shoot you myself. At least you could've warned me."

Killing me softly with his song
Telling my whole life with his words
Killing me softly with his song...

The face of his father

Montevideo, April 6, 2012

The siren of a distant ambulance sounded. Then the furious engine of a police car. He imagined Lucía being rescued from an accident. He always imagined his dearest ones in the midst of tragedy. Then José Ignacio defending himself from a robbery. Then, as his gaze wandered over the unadorned wall, he thought of the Figari that had been stolen from his office fifteen years earlier.

It was a compassionate robbery. Don Jordi hated that Figari, those poorly painted drummers, twisted like a child's drawing that insulted him every day when he opened the door, as if saying, "Good day, ignorant sir." He had paid a fortune for that daily dose of sadism. The only thing that was clear, not just to him but to the rest of the country, was its value in dollars, and that was the only thing he regretted when he found out about the theft. If he had known the thief was an art lover, he would have reported it without hesitation, he joked. Or pretended to joke.

Comedians are repressed, he thought. He had that painting there to impress the young wives of his wealthiest clients, who always have free time for such things or sigh over those crayons just as they do over a copy of *People* but with less spontaneity. Like when they fake their orgasms under one of those old, pot-bellied men like him.

He thought about the tropical fish that appeared dead one morning. He thought about those same fish flying past his left temple and then, futilely, tried to think of nothingness, of the night, of the world without him. He couldn't. The dead fish were still there, floating in the tank, two years back. It must have been an act of revenge by one of those employees who knew they were going to be laid off to increase the company's productivity.

He thought about the look of sorrow Marina would have on her face when she walked in that morning. She would think of him, the poor old man, who hadn't been so bad after all, but she would think much more about her job, the unpaid mortgage, the kids who would have to start going to public school if things got worse. Marina was too young for both her talent and her sense of responsibility. José Ignacio wasn't far behind in intelligence and in his ability to predict market demands two years in advance. He shared with him not only a passion for business but also incredibly dark eyes, so deeply black they resembled nothingness.

Maybe the major was right

Montevideo, March 17, 2011

At the restaurant on Avenida Soca, he recalled the major's words. "With time and lack of training, memory declines. Thankfully... Imagine if one remembered all the garbage one has stumbled upon in life. What would one be, doctor...? Memory would be a garbage dump..." Back then, Santiago didn't imagine that soon those words would reveal their deepest meaning. The major had serious reasons for saying what he said, and he, Santiago, would discover that even the most spontaneous banalities of a person might make sense if one knew just a single detail of all that they hid.

He himself couldn't remember the face of every corpse he had to dissect in medical school, every patient he'd seen struggle and die. At first, it was hard. Especially forgetting the face and the pale legs of his first body, the prostitute who had been hanged. Then, for a while, he became fixated on the frozen gaze of a dark-skinned man who had died in an accident. On his face lingered the moment just before, as if he had known that was his end. For a time, he would remember this face in the mornings, while shaving. Sometimes, shortly after one of his more recurring dreams: he would be on a plane plummeting into the sea, and as it fell, he would think of his parents and Paulina with profound sadness, not despair. Another time, he would be driving at night down Briancliff Road toward Atlanta, and the lights and horn of a truck coming the wrong way in the opposite lane would end in a muffled explosion that meant his death but not unconsciousness or oblivion. And again, he would feel that deep sadness he knew from other times, thinking of his parents waiting for him, unable to do anything to fix it, unable to tell them that he hadn't suffered, nothing other than that familiar pain of abandonment.

Maybe the dark-skinned man had come to understand that it was the end and, for a moment, thought of his children. That was what it *meant, that* was death: not the fear of dying. Death, that death, was the faces of his small children, the long years of helplessness that still weren't over, all concentrated in the clarity of a single instant lost in the infinite forever.

He also remembered what an undocumented Mexican man told him in Georgia at a clinic where he volunteered. He had an almost complete cut across his right hand, the result of an accident with a lawnmower. He was cleaning the mower when one of those girls who seemed straight out of a movie walked by. It was a second, and he doesn't know how the machine turned on and sliced his hand from top to bottom. His friend tried to console him by saying it was God's doing for looking at what he shouldn't have. Ramón, the Mexican, by then had been sleeping four hours a night and mowing lawns from sunup to sundown because he was paid by the house. He bandaged his hand and hid the blood as long as he could because he knew no one likes blood staining the patio where children might play. But after several days with no improvement and increasing pain, he had decided to quit the job and seek out a doctor. Santiago asked him what part hurt the most, and the Mexican, almost unable to speak, pointed to his chest. It hurt him that his son didn't have his father and that, because of that carelessness, he also wouldn't get the three hundred or three hundred and fifty dollars he sent to his mother every month in a town in Oaxaca.

That memory was another fixation he found hard to shake. Every time he picked up a book, he saw in his hand the hand of the Mexican man. But given the training he had gained over time, he learned to set that image aside"if not forget it"every time it appeared. Yet just when he thought he had overcome that weakness that called his capacity for medicine into question, one day at Emory, he had to work on a woman who looked like Julia Roberts. The resemblance turned the stranger into a kind of familiar figure. And still, he had to cut as if she were waste material.

As a good doctor and even better student, he underwent therapy for six months. But he eventually quit when the doctor in Atlanta, Dr. Richard Gomes, a Puerto Rican who had extended his fame to Princeton University, chose to explore the vein regarding his father's abuse. The sessions began to remind him of the psychologist in Villa Devoto that had ended in the nuns' school. Dr. Gomes in Atlanta, like his parents, was from the school of thought that believed in the monopoly of the church and the military to correct spiritual ailments. And although the doctor had no authority over him, he still showed him what a waste of time it was to drive every Friday from Emory to Atlanta to talk about something neither of them truly understood.

Still, he thought, if the past was complex and unfathomable, at least there was some possibility of digging into it, of looking closely and discovering details imperceptible at first glance. For some inexplicable reason, humans are animals that walk backwards. We can see the past; we cannot see the future that supposedly lies ahead.

MARKED DAY. The Far East

San Francisco, December 25, 2010

Ernest Hatuey managed to hold back his rage until the night, until shortly after Eduardo's friends had left. But when Eduardo thought the afternoon's incident had been forgotten, Ernest approached him and said:

"This is the last time I'm hosting a *barbecue* with your buddies. If you don't respect my people, don't expect me to do the same with yours."

"Alright, I'm sorry," said Eduardo. "But you should admit your friend had part of the blame, no?"

"I'm not interested in calculating percentages or talking softly like the idiots at Stanford do. Fags. If any of you had gone through what Vladimir went through in Cuba, at least you'd shut your mouths. Did you know what the teacher said to his son when she found out he had left on a raft because his own country wouldn't let him speak his mind? 'In this country, there's no place for worms that throw themselves into the sea,' she told the boy. 'The worms that betray our Comandante Fidel should all be at the bottom of the sea.' she said, and the boy still didn't know if his father had reached land or was still fighting the waves, sunstroke, and sharks."

"I don't recall any of my friends approving stuff like that," said Eduardo. "Now, if we're going to look at the problem like it's a soccer match, then we're lost. Leave me out of that twisted game…"

Eduardo dodged the argument as long as he could, but soon the two were unraveling different versions of family stories that seemed buried in time: their grandfather's favoritism toward certain grandchildren, the times Eduardo hadn't answered his emails since starting at Stanford, Ernest's feelings of inferiority that made him see things that weren't there, the deaths in Iraq that weren't counted in four thousand American soldiers but in hundreds of thousands who were also human beings, Hiroshima, not wanting to see what's inconvenient…

Ernest Hatuey had ended that argument with a punch to his cousin's face, so forceful and precise it had split his lip and caused heavy bleeding from his nose. Far from acknowledging the mistake, he had lunged at him, nearly strangling him. If it hadn't been for Mike and Brian, his cousin's study partners who showed up at the right moment, a tragedy might have occurred. The two struggled with Ernest, who seemed possessed by a superhuman fury and strength, until during the scuffle he hit his head against one of the pillars in the room and sat on the floor, leaning against the pillar, as if he had suddenly realized what he had done or had stopped thinking at that moment.

His cousin didn't report him to the police in exchange for him leaving his house. But Ernest didn't return to Georgia or Florida. For two weeks, he wandered around The Embarcadero area until Eduardo himself managed to find him, lying on a *pier* next to other *homeless*, likely war veterans like him, veterans of Vietnam, judging by the khaki pants and gray beards.

Ernest Hatuey returned to the house on Embarcadero Road reluctantly and with the promise that his cousin had secured him a job at a fishing company.

"I'm doing this for Grandpa, you know?" Eduardo told him.

"I don't care," Ernest replied. "If Grandpa could hear you, maybe he'd be moved or something. But I doubt it. He's too far gone."

"When did you become so cynical, Hatuey? You used to be the poet, and I was the jock, remember?"

"Oh, I remember. You even called me 'faggot' because I wrote verses in Grandpa Ramón's newspapers. Of course, I wouldn't write them in Grandma's Bible. Poor Grandma, she was convinced she was one of the saved and was so worried about Grandpa. Imagine loving someone so much and then God decides to send one to paradise and the other to hell for being a skeptic. Could Grandma be happy in heaven knowing her beloved husband was burning every day in the eternal flames of hell? The old man was an atheist or agnostic, a liberal from the old guard who, according to Mom, cried when the Republicans fell in Spain. So Antonio Machado still had permission to write in his unread journals. Maybe I knew what I was doing. The old man, before reading about the misfortunes of Bébé Doc Duvalier on the neighboring island, would read my verses to the princess in the castle at the end of the row."

"The princess kidnapped by pirates who lived beyond the high stone wall, covered in Grandma's vines. You were a better person when you were delirious, you know? I think the Army fried your brain."

"But I was the poor cousin, and you were the rich one. So I had to join the Army, and you got to go to Stanford University..."

Eduardo fell silent.

"And now the jock succeeds as a grad student in the Department of Latin American Literature and Culture at Stanford University, and even has time to rescue a stupid poet, an Iraq veteran, no less, and enough connections to find him a job that, while a bit shady, let's be honest, pays pretty well."

"It's what I found, in the middle of all this craziness. After the Japanese whaler, you'll have to find something more stable..."

"More stable, sure... but look, I actually appreciate it, really. Without bringing up the stupidity of breaking your nose for no reason. You know, I think in Japan I'll start a new life, far from all this divorce mess, the war... I can't get much farther away. Unfortunately, the world is round, and if you go too far, you end up right back where you wanted to escape from. I've always liked Japanese women, those pale faces with small lips, stress-free. Not the kamikazes from the movies but the Japanese you see in restaurants, always so calm, speaking softly... sometimes seated, occupied with something small, especially the elders, folding paper, not saying a word, because it's better they don't, drinking tea or doing complicated things like making sushi, which must be more therapeutic than anything..."

"Deep down, you're still the child poet," said Eduardo. "I hope you don't get a surprise."

"No, I'm not talking about the Tokyo Japanese, stressed out from work. Once I've saved up some money on the whaler, I'll retire to some simple little town. I've been researching, and I think the best place is Hitachi Province."

"Like the TVs?"

"Yes, but you don't know how beautiful it is. It has nothing to do with technology…"

"Let's hope you're right this time…"

On December 29, Ernest Hatuey left San Francisco on the Yellow Sky II, a tuna boat that, as per their initial agreement, left him in Hawaii a few weeks later. With the remaining sixteen thousand dollars, he waited three weeks in Honolulu for the arrival of the Japanese whaler. This was the shadiest part of the deal his cousin Eduardo had arranged. The Japanese whaler operated in an area and in a manner that one might suspect was illegal. But Ernest knew this from the start and couldn't afford to be picky, considering his cousin had managed to get him a job worth nearly a hundred thousand dollars when he hadn't even been able to land a job washing windows.

His father seemed to return in a fleeting visit

Montevideo, April 6, 2012.
When Don Jordi was a child, his grandparents would lavish praise and say he looked like an Egyptian statue—silent, with dark but beautiful eyes, lost in the eternity of the future. Like his father.

"Why does Clarita have blue eyes, and mine are black, Dad?" asked Jordi.

"Because that's nature," his father tried to explain. "Your mother has blue eyes, and I have black ones. When you were born, you got Mom's black hair and Dad's black eyes. That's why you look a little like both of us."

He had forgotten his father. Or almost, which is too much for a father. This discovery moved him. His finger on the trigger trembled uncontrollably, like the finger of an old sick man, as if anxiety or exhaustion demanded an immediate resolution. "You don't need to overthink every little thing," he would tell his employees. "If something requires so much deliberation, it's because it's not worth it. You either do it or leave it aside, or the competition will trample over us."

It had been more than ten years since he'd thought of his father. More than ten years. To be honest, he hadn't remembered, hadn't recalled, hadn't thought a single full minute about his father in the last forty or fifty years. It didn't make sense, he thought, but that's how it was. It was as if his father had died before he was born. Or as if he had abandoned him at birth.

He had recalled the house in Barcelona at some point. Once, he had closed his eyes and seen his room, the map of the Americas on the wall, the bathroom that his mother had adorned with flowers and perfumed soaps (in a store in the United States, he discovered that those soaps were lavender from Provence, probably made in the south of France), the small kitchen, full of tiles, the window where you could see the clothes drying in the sun. The toy box.

He remembered that he was fascinated by trucks as much as he despised them. On Saturdays, early in the morning, he would jump with joy when he heard the roar of the Ford. It was his father. Where had that man gone, that shadow, almost faceless, in the last fifty years? On Sunday nights, Jordi would hide under the sheets to avoid hearing the same snore, which would take Dad away for another week. He didn't remember his face. He remembered his black shoes, with dried mud at the edge of the sole. He remembered them because his mother would always get annoyed about it. He would laugh.

"Jordi, little Jordi, like a little bird, skinny arms and tiny belly," said the black shoes with dried mud at the edge as a giant hand caressed the belly that the shoes called tiny. "This belly needs to eat more…"

For a moment, he thought he saw his face. He closed his eyes. Maybe he imagined it. Did he have a mustache? Yes, he had a mustache, neither too thick nor too trimmed, which concealed misaligned teeth. He must have been a very young man. A truck driver with heavy hands and a cheerful smile. What was he himself doing when he reached his father's age?

He wasn't sure about his face. But he did remember, now more clearly, that every Saturday his father brought him something new he had gotten from his trucking trips, perhaps as a way to make up for his absence during the rest of the week. As a child, Don Jordi wanted to be a truck driver so he could travel to distant and mysterious lands where lavender grew and the moon shone every night. Being a truck driver and Sinbad the sailor were kind of the same thing. He closed his eyes and saw a toy car, a little green car that his father had brought from the other side of the border and which he treasured in his pants pocket until his school friends took it from him; and a box of colored pencils; and a book of stories full of animals and flying Chinese characters; and a harmonica that the owner of a boarding house had exchanged with his father for five liters of fuel. Maybe even the Provence soaps were from the other side; though he never saw it, or didn't remember, it could be assumed, because she, his mother, treasured them with a sickly affection.

One day, his father couldn't stay until Sunday and had to leave as soon as he arrived. That time, he didn't have time to bring him a gift, as was his custom, and he gave him a white peseta to buy a little truck at the Turk's store. The little truck cost two of those white pesetas, and his father had promised him the other one for the following week. He was going to the border to get the other coin, he said.

That night, Jordi fell asleep late and woke up definitively early, at five-thirty in the morning. The first thing he did was grope in the dark until he found the coin, still warm. It was there, between the folds of the sheets. It hadn't been a dream or a nightmare. It was real, the white peseta was there waiting for him. His father wasn't there, as he had said; the white peseta was there, and his transparent smile. He had been smiling at him since the night before, with the same smile, with that careful art that fathers practice and perfect to protect the innocence and tenderness of those fragile beings who step into this un-grateful world with their still innocent little feet, without hard and shiny shoes, without heavy and dull boots.

While eating breakfast, he clutched the white peseta under the table, unnoticed by his mother, who was always so worried about everything, and he defended it with his whole body when at school one of the boys suspected he was hiding something valuable in his pocket. He defended it with fists, kicks, and bare teeth. He earned the teacher's punishment for disrupting the order at recess. But he didn't care, not about that nor his nose dripping blood, because when he put his hand in his pocket, he could feel it there, waiting, waiting for his father to return, as if he hadn't really left.

Marked day. The Russian of Lower Manhattan

Saturday, March 19, 2011

The first Saturday in Manhattan, he went to Glinka's store. If he hadn't gone more often, it was to avoid the excessive famil-iarity with which the old man treated him. He felt uncomforta-ble with peddlers like old Glinka, the Chinese woman in Chi-natown, or the Turks at the Otoyolu Bazaar, who acted cheerful and friendly to sell their trinkets. He felt more comfortable with a waitress in Upper Manhattan who smiled warmly whenever she served him at a restaurant, or a beautiful employee who said *"sweeeeet,"* while trying to sell him a shirt or a TV. The capitalist lie seemed more sincere to him, he would say with a proud, sideways smile. For that, he paid without haggling, so they'd sell him a little joy when he left work. And for that, they paid him too, to show his boss and his clients that he was happy, even if he were dying.

Miguel proceeded the only way he could without the excess of considerations paralyzing him. He placed the box of letters on the little table where old Glinka did his numbers and drank vodka at sunset. He told him he needed them translated, no rush. The task shouldn't be a burden for the old man, who ran that business more to keep himself occupied than out of necessity.

But instead of the enthusiasm Miguel had imagined, he found surprise and perplexity.

Old Glinka hesitated. He wanted to know more. He placed his hand on the little box to prevent Miguel from opening it. He asked who the letters belonged to, if he was sure about what he was doing.

Miguel also hesitated. At that moment, he remembered hearing him say more than once, "why clean the basement if the house is in order." His wife scolded him in Russian, and when she left, he translated for the customers:

"She said I'm lazy... like all Russians."

A long laugh gave the key to how the woman's furious words should be understood, each day more stooped, with the same blue eyes from her youth and the same cloth covering her head but now definitely without the glow of that young woman who used to turn heads.

Miguel admitted he wasn't sure. A deep smell of vodka reminded him of his grandfather's kitchen in his final years. For a moment, his breath quickened; he hadn't fully shaken off the shyness of adolescence, as he'd thought.

He hadn't even considered that translating some old, yellowed letters over eighty years old could somehow be a mistake. They were eighty years old for a reason, and probably just as long since they'd become a tangle of symbols no one could read. There was a reason his grandfather had been so secretive. There was a reason neither he nor his father had ever thought to find out what they said.

MARKED DAY. The silver peseta

Barcelona, February 9, 1939

He remembered the woman holding a twig better than his father's face, surely because he kept that coin for many years until it was stolen from the boarding house in the Old City in 1958, along with ninety dollars. He also remembered (he remembered now, almost as a discovery) his father explaining that with that coin, he could buy the little cargo truck or the ship with two chimneys. He remembered the moment perfectly. It had always been there, hidden, protected by fear or by the reluctance to look so far back.

As it grew dark, his father had approached his bed and asked why he was crying.

"I don't want you to leave today."

"I have to do a job at the border, my boy, I have to go, but I'll be back in a few days."

"You can't go…"

"Why?"

"Because I don't want you to."

His father held his breath. Perhaps he was about to explain something, something only adults understand. But maybe, just for a moment, he grasped the logic that rules the world of the youngest ones. Maybe he wished the world were governed by that way of understanding it.

"Look, keep the peseta, and next week I'll bring another one, and with the two, I promise, we'll go to the Turk's shop to buy a toy."

"Which one?"

"Any one. With two white ones, you can buy any toy. So we'll decide when I get back. Okay?"

"Yes."

"During the week, stay with Mom and look in the shop window and pick the toy you like the most."

"But Dad, on Saturday afternoons the Turk's shop is closed."

"Don't worry about that, little one, I'm sure the Turk will open for me, I'm certain... Besides, it's possible I'll come back a bit earlier this week. Saturday at noon, or maybe Friday afternoon..."

Friday afternoon. He never arrived that early. He couldn't hold back a smile as his father kissed him on the forehead and on one cheek, while saying the same words as always, "my dear little son, my little angel..." But this time they meant something else. They would mean the days wouldn't be so many or so long, that Mom wouldn't peer out the window so often upon hearing the sound of a truck, almost always a truck that wasn't the one she was waiting for.

The promise had left him calm that night. He never knew, could never guess, if his mother waited for the man of the house with the same anxiety, the same fears, or perhaps worse fears, because she was a young woman but old enough to know how fragile life was, especially the life of a woman waiting for her man and protecting her child as best she could.

On Sunday night, his father didn't have dinner before leaving, as was usual. He spoke with his mother in the kitchen for a long while. Then he heard, with the same anxiety as every Sunday, the preparations for the journey and the rumble of the truck that slowly faded into the silence of the night and the slow steps of a horse that never seemed to get any closer.

Jordi fell asleep, and at some point he woke with moonlight on his pillow. It shone right through the window. It was a night he'd spent his life struggling to date precisely, a night in the winter of 1939 in Mollet del Vallès and across all of Europe.

Afterward, as the hours and days passed, a growing anxiety settled throughout his body.

Late at night, they arrived.

His mother said he wasn't there.

"Don't lie, ma'am, we know he's hiding somewhere in the house," said a voice, loudly.

AT SOME POINT, HE DISCOVERED *that he had spent almost his entire life consumed by a single obsession: the future. Only in the past, in those warm and transparent waters he had slowly left behind, could* one read the mystery of existence. *The future might be full of prom-ises, of novelties. But only the past was truly an ocean of concrete, fulfilled things. The future, on the contrary, was something that was always behind, something the eyes could not see. So we spend our lives trying to guess, with anxiety, like someone walking backward who doesn't know when they'll fall into an abyss. The past, however, is something that lies ahead because it can be seen. There we find the record of all human existence, even if we're incapable of understand-ing it even to the slightest degree.*

He tried to think, to remember when the illusion of the future had ended. He couldn't pinpoint it exactly. Maybe when he began to suspect that all the effort to stay afloat was pointless? Or when he suspected the sinking was imminent and inevitable? Yes, it wasn't long after that he began to suspect the great universal fraud: the fu-ture wasn't ahead; it was behind.

Lucía had been waiting for him

Montevideo, Saturday, February 5 or 12, 2011.

He went to the bookstore several Saturdays in a row. The fourth time, Lucía told him not to bother disguising himself as a worker because it didn't suit him. Santiago conceded. She asked him what he was looking for there that he couldn't find anywhere else in the city.

"If you're looking for a little fling," said Lucía, "you're wast-ing your time, because I can't stand cleaning up after the kids from Carrasco. Last summer I worked in Punta del Este babysit-ting spoiled brats who nearly got me committed. I'm tired of hearing about how kids today are smarter." They're neither smarter nor dumber. Their parents make them dumber by making them believe they're smarter. No, I'm no good at babysitting. Now, if you're looking for a virgin for marriage, same thing. Don't be fooled by appearances. About three years ago, I had a boyfriend from Cerrito who didn't like school as much as I did. All he could think about was that, and he managed to convince me. I can't really complain, though, because I was Snow White, and he was something like a dwarf of normal height. So you won't get anywhere that way, and I'm already cured of sweet talk.

The following Sunday, against all his expectations, Santiago returned to the bookstore. He browsed the section on 19th-century French sociology because he had discovered that under that label were the old medical books that had founded several disciplines. He found one that classified the Ibero-American race as proof of the inconveniences of miscegenation: South Americans, despite being a young race, had reached decrepitude in just a few centuries. He was struck by several drawings of cranial cross-sections analyzing the different diameters and the typology of the vault of this particular race, destined to disappear in the chaos of their picturesque republics.

As he passed the cash register, his gaze lingered on her, on her hands over the numbers of the register, on her profile as she checked the price on the small green screen. He looked at her with genuine admiration, waiting to be caught. He intended to pretend her gaze unsettled him, but he couldn't. The young doctor who had passed all the most difficult tests, who was capable of managing his nerves and emotions with cold precision, even in situations that would normally induce panic in others, now received an electric shock from those eyes that seemed to either ignore or had forgotten doubt and modesty.

When the previous customer took his bag of books and left, she seized the moment to say:

"Sir, did you find everything you were looking for?"

"Everything, except being treated like a still-young guy."

"Do you need us to address you informally?"

"Would that be too much to ask?"

"No, it's not too much. It's better to tell you straight out that you're a bit annoying and a little ridiculous, but if you're not a psychopath, you could end up being amusing and, in the process, spend a bit more on some books I'm trying to clear out. For example, all that French junk from 19th-century medicine... Thankfully, there aren't many readers coming to sell this kind of book anymore. Single uncles with magnificent libraries aren't dying off as much these days."

Lucía's words took Santiago by surprise, but at the same time, he knew they were inevitable. In some way, he had provoked them himself. He just wasn't sure how to respond or anticipate them, which meant he had no calculated memory of the possible options.

"Is that section going to disappear? Aren't they planning to restock it?" asked Santiago.

"No. Why would they? In our era, we have our own junk. Little by little, Harry Potter books with marked-up pages are starting to come in, as if there's anything worth highlighting in all that *fast food*.

"*Fast reading*, more like."

"I don't know, something like that. My English isn't up to that level. *Fast reading, fast selling, best reading*, whatever."

For a moment, he felt as if it wasn't him inviting her to lunch at a restaurant on Calle Colonia, one on a corner, though he couldn't remember its name. No one cares about the names of restaurants in Montevideo. There are so many that you have to identify them by the two streets they're on.

"Colonia and…"

"Any of them," she said. "They all serve the same thing. Galician food, maybe Italian. I don't know which is worse, but when you're hungry, you have to admit they're the best cooks in the world."

She told him the bookstore closed at noon, at twelve. He returned just as Lucía was lowering the shutters and putting on the padlock. That custom of closing and resting at midday still survived in a few businesses, thought Santiago, nostalgic for what was barely hanging on, like waiting for the end of a loved one lingering in a hospital.

As Julia bent down to secure the padlock against the ground, he looked at her slim waist, at her hips disguised by pants that were too loose. The lines suggesting the rest of her deeper sensuality were as attractive as those of any woman her age, because youth makes almost every woman beautiful, he often thought. Her back and her buttocks, which merged into the legs of a healthy woman (fragilely healthy like everything else), evoked more affection than desire in him. He thought she dressed like all the girls her age, as if being pretty and loved by everyone was an obligation or a need that women confuse with their own freedom.

"I accept because I'm starving," she said, "not because I'm giving in to you. I already told you it's obvious what you're after, and I have no problem sleeping with you if you insist a little more, if you play your part right, like in the movies."

"Don't act all revolutionary," he replied. "There's no need. I don't care either. It's just that eating alone isn't as good as eating with my favorite bookseller."

She laughed to brush off his remark. They walked in silence until they reached the café on Colonia and Ejido. When the waiter left to get their milanesas napolitanas and Russian salad, she put her elbows on the table, leaned her face closer, and said:

"What do you want? Are you going to spin a thousand stories until I melt and say yes?"

"Why do you say that?"

"Because I know you're hiding something from me. I can feel it, I can smell it."

"I'm not inviting you to lunch to sleep with you. It's not that I don't want to. I imagine I'd never refuse something like that. But it's not about that."

"Then what is it? I already told you that if you're looking for a virgin, you're wasting your time. If you're looking for a woman for something more serious, that too. I'm not planning to marry for the rest of my days."

"No, not that."

"Then what?"

"I don't know. Look, once, a friend of mine who lives in the U.S. told me a story that, believe it or not, could have happened right here. My friend had met a man, neither successful nor a failure, who went to the barber twice a month even though he was almost bald. Because it was the only way he knew to buy the touch of someone who wasn't a prostitute. It was true: no one can tickle themselves, because the brain is wired to feel ticklish when something or someone else touches it. That's what the studies from Princeton or some other university always looking for a problem said. On his own, he had discovered long ago that no one can caress themselves, at least not in the intense and real way someone else can. The barber, perhaps without realizing it, would run the comb through his hair and just barely graze his scalp. And it was like someone showing him a gesture of affection, of friendship, in a polite and automated society where getting closer than a meter is seen as disrespectful."

"Poor guy…"

"At first, the discovery horrified him…"

"He must have been some macho Latino or a Southern conservative, one of those who preach against gay marriage in church and then hire male prostitutes when they're possessed by the devil."

"Probably. But the point is…"

"The point? Why are you talking like that?"

"I mean, the thing is, he spent several nights after work looking for a male barber."

"He probably thought what everyone thinks, that only gay men are capable of real emotions."

"One night, he found her. It was the best money he ever spent, he thought. But it turned out she was just filling in for a barber who had gotten sick. So he followed her for days, until the poor woman reported him for harassment, and the idiot ended up in jail."

"Very interesting. I'd like to believe you."

"Man, you're so skeptical. You don't believe anything I say."

"I don't know why. I believe the story. I don't believe it's true. Maybe you just made it up, but I believe the story's message, it's right…"

"No, I didn't just make it up. I thought of it once when I went to the barber."

"Did you like the barber?"

"Don't be silly. It occurred to me because it was like a metaphor for what I was going through myself. You're so oppressed by responsibilities and by being this perfect, respectful man that you can't even touch a friend anymore. I don't even touch my friends anymore, and I'm grateful when the dental assistant puts a hand on my shoulder while the doctor injects anesthesia into my gums. I know that gesture is calculated, but I still appreciate it. Maybe everyone's become like one big brothel, a respectful brothel, for civilized people."

"What dentist do you go to that has an assistant?"

"What's with the question?"

"Because it reminds me of stories from a friend who lives in the U.S."

"Not just in the Empire do dentists work in pairs. You keep going back to the same topic. You're chasing yourself. I'm not trying to lie to you. I'm also not trying to get you into bed. I'm not interested, just like pornography doesn't appeal to me.

"What, you've never watched porn on the internet?"

"Yes, like everyone else. Some scenes are well done. But you know that all that junk, which is fine to consume occasionally, like McDonalds, won't kill you if you don't rely on it exclusively.

"Because all of it just confirms what we're missing people who want to touch you and don't want to sleep with you the next day."

"Yeah, easy sex kills the magic and a lot of other experiences."

"You're about to get your way. Keep going a little more..."

Santiago pursed his lips and called the waiter.

"The truth is, I've never been good with complicated ideas," he said."

The waiter approached, and he asked for the check.

"You really did well," she said. "I also wish someone would comb my hair, like the Paraguayan nanny I had since I turned fifteen did."

"Your dad gave her to you?"

"Now that you mention it, I think it was something like that. My dad gave me a Paraguayan nanny... Incredible, poor guy, he was always so busy. And I loved my nanny so much. Truly loved her, not like the alienated guy in your story."

"What happened to her?"

"What happens to a lot of people. She died."

Santiago wanted to change the subject.

"Are you writing something?"

"No…"

"Don't tell me that living surrounded by so many old books, you've never felt the urge to write some story."

Lucía's expression had changed. Suddenly, it had turned darker, but at the same time more transparent, Santiago thought, though he couldn't tell if the change was due to the memory of the Paraguayan nanny or the question about something that's usually kept hermetic among some book lovers.

"I'm not going to say no," said Lucía. "I didn't get into poetry. The first one who really shook me was Dostoevsky. Then Kafka, the sweetness of Sartre, the bitterness of Sábato, the loving touch of Benedetti. And that's it. I don't know what happened after. It's like I died when the century began. Maybe writers are lost on Facebook or who knows where, and they don't have time to write anymore. Or maybe they just don't write things like those anymore, as if human nature suddenly changed forever."

"Can you share something, a sneak peek…?" asked Santiago.

"Nothing worth sharing," she interrupted. "I'm torn between giving up on trying and restarting the first chapter for the umpteenth time."

"Your problem is perfectionism. Maybe if you let someone else read it…"

"Definitely not."

"At least a sneak peek?"

"You're so annoying."

"It's just curiosity. I'm into scientific books… I would've liked to be a doctor or an astronomer."

"For the last five years, I've wasted time writing something like science fiction. But it's not really science fiction. It's about a world where people don't die unless by some accident."

"I've always wondered what it would be like to live five hundred years and possess the experience of centuries."

"No, in this case, after a normal life, normal as we know it, that is, after fifty or seventy years, people would move to other neighborhoods or cities and start forgetting everything to the point of building a new life from scratch. There weren't graves to mourn but distant pasts to barely remember. Often, someone who had forgotten their previous life would stumble upon what they had done a hundred years ago and remember it as if someone else had done it."

"So the fundamental tragedy didn't exist, only a few *déjà vus?*"

"No, there was no death, only forgetting, and just a few *déjà vus* to make life more interesting."

HE HAD FALLEN ASLEEP as he did every day, soon after sunset. The sea was so calm it was scary. It looked like one of the mirrors that filled one of the rooms downstairs, but it was a fallen mirror, infinite, soft but unchanging.

He was scared because he doubted. For a moment, he thought if he jumped into that surface, he would walk on it. Then he realized the deception and tried to think of something else. Loneliness had shown him that even more dangerous than the storms and the violence of the sea was that unsettling, unpredictable presence that often appeared when the sea was calm. That terrible ghost was (perhaps he never quite discovered it) himself. It was something worse than his own reflection in the mirrors, always threatening to reveal itself. It was something worse, something unseen because it was inside him. Something that could one day make him walk to the prow and hurl himself into the much-feared void. He feared this something when he was awake, more than when he slept and dreamed of ghosts.

The eerie calm of that night was broken by a kind of explosion, something like the sea rising to the sky and then plunging into the depths of the abyss. He awoke amid screams, like the ones he had heard the day before when he discovered that in the ship's hold, his voice multiplied several times.

He woke up and heard nothing. For a moment, he thought the beast, which sometimes accompanied the ship and of which he only knew the back and a certain undulating movement, had decided to end its aimless journey. It wasn't that anything else could bother the beast in such a limitless space. It was the boundlessness of things in time that could unsettle the beast, just as they unsettled him without him being able to avoid it.

But no; everything was just as still, but the strange glimmers on the sea announced it. He raised his eyes with great fear and saw it there above, enormous, white like a giant coin, glowing with its own light.

Gradually, the terror the sky had prepared for him turned into admiration, and perhaps into a kind of absurd love, like all fixations.

He looked at it carefully, noticing its details, its spots, its glimmers, a certain weight that made it slowly descend toward the sea.

The thing returned the following night, and the next, and each time it was as if it were dying. Until the clouds covered it, and he had to wait many more nights to see it again.

Suddenly, the beach had turned white, timeless.

Punta del Este, Friday, February 18, 2011

"Just imagining the loneliness of a coffin gives me claustrophobia," said Santiago, leaning his head back and sinking his feet into the sand.

The sun made him close his eyes.

"Don't be ridiculous," said Paulina, with a less than convincing smile. "Why are you thinking about things like that?"

"Nothing. I was thinking about my retirement. I was thinking about buying a house in Punta del Este for when there's nothing important left to do. Then old age and all that came to mind... Sooner or later it will be a reality, won't it?"

"What does that matter? Are you already thinking about retirement? Aren't you even halfway through your productive life and you're already thinking about retiring?"

"No, it's not that..."

"When the time comes, you won't even notice. Could you try not to ruin my vacation?"

"What if I wake up in the middle of the night like it's happened to so many people? I've often dreamed something similar and woken up gasping for air. Did you know that one version of the saying "saved by the bell" claims the bell was those placed in the nineteenth century, with a string so that the resurrected dead could alert people to dig them up?"

"I thought that saying came from boxing."

"That's very likely. Besides, I don't think the little bell would've worked. With the shock, the resurrected would probably die before anyone could rescue them."

"Why are you thinking about these things now?"

"If you want, I won't mention them."

"It's not that. I asked you a question."

"It's just that this sunlight is so wonderful... and last night I dreamed something like that."

"As you always say, it's logical, isn't it?"

"What's logical?"

"If you felt suffocated for any other reason, it's logical you'd dream about situations like that."

"Sounds very logical. It's pre-Freudian psychology in its purest form. Dreams depend on whether you ate apples or pork for dinner, if you went to bed late or didn't give your stomach enough time to start a normal digestion. That's why Eskimos always dream about the Caribbean and Bedouins about mountains of *Coca-Cola* nice and cold."

Paulina turned her head toward Santiago and looked at him for a moment from under her straw hat. Then she said:

"Yesterday I was with Clara."

"Which Clara?"

"Clarita, Andrés Taranto's sister."

"Oh, what did she say?"

"She's working at a law firm in La Plata."

"That's great. I didn't know she had moved."

"She told you at the meeting at El Congo."

"Well, I didn't remember."

"We were actually talking about you."

"Hold on, Catalina, there's a curve coming."

"About how much you've changed since you came back from the United States."

"Women talk."

"Don't act like a joker. I'm being serious."

"Yeah, yeah. No need to raise your voice."

"You're going to ask me to talk to you…"

Santiago couldn't stop thinking about Alejandro, about la Negra, about the kid. What was that little devil's name? The first time he saw him, the kid almost took out Santiago's eye. He had approached him with a spoon, dead set on leaving him one-eyed. His mother was almost dying of embarrassment. "Kid stuff," Santiago said. It didn't bother him that the kid had tried to take out his eye with a spoon; what annoyed him was that he didn't let them get two sentences in without interrupting.

"Poor little devil," he thought, squeezing his eyes shut with a pained expression on the rest of his face. "In a year he'll have lost his father. He'll have survived his mother's grief and become the shyest little devil in his class."

"Damn it," said Santiago.

"Now what's wrong?"

"Nothing. It just slipped out. I remembered I forgot to pay the electricity bill this month."

"If you were more organized, you'd be less stressed. You don't even relax when you're at the beach."

"The little devil…", Santiago thought, "but what's his name? Soon he'll be thrown by the unpredictable hand of fate into helplessness, as if thrown into this sea, so bright above and so dark below."

"I put everything I need to do in my email calendar. I never forget anything because Google reminds me."

Santiago dug his feet into the sand, leaned back on the beach chair, closed his eyes, and remembered that salty breeze on his lips, the sound of the waves, that moment he had lived forty or fifty years ago, before he was fully born. Being born must be like a terrible blow to the soul, he thought, almost smiling; one forgets everything, remains dazed for a few years until slowly starting to remember and think again. He had lived that moment before, but not there, he thought, but on the shores of the Mediterranean, in the south of France, he was sure. A beautiful woman, whom he admired more than loved, was telling him about a party on a boat.

"Danielle wrote to me," someone said. "She's in Tangier."

Santiago looked at a photograph in the magazine. It was a beach from the movie *Summer of '42*. He remembered the film's music as he looked at a photograph of a beach with waves that might have taken place in 1942, or somewhere in Massachusetts or Connecticut, in 1971. Jennifer O'Neill, her eternal smile, the same sky in her eyes. There was the sea, the beach, those eternal landscapes, always the same, regardless of the twists and turns of human history. The same pearls, the same glitter of the sun on the water's surface, the same seashells with the same patterns from a hundred million years ago, as if nothing had happened, as if nothing ever would, as if Jennifer O'Neill were still there, beautiful, just as young, finally saved from time by the gentle intervention of art...

Old Glinka had suddenly fallen ill

Manhattan, Friday, March 25, 2011

For just over a year, Miguel had learned to buy whisky and *kapusta* at a store in lower Manhattan. He spent his free hours reading the latest news with the smell of coffee at the Barnes & Noble bookstore. He became addicted to the *Wall Street Journal* and once had the intuition that he had discovered the geometric logic of the Dow Jones. When he wasn't in *Union Square* with his *iPad*, he would stop by an Apple store and entertain himself playing with the latest gadgets. There was always something new in the digital world, he thought, but in the end, it was all the same.

"Among the infinite variations of the same," he thought, almost amazed at what he was thinking, "like an Andy Warhol painting, nothing is different. These tidy people will never know what it's like to smell a mud ranch in the Pampas, with a wood stove and kerosene lantern light."

He had barely finished writing that in his email when he deleted it. Who could he send it to? To himself? Yes, that's what he did most of the time, sending emails to himself. But he deleted it.

He did things more out of obligation and less because he wanted to. That's why, he thought, he did them better. He didn't make mistakes. He didn't get depressed or bitter over any failure. And if any nagging doubt visited him at night, he chased it away with a good Johnnie Walker, which was why he worked—so he could be left alone when he wasn't working. Some idiot living in Santiago, Chile, once told him he was becoming too Americanized. Like all idiots, he arrogantly claimed the right to moralize about other people's lives and felt superior because he had failed in every attempt to do anything with his own.

When something went wrong, he chalked it up to probability or a miscalculation. As they say here, a "lack of judgment," though in Spanish, that means something else. How do you say "lack of judgment" in Russian?

One day he returned to Glinka's store. If he hadn't gone earlier, it was due to an excess of speculation, a small existential crisis, typical of those in their 33rd or 44th year. The old man had had a heart attack and was recovering in a dark corner, among bags of rice and curry, dates, and dried figs he had brought in to meet the growing demand from Arabs in the neighborhood.

He had taken on the moribund aspect of Grandpa Mijail. The same straight nose, lips slightly resigned, eyes hidden beneath heavy eyelids, the same clear forehead faintly outlined by sparse white hair. The same absence of energy to smile. That was the grandfather he had known. He hadn't imagined—now he discovered—that the real one, the grandfather he had been for

171

most of his life, was someone else. Someone else, perhaps more energetic, perhaps as insensitive as he was in his forties, a tireless lover of women who didn't love him back at twenty and a young poet who enjoyed the evening lights of Moscow in his early adolescence.

The old man Glinka motioned to him with his hand. Miguel approached.

"*The letters,*" he said.

"I didn't bring them," Miguel replied.

"Bring them" Glinka said, issuing an order without authority that sounded more like a plea.

Miguel didn't answer.

"I owe you a favor," the old man insisted. "Not a day has gone by without me thinking about it. I don't know how I could refuse…"

Miguel tried to console him. As always, he thought, one only knows how to console others.

"Now it's you who must do me that favor…" the old man insisted.

Miguel promised to bring the letters by Saturday.

"No, not Saturday. I'll be very busy on Saturday. Friday…"

On Friday, just before six, Miguel brought the letters. Glinka ordered his five employees to close up and leave.

The two of them sat down at a small table in a corner, beneath a dusty yellow light.

The old man Glinka opened the cardboard box as if it were a sacred chest or a delicate archaeological find. Miguel attributed it to age and fatigue: not to the importance of the letters. The old man skimmed through them one by one, arranging them like a deck of cards. Miguel asked if he was sorting them by date. After a distracted "no," the old man said yes. It was the dates. "More or less," he corrected himself.

Over the course of two hours, the old man Glinka read laboriously and translated from Russian into English, line by line, fumbling for the best words, correcting himself, sometimes groping like a blind man for the meaning behind so many obscure expressions.

The content of the letters was somewhat disappointing. Nothing important, no secrets that would shame his grandfather, no extraordinary inheritance still unclaimed. Reality is often quite boring, Glinka consoled him. Or seems to be. Perhaps if he looked with more care and feeling at those distant events, those recent confessions, he might discover what only a biologist is capable of seeing in a monotonous cell.

Almost half of the letters were full of metaphors. Nine had been written by Grandpa Mijail, had served as drafts, or had been returned. Nearly all were addressed to his mother, Karina, except for one that seemed to speak to a brother. Eleven letters were from his mother, all longer than his grandfather's and easier to read. They were full of motherly advice, Miguel thought. They offered nothing new, apart from warnings about the benefits of good nutrition and certain instructions on how to guard against ear infections, which, according to his mother, were a Polzin family trait—a torment Miguel had suffered in recent years and had attributed to the cold of New York.

The Polzin family had not belonged to the nobility, but neither had the grandfather been the poor man he'd claimed to be before becoming a prosperous builder in Buenos Aires. He had some disagreements with the new Soviet regime, which, it was known, would in a few decades come to dominate the entire world, but politics was not his strong suit, nor had he ever been interested in it. Even less in ideological debates. He said that ideas led nowhere and that all of them were preceded by the actions of pragmatic men like himself. The grandfather didn't consider this to be an idea. Miguel thought that his pragmatism had saved him from all the regimes of the time, though not from the pride of fools who died for certain ideals. In this, he greatly resembled Miguel and not at all his father, who surely must have suffered with the grandfather as much as Miguel had had to endure his father's philosophical moralizing. The ideological silence that characterized the grandfather was due to this disinterest and not to the stoic protection of a secret past that he'd cleverly allowed others to believe through a series of misunderstandings.

In short, the grandfather's life had been quite simple. It was almost devoid of interest.

Around eleven at night, the old man Glinka struggled to straighten his back. He sighed wearily, and Miguel suggested they leave it for another day. The old man agreed. Only two letters remained. The most difficult ones, he said, because of the handwriting. They decided that Miguel would leave them for him to study better and at his leisure, in the daylight.

THE DAYS OF CALM rarely allowed stillness. When the waters turned flat as a mirror, when at midday one could see the sun's gleam playing in the depths without end, when the wind vanished and the air was neither cold nor warm, neither dry nor humid, a storm brewed inside him. Then the memories flowed like hurricanes, vanished things, shadows that screamed or whispered with a clamor. Then the silence is so profound that it hums in his head and only calms when he leans over the bow to see the clear abyss and hear an echo like a white moan, like the lament of a great whale lost in the depths of the sky below.

He knows by heart the list of his speculations, which rarely changes: one: there was something before him and before 00λ; two: 00λ heads toward an established destination, following a route designed prior to all his memory; three: other men like him and other women like the women depicted in the books and magazines of the second level await unnoticed the arrival of 00λ and the encounter with its sole inhabitant; four: 00λ and its inhabitant have an end, though, like the beginning, it is necessarily unknown; five: perhaps the path does not end with 00λ nor with the meeting of the vacationers but with a prior sinking, that is, the long-dreamed-of harbor is not before the destruction of 00λ but after, beyond the horizon, beyond the waters, beyond the depths of the abyss, beyond the world.

This last possibility has always troubled him, and he has always tried to accept the idea that the destruction of that world"solitary, silent, sometimes loudly creaking, battered by thunder and giant waves, by suns and entire days without nights, floating in the transparent waters of the tropics, in the stagnant air that prevents time from flowing anywhere "is necessary and inevitable.

On these days, when the mystery accelerates and time stops, he writes. He does not write what he says because he is unaware of the need to speak. Nor does he write what he thinks because his writing is very rudimentary. He knows that writing is an innate skill (he has written for as long as he can remember), but at times he feels he has not had enough time to improve that skill, as he would have liked, as it would have been more useful to him. So whenever he can, he writes, and whenever he writes, he describes memories or things he had seen, because at some point, glancing distractedly at his writings, he has recalled distant days, with their respective emotions and inevitable nostalgias. Since then, he writes with some irregularity and reads what he wrote months before, being incapable of deciphering the symbols in the books and magazines of the second level.

00λ—the name or symbols barely visible among the rust of the hull that seem to identify the vessel—is shaped like a fish. From the drawings, it looks like one of those futuristic ships that once sailed the skies and outer space. It has something of the spaceships depicted in various books, surrounded by symbols illegible to its sole inhabitant. It could also have been a submarine in distress that has surfaced, like a ship sinking in reverse. At the peak of its occupant's maturity, 00λ still retains some of its engines. The only purpose of all that metal down there, he thinks, is to stabilize the drifting remains somewhat, to prolong their agony on the surface, and, above all, to keep the sole passenger occupied, who has always lived obsessed with the enigma of those engines surrounded by twisted pipes that interlock with mysterious precision, remaining there motionless as if in a coupling interrupted by sudden death.

But 00λ does not stay afloat on its own. Its sole passenger and crewman spends his entire day ensuring it doesn't sink below the surface and head toward that harbor he's dreamed of since the beginning of time. For that, he must bail out the water that accumulates in its belly every day. For more than nine moons, for his entire life, he's managed to keep that mass of rusted metal afloat. On rainy days, he collects freshwater; on stormy days, the task of reducing the water in the hold is delayed, sometimes beyond tolerable limits, according to his calculations.

Carlos II and Willian are occupied with Paulina.

Montevideo, February 19, 2011

From the bar on Misiones Street, they saw her rush past, her heels clacking as usual. Willian followed her with his gaze, and Carlitos said:

"That chick gets hotter every day."

"You know her?" Willian asked, feigning surprise.

Deep down, Willian knew that Carlitos knew everyone, because people from small towns develop that skill of prying and remembering the life and deeds of every individual who passes by twice within fifty meters. It wasn't a matter of how many people lived in a small town or a big city like Montevideo, he thought, but of skills and interests. In small towns, like Rivera, others are always a matter of interest.

"I knew the old man, Dr. Aguirre. He had his office right here, just a few blocks away, right across from Plaza Matriz. Next door was the office of the notary Juan Rossi."

"Did the quack die?"

"About three years ago. They probably haven't even buried him yet. When I met this girl, she must've been eight or nine."

"Does she remember you?"

"Not a chance. I crossed paths with her a few times on Sarandí Pedestrian Street, and it seems she was even disgusted that an old man looked at her."

"She's really pretty, the brat."

"Yeah. But I was watching her in case she happened to remember me. One day I almost greeted her but didn't dare. She might've snubbed me. She's always been stuck-up. Her boyfriends were all from Carrasco, and if they weren't driving a BMW, it was a Mercedes-Benz. Now she's with a doctor from the American Hospital."

"And how do you know so much?"

"Things you hear."

"You can't deny you're from the sticks. Years go by, you see yourself getting old, and you don't lose the knack you picked up as a kid."

"On the contrary. There are things I don't forget. I always liked her mother, Dr. Aguirre's wife. Don't make that nosy face. I never crossed the line. If anything, Grace Kelly did it a couple of times. Because women love to set your head on fire and then leave you drooling like an idiot. She and Grace Kelly were like two peas in a pod. She must've known it too, because she acted just like her."

"And you grow old and don't learn."

"Worse. You grow old and get dumber. But God bless those goddesses. After all, we're the fools, and if it weren't for goddesses like her… what would life be?"

"We'd have to pay a tax to make sure they don't disappear."

"Grace Kelly—who was actually named María José—drove me so crazy that I often went to the notary's office just to see if I could be lucky enough to run into her in the elevator. All for nothing. Like life, you know?"

"And? Come on, mate, don't just sit there nostalgic and silent…"

"This girl, Paulina, who back then was just 'Pau,' must've learned all those tricks from her mother that the weaker sex invents to enslave brutes like us." Worse than her mother, they used to say.

"Who said that?"

"Dr. Aguirre's employees, who were all buddies with the notary Rossi's staff. You need something signed too, damn it?"

"Alright, alright. Don't get worked up…"

"How much of a carbon copy she is of her mother, she decided to give one of those clowns hope…"

"Which 'clowns'?"

"One of the notary Rossi's employees… I used to know his name, but I can't remember now. A skinny kid, freckled, with broad shoulders, like one of those Mexican or Filipino boxers but freckled, like a featherweight."

"And?"

"The girl had rejected him in a really bad way. Really bad. Humiliating, they said, but I can't confirm that last part. Apparently, he... Germán. That's it. His name was Negro Germán, though he wasn't black except for his tight, wiry hair. Apparently, he had waited for her one day at the entrance of the office building, with a rose."

"Stop, I don't even want to imagine it... I'm already feeling secondhand embarrassment."

"Yeah, it was something that stupid. But how do you tell an idiot to stop?"

"And what happened in the end?"

"I don't know the details. I only know that the doorman was there with the other employees of the notary who had come down to witness this poor devil's cheesy love confession. She must've said something to him that had the consequences it did. Apparently, she called him a beggar or a starving loser or something like that, because he shot back that a princess like her might despise a beggar like him, but deep down that's exactly what these snobs wanted, some rich guy to marry and a lout like him to screw them good, some uneducated starving guy to help them endure their marriage. She laughed, and it seems he promised her that one day she'd swallow all the cum from his balls. That's when one of the doctor's employees punched him in the face, leaving his mouth bleeding. I don't know if this was before or after he told her she'd swallow it all, and with pleasure, but that's roughly how it went."

"A bit over the top, that Germán guy."

"Yeah. But you have to see what a humiliated man is like. The guy quit his job at the notary's office—he wasn't fired over the incident—and got a job as a cook at the restaurant that's still on 18 and Ejido."

"La Pasiva. The old and beloved La Pasiva."

"That's the one. Now there's a Burger King there, but back when this happened, it was still the famous La Pasiva. Negro Germán spent six months struggling in that job until she showed up with some guy who eventually turned out to be the last boyfriend this chick has, some little doctor who works at the American Hospital, though this one doesn't have a BMW."

"You know doctors aren't what they used to be. Now they're just like us."

"She ordered a salad, and he had a napolitana milanesa. After all, the little doctor wasn't that snobby. Napoli, not sushi or anything weird. Then they were served by an old waiter from the place. When they finished and ordered dessert, Germán went to the bathroom and jerked off as much as he could into a little cup, which he then used to top the chocolate ice cream."

Carlitos gestured toward the bar and said:

"One chocolate ice cream crowned with the waiter's sperm, please."

"What a bastard. You're going to make me vomit."

"When the boyfriend asked for the bill, the crazy guy showed up. 'How was dessert?' he asked. She opened her eyes wide, like this. Then the guy asked again. 'Miss, did you enjoy the dessert? It's a house specialty. The secret's in the cream.'"

"A real bastard, that Germán guy."

He thought about that absurd story

Punta del Este, Friday, February 18, 2011

Suddenly, he remembered Lucía's novel. Or rather, the novel she claimed to have started a hundred times but couldn't get the tone right. The tone, the key. He couldn't remember the exact word. The idea was the best part. Well, there wasn't something concrete, which in art must be like a scientific theory supported by the existence of angels and demons. But there was an idea. Or he had imagined something about the novel based on that idea. He didn't know if it was science fiction. It was something else. It was about a parallel world or time, like dreams.

"Don't bother," he would've liked to tell her. People don't read other people's novels anymore.

Paulina's phone rang. It wasn't a call, just a new text message. He took a deep breath and dug his feet deeper into the sand. He heard the protest of a seagull that drew a swift curve near his head. He didn't open his eyes.

In that world that still had no name, people were deprived of one of the two most important experiences of our lives: death. Or rather (she had tried to explain) death could occur sometimes, but it wasn't the inevitable end of someone known. It was more of a very rare experience that only happened during wartime, and the dead almost never appeared to be mourned before being forgotten by others. Instead of death, there was forgetfulness. An easy and merciful forgetfulness. People disappeared; they didn't die, and therefore, they were rarely born. A peasant in 1216 France would go to the forest one day in search of firewood and never return. His wife, who waited for him with five crying children, would receive a visit from another peasant who, seeing her so sad, would try to help her and eventually, as is so predictable in any dimension, fall in love with her, and she would completely forget the father of her children, who had suddenly been lost in the forest. Because everyone knew and accepted that the world was a labyrinth, and there were certain moments when people got lost in such a way that others, for some unknown reason, began to forget them or barely retained memories that gradually faded until they disappeared—perhaps because memory itself was also a labyrinth. Then, the man who had been lost in the forest might, by chance, return to his old home and ask the owner's permission to gather some branches for his family waiting on the other side of the mountain.

This same man could be the one who in 1447 stowed away on a ship in an Italian port and, after being discovered, was thrown into the sea, where he probably disappeared forever without ever having witnessed death, only the repeated forgetfulness, that very human form of nothingness. Because, in the end, death and forgetfulness are the same thing, with the difference that one is unbearably tragic and the other is sweet nothingness. Almost as sweet as infinite memory that no longer worries about what is to come, that has forgotten the uncertainties of the moment and, therefore, inevitably transforms into pure nostalgia.

Or perhaps it was that other man walking down Les Champs-Élysées in 1966, in high heels, with painted lips, waiting for another man who wouldn't insult him, who wouldn't call him a son of a bitch, a lying cross-dresser, a fraud pretending to be what he wasn't. And one night, after violent sex in a Paris hotel, completely drunk, he fell asleep only to wake up in a hospital, remembering not a single moment from the night before, hallucinating about someone pushing him into the sea from a ship, and then waking up nearly drowned with a load of branches on his back, descending a mountain to a humble house where five crying children waited for him. Then, he'd wake up agitated, and the doctor would tell him to calm down, that it had just been a dream, that he should rest. Then, the man would lie back and tell himself that he needed to recover from the accident to go to California, where he planned to fulfill his dream of starting his own Harley Davidson motorcycle parts business.

He thought he was still too young

Montevideo, March 15, 2011
Alejandro Spinelli took almost his entire life to confront his truth. It wasn't something he had to suffer from childhood, or even adolescence. In that same brief period of one year, he discovered his illness, the cause, and the consequences of a poor solution for his partner's suffering.

The brief story of that last year began on a Tuesday when the doctor opened the envelope, unable to avoid a slight tremor in his hands. At the time, Alejandro attributed the tremor to age, not the circumstance. Doctors don't get involved with their patients, not even in the worst cases. If they did, we wouldn't have doctors, he thought. Luckily, he wasn't a surgeon.

He pulled out a sheet, read it quickly, and put it back. He took off his glasses, and Santiago saw his tired eyes.

"Any news, doctor?"

The doctor didn't answer. He adjusted himself in his chair and pulled the paper out of the envelope again, as if he had forgotten to read something. He put his glasses back on and read once more.

"Is something wrong?"

"We need to do more tests."

"Did these come back bad?"

"No…"

"But…? I feel perfectly fine… Is there a problem?"

"Life is a problem that needs solving."

"I'm serious."

"Yes, yes, sorry… Don't worry."

"I am worried. I'm worried because when you feel fine and a doctor isn't so sure, it usually means something serious must be going on." Tell me straight: the tests came back bad.

"No… I mean, maybe. The issue is that these tests aren't entirely conclusive."

Alejandro figured the doctor must be over sixty. Maybe he was about to retire. Maybe he was at that point where age weighs more heavily on the emotions than decades of professional experience painfully accumulated. Hence the mechanical tremor in his hands, the stuttering more characteristic of a be-ginner than a veteran hardened by the misfortunes of others.

"Not conclusive? Conclusive for what? Do I have something serious?"

"We don't know yet. We need to run more blood tests. I'll give you a referral to another specialist."

"Do I need a second opinion?"

"Yes, maybe."

"Dr. Ignacio Rovira will give us a definitive diagnosis."

"Is he another neurologist?" asked Alejandro.

"No, he's a highly regarded oncologist."

The lake's mirror reflects the moon and hides the monsters

Piriápolis, March 26, 2011

Sometimes I try to imagine what the world would have been like in the Middle Ages, said Santiago. I don't mean how it looked, obviously that's child's play. I'd really like to know —like feel, even for a moment—what it felt like back then. The most basic pleasures and hatreds couldn't have been very differ-ent from ours, but maybe that daily map, that persistent emo-tional state, was different from ours. Every individual had an assigned place, with few or scarce chances of changing. A very unfair and boring world, of course. But on the other hand, they didn't have to experience what we do. That permanent sensa-tion that we're on a ship hiding a crack, a hole somewhere. So we have to work obsessively just to stay afloat. Just to stay afloat while we drift toward somewhere. Very interesting, I won't deny it, but at the cost of anguish and despair. It's enough to lose your job, to miss a debt payment, to lose a document, for someone in government or a big corporation to make a decision that will turn everything upside down—us and our entire family. Maybe the only uncertainty for men and women in the Middle Ages lay in not knowing what to do in case of illness, in not knowing when inevitable death would come. But in truth, our case isn't so different. We don't know what terrible illness will torture us in the near or distant future. We don't know when we'll die. We don't even know what will happen to us after we die. Those backward people, at least, had a clearer idea. Maybe they were wrong, but they had a clearer idea and probably didn't anguish over the future and the loss of the ground beneath their feet, like us, who, with growing obsession, keep bailing water out of our solitary ships, drifting aimlessly toward somewhere."

Uncertainty. That's the only word that defines and sums up our era, this damned 21st century. Fear of losing our job, our home, our identity. Fear of losing our sanity, of losing what we love. Fear of losing the fear itself, like someone who falls asleep at the wheel and jerks awake a second before crashing into another car stopped in the same lane. Like a patient forgetting to take the medicine that keeps them alive. Like a stranded survivor, trying to keep afloat with air in a life jacket, not knowing which way the shore lies. Like a ghost ship adrift in the vastness, battered daily by deafening uncertainty.

MARKED DAY. His father had condemned him

A Tuesday in July 2011

He mentioned it to Santiago over the phone, as if expecting his friend to correct the diagnosis—or, rather, Dr. Moreira's suspicion at the Hospital de Clínicas. Santiago slumped into his office chair and looked out the window at the birds chasing each other in what might have been an erotic game, as always at that hour in the evening.

He remembered that when Alejandro was a child in Villa del Parque, his father had built him a shelter in the backyard, on the other side of the small, sometimes nonexistent garden that his mother tended with such care.

"Actually," Alejandro had said, chatting with Quique, his blind stepbrother, over beers one afternoon at a restaurant in Parque Rodó, "actually, the two of them had built it together, him and his dad, back in the summer of 1981, with the radio hanging from a tree and narrating the events of the River-Independiente match." And since he was an Independiente fan, he had spent the afternoon juggling both things, rooting for the reds and watching that little shack grow, which would become one of the most important, inexplicably important things in his life. Every now and then, his mom would bring them two glasses with ice and orange juice and tell them they were crazy, working under the sun like that for no reason. By the time evening fell, only the roof was missing. And because Alejandro had insisted so much, they finished putting it up by moonlight, long after the commentary on the match—whose outcome he couldn't remember—was over, between the half-hourly news bulletins from *Mitre informs first, two minutes of news* and the songs of Mercedes Sosa between seven and eight. But they managed to finish before the old lady got furious because the food was getting cold. Alejandro talked about his mom's bad mood that night with a nostalgia that would be incomprehensible if you didn't know him or the importance of that shack at the house in Villa del Parque.

From then on, those hours became almost the entire summer of 81 for Alejandro and nearly all the summers that followed, until his father died in 85 from a heart attack, likely brought on by the stress of mortgage debts. By 89, they no longer had the house in Villa del Parque, but his mother had married Sosa and they moved to Montevideo. In 94, Alejandro met Negra Laurie and left his stepfather's house. His father-in-law had gotten him a job as a traffic inspector at the Montevideo city hall, which allowed him to keep studying for a while longer. For three years, he was a traffic inspector and a medical student, influenced by Santiago, until Albertito was born and the temporary abandonment of his studies turned, as was to be expected, into a permanent one.

The refuge, the famous Refuge of 81, was a bit of a primitive shack, Alejandro would say, a caricature of his own house, eternally unfinished and with holes in the tin roof that during the day let tiny rays of sunlight filter through during siesta time and at night projected indecipherable little white dots in the silence inhabited only by his mother's soft voice and his father's rough snoring, which always comforted him when he was scared. For Alejandro, problems didn't exist when his father was alive. In truth, the old man absorbed them all. He was like a wall that kept worries about debts, lack of money, humiliations from his boss, threats of layoffs, and threats from the crazy Ramiro—a small-time criminal who had threatened to kill him for reporting a minor theft of some public streetlights—from getting through. Sometimes, the old man would rub his chest and, to hide it, twist his mustache. Alejandro's mother would tell him he needed to eat lighter, that she'd take care of changing his diet, since wine and food had become the justification for a whole day of hard labor and carrying all sorts of loads, the old man had overindulged in these two pleasures. But surely it wasn't the food, Santiago thought, years later. A simple warning, a little notice here, just in time, could have extended his life another ten or fifteen years. A dog's lifespan, he thought.

The shack from 81, as Alejandro called it, besides recalling the year, also heavily resembled the house of TV's Tarzan. For a long time, it stood on four wooden pillars. It had a door that closed with a small rusty padlock on one side and two small windows on the other. It was the best house Alejandro had ever had in his life, he said, and Santiago believed him. It had been a real refuge where he kept an old, tattered copy of *The Thousand and One Nights* and another even more aged book by the Brothers Grimm, inherited from a nun cousin, the smell of a lighter he called a "flint striker," the songs of Camilo Sesto and Leonardo Fabio on a *Spica radio ("Mitre informs first. Two minutes,"* "*Empanadas, empanadas. Tapas disco de Oro, the best,"* "Colonia

Radio informs, the most left-leaning station on your dial," "Fravega *invites the city. It has everything you could imagine for your taste,"* "There's more informaaaation for this bulletin"), the incomprehensible idea that this space wasn't in Buenos Aires or the year 1981 but on an island in the Pacific and in a time already lost in the labyrinths of history, 1963 or 1936. Santiago believed all of it and, perhaps because of that, they were such close friends, like brothers.

In the unbearable summer of 1985, shortly after his father's death, while radios repeated *All I Ask of God*, that song they had once sung together a few months earlier, Alejandro expanded the shack by himself, adding two more pillars and extending the roof with several leftover sheets from the original construction four years prior. In this way, he was able to set up a small study table and a bookshelf that soon filled up with physics and philosophy books, from *Metric Geometry* by P. Puig Adam, with its Greek columns on the cover, to the *Introduction to Mathematical Analysis* with Newton's binomial theorem (which only Clarisa mastered), its matrices and endless series. In his early youth, he thought the author of that book—which smelled new and had cost him two months of begging his father—was a kind of Galileo Galilei, a demigod who had punished and made thousands of science-oriented students dream, until one day he met him at a lecture in Once. Then he found it hard to accept that the author of *Analysis* was just a man like his father, like anyone else, even if he was alive. In the same way, over time, he had to face the painful experience of acknowledging that *The Refuge* was, in reality, and had always been, just a sheet-metal shack, like those in a slum, or not even that, and not the setting for the dizzying reveries of Sinbad the Sailor and Michael Faraday, the inventor of induced current, who seemed to watch him from that beloved physics book with yellow covers, with its formulas on magnetic currents, $\varepsilon = -Blv$, or from volume F of the Encyclopaedia Britannica, which he had never returned to the municipal library and which, for some bureaucratic reason, no one had ever asked him to give back.

That had been his refuge, as Santiago had rightly called it, the place where he felt distant from the rest of the world, safe for a few hours from the sea of faces at school, from the sarcasm of Professor Rebles, from the mocking laughs of the heavy-hitter Aguirre, the long-haired Riveira, and the traitor Chino Kaplan, away from the girls with perfect smiles and fashionable pants like Fátima and the blond Carina Ferrari (adorable and perfect, so beautiful and unattainable, who nonetheless once looked him in the eyes and said, "I like smart boys," as a thank-you for having solved her inorganic chemistry assignment, a comment Alejandro cherished for many years, like the book of the *Thousand*, until at some point all that emotion and all that vertigo vanished into thin air like a soap bubble when she appeared pregnant, four or five months along. The refuge was far from the teachers who lived thinking about the unsolvable exam, far from his father's bitterness every time he received a letter with a blue seal and the national coat of arms. Then, he'd go into *The Shack of 81* and imagine himself sometimes as a castaway, other times as the discoverer of penicillin.

The refuge had withstood every summer storm and some winter hailstorms. Other times, he'd had to repair it, cutting and trimming some of the asbestos cement sheets. The pillars were made of everlasting wood that his father had bought at a sawmill in Avenida Nazca. It had strong walls, built with cured planks that kept out insects, worms, and any kind of rot. It had a rigid corrugated roof that barely insulated against the summer heat but made a pleasant sound during rainy siestas. Alejandro believed in the psychological effects of rain long before Santiago spent three weeks at Emory writing a *paper* for psychology, which he deliberately titled *Rain on a Tin Roof.*

He didn't know it. His father didn't either. At that time, almost no one knew that the asbestos cement of *The Shack of 81* and his little room in his parents' house, the one that threw mysterious moon halos on certain summer nights, was made of asbestos cement, a substance that produces cancer with almost no exceptions. Alejandro found out when he was studying medicine but chose not to remind his mother, because they no longer lived in that house, and the shack had probably been destroyed.

You never know (thought Santiago on March 24, 2012, closing his eyes while listening to the soft, persistent sound of the waves breaking on the beach), all that's behind each thing you do every day. Especially when it comes to the most important things in life. Like going to the forest in that novel by Lucía, going to the forest to gather wood without knowing that one will get lost in time and never return again, at least not as the person they were, in the time when they had been something else, someone else.

The day Alejandro's father had gone to the lumberyard and instead of buying zinc sheets had decided on asbestos cement because he thought they'd be cooler in summer, it had marked that day and the rest of Alejandro's life, Negra Laurie's, and many others. But what blame did the poor old man bear? Those are the marked days, thought Santiago, one of those days when one exercises a high degree of freedom to save something or plunge it into the worst catastrophe. All other days are days dominated by the causes and consequences of logical and practical processes, by reflections and melancholy, by contemplation and storytelling, by laughter and tears, by vomiting and sex, by the pleasure and pain of being alive, by other mysteries, perhaps, like the infinite mystery of consciousness and inevitable ignorance. On other days, things happen in a comprehensible and necessary way, almost like how plants grow and stones fall. Consequences unfold in secret or in inevitable ways, things occur or simply wait for the moment, but in no case are they a supreme act of freedom based on wisdom or ignorance that one day, in a sometimes imperceptible moment, decide the life or death of one or many people.

There is no fate; there are bad decisions, Santiago told himself on the following April 6, watching the clouds twist very slowly in the sky, like someone who recognizes a truth but knows it will serve them little, because the world is an unfathomable complexity or because their own apathy had the capacity to survive many decisions, no matter how radical they were.

Alejandro's father had been slowly killing his son, unwittingly, unknowingly. Since November 2011, all his work,

Alejandro's work, was reduced to leaving something to Negra Laurie and her child, making the transition as easy as possible, and hiding from both of them the true causes of the problem of so many changes.

The waves kept breaking before reaching the shore, the foam kept dragging over the shells of five and a hundred million years. There were no problems there. Only truth, a truth he could touch with the tips of his toes, thought Santiago.

NOT DESPITE HIS LONELINESS *but because of it, there were few days when he could rest. Especially after the fourth moon, when the level of low waters surpassed its usual mark and he couldn't find enough strength to return it to the mark of earlier times. Since then, he felt more tired, or tired more quickly.*

There was always something urgent to do in 00λ, so resting was part of the plan, part of 00λ. The few and almost exceptional free hours he had to invent for himself in the absence of clear signs that everything was going well and without needing his care, he spent lying under the green tarp of the third level. He was drawn to the stains that came to life depending on the different suns and moons that penetrated it. Sometimes they resembled sea monsters. Other times they were like gods descending austerely from the sky or rising sensually from the waters. They were waters of rain and storm, flesh of the sea, and certain death. From the sea he drew his food, and one day in the sea he would be food for other beasts.

When he allowed himself the privilege of resting at noon, he often had daydreams that blended with the excessively illuminated landscape of the tropics. When he let himself be carried away by those images, as if he were a twenty-year-old boy traveling through the tunnel of time to a place that no longer existed, he would fall into a deep sleep that not infrequently returned him to reality while walking on the edge of the third level, risking falling into the waters, smiling senselessly or uttering sounds with his mouth as if he were writing to someone who was there at that moment.

He was obsessed with the image of a woman he did not know but who, for some reason, felt familiar to him. At times she was very similar to the woman in the photo in the engine room, the woman with black glasses. Her perfect smile, the way she tilted her head slightly back, her clear eyes, long and curly hair, probably red. The same woman appears in two other photographs, between the pages of a green-covered book, among the small labyrinth of a messy cabin, number 23, to which he'd hardly given any importance in his entire life. He had always been fascinated by cabins 45 and 89, and he wasted entire months in the crew command, where there were books full of giant explosions at sea, charred bodies and worried faces that entered his dreams and never completely left them.

The woman from cabin 23 was the image that most often repeated itself in the reflections on the green tarp, especially when exhaustion overtook him in the afternoons and he collapsed, spent, drunk on sweat and satisfaction from having reduced, in a fit of fury and weariness, the water level in the holds to the same point as the last five or six months. When this happened, he felt happy with those achievements, which kept him from seeing that in terms of water levels, each minimum was always higher, that every triumph, every repair, couldn't completely reverse the inevitable process of sinking.

Deep down, he knew it. Perhaps that's why his rest hours were few and strictly limited. He knew that if an emergency found him exhausted, it would be the end of his days. His mind had to be clear and alert; his muscles always ready to spring into action and endure long hours of tension, climbing up and down the stairs to reduce the water, holding the ropes so the wind wouldn't carry away the antennas, as it did with the windows of the command, or ensuring no piece of metal could slip overboard. In his life, he had often thrown himself into the sea to rescue insignificant bits of wood, plastic boxes, bottles, and even a chair, but he knew that any piece of metal that fell into the water, any tool or even a simple bolt, wouldn't stop sinking at the speed of a whale's moan, until it was lost in the darkest infinity. Every piece of 00λ that was lost forever provoked a deep feeling in him, a kind of ancient melancholy.

Quique confessed to him how he had gone blind

Canelones, autumn of 1989

The story of Enrique Sosa was resolved much earlier, and he managed to survive it. Under other circumstances and with a greater dose of ignorance, nothing would have happened. Neither the tragic outcome nor the revelation would have dared to lift its head even a centimeter to destroy two or three lives.

At some point, it became known that Alejandro Spinelli's stepfather had been worried about his first son, Quique, since he turned nine. He had started looking for his own features in the boy's face and had concluded that, without a doubt, he was his son.

But the child cried more often than usual, still wet the bed after a couple of corrections. At school, he preferred to sit next to a girl, and during recess, he recited Martí's verses, which the teacher had assigned as homework, instead of playing cowboys, cops and robbers with the other boys. At fifteen, Quique had shown some interest in music, more specifically the piano, and at seventeen, he came home one day saying enthusiastically, as if he had received a prize, that Maestro Carmona had seen good potential in him for opera singing.

"Baritone or soprano?" his father had asked.

At eighteen, Mr. Sosa enrolled Quique in the army, which had the added advantage of paying for his studies.

MARKED DAY. Alejandro thought that at least he had a plan

A Saturday in November 2011

From the moment he found out he would die soon, he stopped caressing her the way he always had. After a week, la Negra began to worry. But she hid it. At first, because these mood swings in Alejandro weren't uncommon. Always worried about everything, as if the fate of the world depended on what he did or didn't do.

Then, as always happens, suspicions take unpredictable paths. She began to feel that her virtues as a lover had declined, just as Alejandro's energy had declined from overwork at the pasta factory or from a progressive sadness that had crept up on him in his thirties, like it had with his father. But his father had a good reason not to smile… Didn't he?

He looked at her without thought. At times, he looked at her with that sweet distance with which some young people see reality, as if it were a work of art, suspended in time, free from any obligation to reality. There she was, lying on the bed on her side, enjoying one of those rare moments of deep sleep. He gazed at the profile of her shoulder, the curve from her abdomen to her hips, softly undulating with her breath, like a bay on a breezy afternoon. He looked at that bare back that he had caressed in so many ways and couldn't remember when the passion of the early years had turned into this deep, nameless love that had endured every failure, even weekends with an empty fridge.

The fresh breeze of a summer that had arrived early occasionally rustled the papers that la Negra had piled on her desk, by the window overlooking Maciel Street and the promenade.

But reality also exists, he thought, without articulating it into words. Then, suddenly, the freshness of seeing and perceiving things transforms into understood things, into obligations not to forget, into that endless list of "I have to" that responsible men like Alejandro follow, into that interminable list that numbs life with the mere promise of avoiding pain, hunger, or failure. That long, endless list of worries that consumes one as if one were immortal.

She poured so much love into her drawings… thought Alejandro. If she put more passion and less love, she would be a recognized artist. Gloria Echenagucía, from the Constituyente gallery, the only *dealer* who had shown interest in her, would respect her more than the money he discreetly sent to her gallery in the form of donations. Yes, la Negra loved more than she desired. Her love for her two men, for the things she did, for Alejandro, for her child, for her paintings, was worth more than her art and all her abilities to express it. But only Alejandro suspected this. Sometimes, not even he. That is, la Negra's love wasn't worth much. On the contrary, perhaps, it was a hindrance. That was the explanation for her failure, thought Alejandro, and he was surprised by the word that had just crossed his mind: *failure*.

She had more projects than finished works. Her latest consisted of a series of sculptures, more like bas-reliefs, geological cross-sections like those where you can see fossils of fish or plants that lived millions of years ago. She intended to create a series where the fossils were replaced by firearms. She wasn't sure exactly what it meant, but it was a strong enough idea to excite her and not leave him indifferent. The problem was where to find decommissioned firearms. As staunch opponents of such things, neither of them could imagine searching for old revolvers and pistols at some flea market or antique gun store. Besides, they had to be expensive objects.

"Can you imagine if in a hundred centuries others find a Colt or a Winchester fossilized beneath layers of geological sediment?"

"Centuries? You're very optimistic…" he had said.

The question would be whether those men and women would see those instruments of death with the same innocence

that today's archaeologists unearth little arrows from our ancestors.

"*By then, they'll have either overcome those flaws or developed
them to the point of seeing a revolver with innocence…*"

"*I don't think in a thousand years they'll see anything, because if
instruments of death continue to advance at the same rate, long before those men and women of the future, there'll be no one left to
unearth our technological feats.*"

No, la Negra wasn't a failure, he told himself, almost out of
obligation. Perhaps the Little Negrita hadn't managed to become what she wanted, what almost all artists want, talented or
not: to have a painting in the Parque Rodó Museum or, at least,
in the downtown galleries or the Biennale di Venezia. Dear Italy
will remain an old dream, at least for him, probably for her too.
Soon she would have to leave painting behind.

*ON RARE OCCASIONS he allowed himself the dangerous distraction of
looking through the magazines that were in λ. There weren't many,
but he treasured them because they were sacred. Although they were
written in some dead language he had never fully grasped (he knew
that symbols are like clouds and stars; those who can read them can
know the present and predict the future), still, he could understand
their images. A beautiful woman, her hair the color of fish and
dressed in coral red, dominated from the cover to the center pages. She
was almost naked, and he adored her like the sun, which is why he
only allowed himself to admire her on full moon nights, since it had
been a moonlit night when he discovered her and a moonlit night
when he felt his entire body trembling at her fleeting, mysterious*

presence, perhaps unreal like dreams, and his penis spilling semen, which he confused with thick urine, but never with sin.

When he saw the photos inside, he knew it was her, the same woman in different poses, in different moods, but always beautiful, always cherished to incomprehensible extremes.

In every magazine, there were women and men like him, almost always smiling, lying on the sand of a beach (that place where the world ends and Paradise begins) or walking through a vast hallway surrounded by very tall buildings. There was one that struck him particularly because it reminded him of dreams he had long before discovering the magazines. It was the image of a city with very tall buildings, seen from the sea. He always imagined that one morning he would wake up and, looking toward the horizon, he would see the city rising from the calm waters of the West. And she would be there, waiting for him.

One night he realized he had two options. One, to overcome the rising waters from the reservoirs. Two, to steer 00λ in a single direction. Suddenly, he understood that, despite having invested almost his entire life in it, the first option was not attainable. On the contrary, his physical strength was already showing signs of fatigue or decline, while the waters seemed to grow stronger. They were because the hull of 00λ was aging just like him. The rust had never stopped advancing, though this process had been so slow that it had gone unnoticed. The second option, though somewhat fantastical, seemed more logical. If there was solid land somewhere in the sea, it was more likely he would reach it by holding a steady course. Since he had no idea which direction was the best, the shortest, he realized that any direction was better than none.

He probably let this new idea mature, which in the night's light must have seemed fantastical. But the idea, a rare occurrence by nature, survived the light of day and the days that followed, so he moved on to solving the practical aspects of the problem. The old ship books held the answer, and his intuition, honed by the winds of the sea, allowed him to interpret them correctly. For weeks, he almost abandoned studying Ann and the pleasures of the green canvas to focus on two tasks: maintaining the low water levels stable and building the great sail with the canvas and sheets that were plentiful in the cabins.

The first sails were a failure. They were neither strong enough for the strongest winds nor large enough to move the ship significantly. He was absorbed in this process of trial and error for many weeks. Inevitably, he discovered that the sail had to be folded in bad weather and unfurled to take advantage of the more moderate winds. He discovered that multiple sails were better for this function than one giant sail. Little by little, he perfected a system of ropes and pulleys that made it possible for one man to perform this Herculean task. Since he never mastered the mathematics of the stars, he decided to steer 00λ westward, which was more reliable than the sunrise, as it offered him the comfort of pursuing the light, not the darkness of dawn.

According to Lucía, space no longer existed

Montevideo, May 20, 2011

She said she was writing a novel where the actions do not take place in space. Not in a concrete space, she meant. Have you read *Don Segundo Sombra*?, she had asked. No, he replied. Well, it's a bore, she said. I always wondered, she continued, how a novel so famous could have aged so badly. Today it's worth more as an archaeological piece than as literature. Yet, almost simultaneously and not far away, works like *El Pozo* by Onetti or *La Isla Desierta* by Roberto Arlt would emerge, two brilliant works from the literature of the Río de la Plata that still have a pulse. Not to mention *La invención de Morel* or *El Túnel* by Sábato, or any of Borges's short stories, light-years ahead of Guiraldes and gauchesca literature. In *Don Segundo Sombra* nothing happens, she said, stirring her coffee while watching the people waiting for the bus on the corner near the café. There, everything is space: a thug in a tavern, a boy who some-what resembles Lazarillo de Tormes but without the brilliance of that anonymous work, a troop whose only action, as the novel itself says, is to walk, walk, and walk. Now we are still waiting for the step that surpasses sixty or seventy years of an era inaugurated by *La invención de Morel* and *El Túnel*, just as both those brilliant little novels advanced so quickly beyond those anachronistic, fake chronicles about gauchos and tapes. "What would that novel be like?" he asked her, because he knew she must have the matter well thought out. Truthfully, he didn't care about the fate of any novel but the depth of her eyes, the tender fleshiness of her lips, that something sweet and loving that some women radiate when they speak and that someone like him, like any man, less subtle and sophisticated, would only manage to cover with kisses. A novel without space, she replied, a novel of *no place*, to put it in a more distinguished way, built entirely of time. What was the point of the proposal? Well, to the spirit of the times, to the *zeitgeist*, she told him. Our time in the Digital Age is the time of *no places*, the non-places, where what happens matters more than where it happens. Airports, *shopping centers*, or *malls*, as they say over there, virtual spaces, all of that is pure non-place, as a fashionable French philosopher once said. So, she went on, the new art or the new novel should reflect or deal with all that, pure time, the fragility of things, the insignificance of causes, the virtuality of nonexistence, the vertigo of narrative in contrast to the descriptiveness of regionalism. Places are merely anecdotes on social media, in the world of ego consumers, in the world of zombies. That sunset in San Francisco, or in Shanghai... What does it matter if María met—that is to say, consumed, devoured—Ernesto or the King of Jordan in Jordan or in the United States? What matters is that she's there... Polishing her ego, exposing herself or cannibalizing someone else, he added. Yes, whatever you say, she said, but in any case, the place doesn't matter, unless it's as an anecdote.

La Negra, nothing else mattered to him

Montevideo, March 2011

It wasn't a failure. No, La Negra, not at all. Her only problem was that she still hadn't managed to support herself by her own means. He had wanted her this way and had never considered how terrible it would have been for her to have to fend for herself with the child in a world in perpetual crisis.

"Dear Negrita..." he said, almost in a whisper, moving his lips.

He wasn't calling her. He was calling himself. An instinctive movement led him to wrap an arm around her, but he held back. Now, more than ever, he had to rely without exception on the virtues that had characterized him over the last ten years. Virtues, no—defects, as she called them when she got furious. That habit of always going for the practical, of calculating losses and benefits in every decision, without putting his heart into it, without ever shedding a single sappy tear. That sickening rationalism, Laurie said when she was angry, that doesn't speak just to speak or argue just to argue unless there's a solution to the problem in it.

But Alejandro hadn't been so thoughtless after all. La Negra would have around ten thousand eight hundred dollars left in Banco República, which, according to his calculations, would last her a year or a year and a half. What would Negrita do in that time? How would she manage? Would she remarry or get together with some good Samaritan? What would Dieguito think of his absence? Would the good Samaritan treat him well? Why not? It was even likely that he'd treat him better than he himself had. He'd been a tough father, always worried about Dieguito learning what was necessary to survive in this harsh world. Although, perhaps, he'd gone too far, he admitted with unrelenting pain, like that time he'd lost his patience and tugged on his ear. It wasn't just once, but he remembered one time as if it were all of them. Now he remembered Dieguito's face, crying desperately, perhaps more because his father had punished him than because of the pain in his little ear, which had turned as red as a tomato. That day (when was it, where, exactly?) La Negra got furious, and he gave up disciplining Dieguito for several days, for weeks. Who knows what the boy had understood, he thought, because he'd come back slowly, over and over, as if begging for something, saying, "Dad, I was bad," and he couldn't tell him the truth without undermining his authority: "Yes, son, you were bad, but Dad was worse with you."

I hope, he thought, he never remembers any of that, because it will hurt him, and it's not fair; because the little one isn't to blame. And no one was to blame. Life just plays with us like that.

He turned over and lay there staring at the ceiling. At least he had a year left. Alejandro had taken his role as Sales Manager at the factory seriously, and he measured all his worth by the number of ravioli and agnolotti he reported to his boss on the last business day of each month. Thanks to *La donna mobile*, they had saved themselves from hunger and the humiliation of being supported by her father. It had taken him almost three years to rise to Sales Manager, almost as long as it had taken to salvage the last subjects of his abandoned medical degree. He had discovered, he said, his true calling. He had become what he did, said La Negra, somewhere between praise and criticism.

Dear Negra didn't understand, Alejandro thought, that numbers weren't just numbers. They didn't even just mean more money and more food in the fridge, which wasn't a minor detail, but they also meant that things were going well, that he was doing well. Every new sales strategy translated into cold numbers, but those numbers represented the recognition of all his creativity, which was put to the test every month. So, they weren't just numbers, and they weren't just ravioli. Artists could afford to have no one buy their paintings or books. Many of them even took pride in such things. A ravioli seller, inevitably, needed to sell his ravioli to at least think that the work had been worth it, that all those hours spent thinking up new strategies had been useful to someone, that he had succeeded in his field, like a writer who measures his worth by the thousands of books sold, like an artist who sells a painting for thousands of dollars—and it's not just about the damned dollars, but the reassurance, the comfort of knowing he's not a mediocrity with a paintbrush, pretending to be something else.

Grandfather's Secret

Manhattan, Saturday, April 2, 2011

Later he learned that a letter, dated March 25, 1928, was from someone named Aleksandra. It was filled with questions about his grandfather's journey to America. Aleksandra had been his grandfather's girlfriend or lover for almost a year.

Apparently, his grandfather never replied to this letter. Instead—Miguel speculated—he drafted a lengthy prose poem. Miguel thought that the mere form in verses would have embarrassed his grandfather. But he did not feel shame—perhaps he foresaw that his confession would not be read in his lifetime—when he confessed that the most beautiful woman in Russia had given him the best year of his life. A woman can only give her best year once. They loved each other in the finest hotels, in the cheapest pensions, and even in the parks of Moscow.

They loved each other like mad in winter and summer. His grandfather had never forgotten her perfect face, her twenty-year-old body, her fantasies of a happy marriage, like a princess, like a fairy tale. That whole absurd madness had lasted eleven and a half months, and afterward, according to his grandfather's poetic confession, there was no way to return to reality without dying. But he had decided to keep living.

"Typical 19th-century romantic love," Miguel commented. "The love is so perfect that the lovers or fate decide to end it... I suppose by 1928 all that sentimentality would have already gone out of style in Russia."

Glinka smiled. He wanted to be complicit in Miguel's criticism. In fact, it was an incontestable criticism; it was true, all of that had passed.

"Men do things that have no explanation" old Glinka admitted. "If we were more sensible, we'd be less happy, but we wouldn't suffer as much."

And that description of the eyes blue as the sky, Miguel thought, was terribly bad. Good thing his grandfather hadn't dedicated himself to poetry. He wouldn't have made much.

"Cheesy," Miguel declared.

The old man didn't reply. He pressed his lips together like presidents do when delivering bad news or admitting some infidelity.

"She betrayed him, Miguel said.

"It's not clear," the old man said. "In her letter, she defends herself. They had been rumors from her brother. Apparently, your grandfather punished him too, or tried to punish him with silence. Nowhere is it seen that he responded to her letter."

He searched for one.

"This one," said old Glinka, holding up one of the letters. "This is the letter where your grandfather's brother mentions the story of the girl with her boss at a restaurant... According to her, it wasn't a private lunch but a work lunch. The other employee was in the bathroom when someone they knew (what was his name?) passed by."

"I'm sorry to have wasted your time, Mr. Glinka," said Alexander.

The old man looked at him as if he couldn't quite make out his face in the darkness.

"What did you say?"

"I apologize for wasting your time with these silly things."

The old man did not respond. He leaned on Miguel's shoulder, moved toward the counter, and sat in his usual chair.

"We'll finish tomorrow," he said. "It's very late, and these bones can't stay upright much longer."

Miguel took the letters, except for the last one that remained untranslated, thanked old Glinka with a pat on the back, and left.

A Day Marked. Where Men Are Made

A Saturday in June 1989

In the same year he enlisted his son in the army, Emualdo Sosa did what his father had done with him in Rivera thirty-three years earlier. He took him to a brothel in Ciudad Vieja so he could become a man before the other recruits took advantage of his shyness. But the madam who ran the place noticed that Quique seemed underage.

"How old is the boy?" she asked.

Sosa wasn't exactly sure what the legal age of adulthood was, so he cut to the chase:

"Twenty-one," he said.

"Of course he's not twenty-one," the woman said. "Do you think I was born yesterday? I've been sucking on something else for forty years, and I know when daddies bring their little boys to be turned into men. I've seen more than one of these kids, and I can recognize one who just lost his baby teeth."

"Nineteen. Fine, he's nineteen," Sosa said.

"Not twenty-one, not nineteen. The boy's barely sixteen. What do you expect me to do with one of my girls? He's got nothing. Wait until he's a real man before you bring him back."

"I'm eighteen," Quique said, momentarily snapping out of the terror provoked by the idea of making a fool of himself in front of a naked woman, "and I do have something. I've got enough to handle any of those whores and you too, with all the rides you've got on your record."

"Don't make me laugh, little baby. Finish drinking your milk, and then we'll talk. And you, sir, out of respect for having once been one of my clients, if I recall correctly, I'm asking you to take this chick out of here. I don't want to have any more problems with the police, understand? And because I know you,

I know you're not one of those too-sneaky types, but I don't want to risk anything. I want to retire soon."

Sosa, smiling to ease the tension of the situation, asked for an exception for the boy until the madam threatened to call the police. Sosa laughed out loud. He knew more than one of the girls was working illegally, but he didn't want to push it. Quique had turned pale, and Sosa thought he was shaking, if not from fear, then at least from anger. That's where he took after his father, he thought—hard to control.

On the way home, Alejandro didn't say a word. He just listened to his father's fragmented monologue, congratulating him on his intervention ("those whores deserved it") but didn't fail to point out other shortcomings, like folding at the end, "like a wet chick," he said.

Quique would forever remember the face of the woman they called "La Colo," because she was Colombian and always dyed her hair red. He would remember her dark circles with wrinkles, her hair dyed a straw-like red, and her full, but not entirely sensual lips. Those red lips that had spat in his face, "you've got nothing," as confirmation of what he had always suspected. He wasn't man enough for women who knew what it was to be penetrated by real beasts of burden.

Antonio Tejero, Fernando, and Isabel

Buenos Aires, February 24, 1981
In a bar on Corrientes Street, he ordered a coffee, the newspaper, and took out the new pen a client had given him, a black

Parker 51 with gold trim, and he thought about the smell of Buenos Aires, which reminded him of his early days in Montevideo. It was the smell of a city and its different people. In that way, they were alike: they were different and, therefore, they had a smell.

"All the important things were signed with a Parker," Mrs. Robertson had told him.

Don Jordi had wanted to be like Ladislao Biro, that Hungarian who discovered, in an Argentine magazine on the ship that took him to Montevideo in 1953, Biro, the inventor of the ballpoint pen, the Jew who fled to Argentina to found the Birome company. The Americans bought it in 1943, the following year, as expected. Because Americans may be anything "said the Brazilian who accompanied him to Rio" but they're not stupid, especially when it comes to business. They were born making good deals when they bought Florida from Spain for a pittance they never paid, when they doubled their territory with the Louisiana Purchase from France, and didn't stop until they bought Alaska from the Russians. And when they couldn't buy something, they took it by force, as is fitting when one can, as the Brazilian who almost convinced him to stay in the land of carnival had said.

At first, the invention of the Hungarian Ladislao was not taken seriously. In Buenos Aires, it was sold as a toy for children, not because it lacked usefulness but because it was too cheap. But it didn't take long for the Biro ballpoint pen to grow up and dedicate itself to serious matters. Very serious matters. Since then, everything was signed with a Parker pen. Wars and peace, profits and bankruptcies.

Jordi was going to write something with "the most coveted fountain pen," but the gold trim on the pen distracted him. He jotted down on a separate sheet the prices of the printers he was going to sell to the newspaper *El Día*. He noticed that he wrote the 5 and the 9 like his father. The 5 in a single stroke, extending beyond the bottom margin. The 9, also in one stroke, starting from the center and curving down like a hook. He thought of his mother, cursing the Republicans in front of her children, like someone who jabs a needle into their hand to stop it from speaking. He thought of his sister Clarita, denying to her children that she and her husband had been collaborators and believers in the regime of General Francisco Franco.

"One day, democracy will come to Spain," the Galician Suárez had said in 1973, the young waiter who brought him coffee every morning and with whom he hardly exchanged a word, until he disappeared in 1976 and no one asked about him, then, the leeches of the regime will deny what they've been. Not because democracy threatens them with death, as the Falange did, but out of the shame of having been what they were. Coffee distributors *CAFE*."

"As time goes on," Jordi remembered one of his recently divorced employees saying, "we grow to resemble our parents, our grandparents more and more. The wife starts to resemble the mother-in-law, as they say."

"Every day we become more like our elders," thought Jordi, balancing the Parker pen on his index finger, "especially because we learn nothing from this inevitable fact and, consequently, we cannot be anything else. What sets us apart from our elders are the least important things, the most visible: we dress differently, speak different dialects, live in different places, know how to do other things. The deepest emotions, the ability or inability to love and to hate, frustrations, the fear and desire for death, meaningless drunkenness and questionable sobriety, jealousy and indifference, that is, what truly matters, what barely flickers on the desolate horizon of the human soul, that, that hasn't changed much. If it has changed at all. Because all our wisdom boils down to a few toys, to going to the Moon, exploring Mars, flying over a city and drilling through a mountain."

Almost everything we know about the world and the Universe remains unchanged. The little we know about the eternal struggle between happiness and sadness dies with each of us. What did he, Jordi, know about his father's dreams when he arrived in Barcelona? Would he have tried to invent the amphibious car that could finally reach the Balearic Islands, dehydrated paella, or the deferred check before the Uruguayans thought of it? Would he have dreamed of a prosperous freight company, of a fleet of a hundred trucks? Had he harbored any illusion of becoming a deputy for the Republican Left of Catalonia, being himself a newcomer?

He would never know, he thought. But perhaps, deep down, where truth resides, those distant dreams and his own were no different, despite time and distance. Those dreams, those hopes, all these frustrations…

Suddenly, a shout in the street pulled him out of these thoughts.

And his grandparents? he wondered.

Perhaps for the first time. A question so obvious, a knowledge so impossible. Why had he never met his grandparents, if they weren't dead?

He hadn't had time to understand it

Montevideo, July 1999

"Almost the entire body of a woman is sex," thought Alejandro, as he tasted something salty in his mouth, as if he were still in Punta del Diablo". "The same goes for a man's brain. Almost the entire brain of a man, at least a young man, is sex. They are more romantic, we are more pornographic. That's why they get lost in a labyrinth of inconsistencies, and we are mortally more practical."

Quique had once told him that his pragmatism had a leak somewhere, because he failed to consider that a woman doesn't need her problems solved—the ones she invents herself as a substitute for the real problems she faces.

"So you're saying I'm wrong when Negra comes to me with a fuss and I solve it for her?"

"Correct."

"Please, I've got enough problems as it is without having to guess that a complaint about poor time management is really about my lack of patience to listen to the argument about poor time management."

"Well, that's your problem. I've never understood how an artist like Negra ended up marrying a relentlessly practical man like you."

"Me neither. But it's worked out pretty well."

"It's worked, but if you'd thought it through better, you'd never have married her. Or am I wrong?"

IT TOOK HIM A LONG TIME TO LEARN HOW TO NAVIGATE using the stars. The movement of the nocturnal stars was far more complex than the simple motion of the sun, and on top of that, he'd taken to sleeping at night, not during the day, which kept him from gaining any understanding of the cosmic order of things far above. For this reason, he knew his navigation might not have always been on course. Perhaps at night he veered off toward another cardinal point. Maybe he retraced the path he'd taken during the day. Only the woman who smiled could say for sure someday.

With time, he dismissed this second possibility. Indeed, on day 5 of moon 9, he concluded he'd sailed toward some part of the universe. During the day, the sun took a different path, more slanted and colder, as if it had aged. As a logical consequence, the waters had cooled and were no longer as transparent as they'd been at the start, though he remembered this with a sweet vagueness, perhaps owed to nostalgia.

A cross for the son

Buenos Aires, February 25, 1981

He'd spent all of Tuesday night and the entire morning of Wednesday trying to remember.

He returned to the same bar on Corrientes Street as if he'd lost the trail of what he was about to find the previous afternoon. He ordered a strong coffee. He asked for the newspaper again, but he barely unfolded it before closing it again. It wasn't the same one, though in the end, all the news starts to look alike.

The children from the previous afternoon weren't there. In their place, a young woman in a white miniskirt waited for the bus.

He started over from the same place. He knew some grandparents lived in Santiago, in Santiago de Compostela, and the others in A Coruña, and that was about it. With some precautions, his parents had managed to dodge all of Jordi and Clarita's questions. Like all children, the siblings took the world of the adults for granted. If the grandparents weren't talked about, it was because there was no need, because no one talked about grandparents at home. If the children had never met their grandparents, it was because they lived far away. Farther than the moon.

As he was nearly finishing his coffee, Don Jordi picked up the ballpoint pen and prepared to write something in the small notebook he'd bought a few days earlier, which remained untouched, all its pages blank.

He hesitated. He thought. You can throw a veil of silence over an inconvenient truth, but there's nothing you can do to silence the logic of events.

He rested the pen on the first page, a small page that seemed to expand like a snow-covered field. He'd thought of something about the logic of facts, or rather, it was a vague intuition he couldn't put into words.

He set the pen down and looked at some children playing on the other side of the window.

If his mother was such a cultured person, he recalled, if she knew French and could play the piano, how was it that they lived so modestly in a tiny apartment in Barcelona, without a piano and almost without windows? Did Lucía's family never accept the poor boyfriend of their renegade daughter? And what about his own parents? Did they never accept a Republican son? That cross and that rosary his mother sent, which Lucía hung in Jordi's room just days before the soldiers arrived—wasn't that a warning? Why send such a cross and such an ostentatious rosary to a son who never went to church and didn't have the habit of praying on his knees? Was that why he'd never met his grandparents? And what did the grandparents say when they found out their son had disappeared? Disappeared, perhaps, after the Falangists traced that enormous package with the crucifix. Disappeared, crucified by the defenders of Christ, by the soldiers of Rome and the masters of the law. Betrayed, in some way, by his own parents.

Carlos II waits in the bar

Little summer of July 2011

And with so many women to bed ("fuckable," to put it in Galician terms, who fucked there and bedded here), and one leaning on the marble table, like an old fool, like a rabid dog sitting on his balls, watching the cars go by, gawking at the girls who go to deposit at the Central Bank and then come back to have tea at the fancy bar on the corner across the street, to talk about the orgasms they deserve and never get in a macho culture that doesn't fuck them properly, and one watching them pass by as always, rich and poor, but young enough to wear what they wear and go out to provoke social uprisings of all kinds. All of them fuckable, but none of them willing. Well, willing yes, more than willing. But not available, and that's not the same thing, you know? The world is just this unfair. Of course, you have to imagine a world where all those twenty, twenty-five-year-old girls, with those perfect asses no matter what they wear, were within reach, not to say within reach of your dick. Imagine if you could just take the one that suited you best, what would happen? Hell if I know, maybe you'd turn gay, I mean, with no restrictions on desire and sated to whatever you can think of, what's left to desire? I don't know. Are prostitutes lesbians by reaction? Maybe the best thing about these goddesses is that they're goddesses, I mean, unreachable asses, unfuckable, untouched tits, untouchable, all that drives you crazy walking around for free out there without you being able to do anything. Because if they excel at anything, it's heating you up from head to toe, but if you look at them or give them a compliment about their most visible virtues, you end up in jail or get slapped, as if they expected something more from you, I don't know, a prince and not a frog-faced worker. But if they only knew what the frog-faced worker has... No, no. They can't know. Because you can't go around boasting about your dick the way they boast about their asses, because you'd be in jail before the rooster crows. Anyway, what does it matter. If you could grab any of those forbidden fruits, maybe the fruit wouldn't look so delicious. It wouldn't be the same. Like, the Lord made us with a little defect, as the priest says, something that doesn't work right and still doesn't. And here you are, watching all those well-dressed hips and asses go by, showing just enough and hiding just enough of what drives you crazy. That's not right, but you know it can't be any other way. So you have to settle for what's there, adjusting your balls and calming the Indian in the middle who wants to come out, calming him, saying, easy partner, it's not your turn, I know it's never your turn but what can we do; and explaining to him what the rules and manners of a civilized man are, having to see so many beauties that turn your head and controlling yourself like the gentleman you are. And the one below has to put up with it. Because if there's a repressed being in this world, it's him.

The subjunctive of Emory's Chilean

Montevideo, May 2011

At Emory, there was a Chilean who was a *teaching assistant* in the *Department of Spanish and Portuguese* " said Santiago, while opening a can of beer and the hiss of the pressure created a pause between *Emory* and *had*, as Alejandro sank into an armchair". He was studying psychological verbs in Augusto Pinochet's speeches between 1971 and 1994. Or something like that. Apparently, he hated Pinochet so much that he decided to make him the subject of his master's thesis, and as random research material, he spent entire nights reading documents declassified in the nineties by Bill Clinton's government. He was obsessed with Kissinger, that Nobel Peace Prize winner who, according to him, appeared in the "*minutes*" of several secret meetings before Allende's victory, conspiring against a government that hadn't even been elected yet. As everyone knows, leftists have a collection of conspiracy theories. I barely suggested it, and this Ernesto or Enrique guy told me that accusations of "conspiracy theories" always came from "conspiracy practices." He wasn't a bad guy, despite his paranoia. I liked him. That night, I traded a first-rate sofa I'd picked up from the apartment's parking meter for a 29-inch TV he had spare, which I assume he'd also found somewhere.

We made some burgers again on a grill at the park in the *family housing* area and started arguing about the meaning of Chilean *cowboys*, whom they call *huaso*. For us, *gaucho* is a form of praise, while "guaso" is more of an insult. That Ernesto or Enrique guy explained something to me about history and the sociology of language, about the nonexistent white horse of San Martín, the Andes, and Charles Darwin complaining about the pride of Uruguayan gauchos despite their poverty, as if being poor disqualified one from having any kind of pride.

But something that stuck with me from that night under the oaks at Emory, next to a Puerto Rican who complained that at that hour you couldn't play Daddy Yankee because the Chinese folks would come out to the balcony to ask for silence, was about a linguistic technicality. I don't know why the hell that got stuck in my head. The Chilean Ernesto or Enrique told me that when we say "I don't think she'll arrive tonight," we use the subjunctive "llegue" because the chances of her arriving are very low. No one says "I don't think she arrives tonight" or "I don't think she is going to arrive tonight." But if I believe something is going to happen, I can no longer use the subjunctive. "I think she arrives tonight" or "I think she is going to arrive tonight." The subjunctive is either a curse in Spanish or a reminder that what we believe is real and what we don't believe is just a miserable probability. What *I* believe is more real than what I don't believe.

But what I believe is still a belief. That is, it has nothing to do with truth. If it has anything to do with truth, perhaps it's by accident. But we'll never know. If around the corner we were to meet a man in a suit and tie holding a book in one hand and vehemently claiming that the world was created by ants, there would be nothing we could do against his faith. For that wise man, the world was created by ants, and it's possible he could convince more than one person before someone convinces him otherwise.

I don't know if I'd call a belief a truth. But it's clear that these are not truths that have any commitment to reason or logic. And this last group of truths is so small that practically we wouldn't have a life if we only accepted the truths born from logic and reason. For an individual who has never been to Asia, the existence of the Himalayas is a matter of faith, not logic. It's not something you can deduce or infer. I also can't deduce everything I know from my parents, from Quique, from Alejandro, from la Negra. I can't deduce almost anything. Or almost anything that's really important.

In short, Ernesto or Enrique said three beers later, our magical realism is more magical than realism, but we assume the opposite. Every time he said something, he'd scratch his head, as if disowning himself.

"Did he have the face of a guaso?" asked Alejandro.

"Now that I think about it, yes," said Santiago.

Alejandro leaned over the coffee table to grab another beer. "I like that guy," he said.

A neighbor of Alejandro

Little summer of July 2011

The dinner with Santiago had left him with more of a Chilean in the United States, whom he had never met, than of Santiago himself. The old friend was still an old friend, but he was different. He was about to think things had gotten worse when Santiago sold out to the empire or the empire changed his head. Of course, that would have been the quickest answer. A comfortable, absolute response. One of those answers everyone needs when faced with questions that remain open like a wound that won't stop bleeding. But the truth was he couldn't say why, what it was that had separated them and why it should matter. Santiago was different, perhaps because he himself, Alejandro, was different. Yes, Heraclitus. But the truth was that all the worries, joys, and frustrations that had built that friendship so many years ago no longer existed. There were no more points of connection. The sets (Alejandro remembered those circular shapes representing "A ∩ B" on the chalkboard of the last classroom in school) no longer had any elements in common, said the teacher, that old guy with Einstein-like mustaches who by now was probably dead, his busy brain and simple heart resting in Chacarita. Now Santiago was a respected doctor, had a girlfriend who had come from some other part of the city, and had gained experience in a country that meant nothing to him. He made a living by curing the sick, and he, Alejandro, was trying to survive like a sick man with no cure. Santiago was committed to a woman he clearly didn't love, and he, Alejandro, loved one he was soon going to destroy.

He had to go through it. He knew that at some point he had to confront that very idea. It had become something recurrent, something worse than death itself.

He turned off the engine. He waited thirty seconds for no particular reason, staring at a wall where what looked like a B seemed to be drawn. He got out and walked slowly toward the building's entrance.

In the elevator, he ran into Silvana. He smiled at her. She responded as usual, with her automatic, unfriendly gesture.

"Good day," she said.

Alejandro raised his eyebrows.

"Good day," replied Alejandro, distant, more annoyed by the coincidence of running into the nurse in the elevator again.

"A bad day?" she asked.

Alejandro was surprised by the question.

"No... Why do you say that?"

"I'm sorry. It was a dumb question."

When the door opened, Silvana rushed out. Alejandro remained thoughtful and had to hurry to put his hand out to stop the elevator door from closing again.

It was the first time the unfriendly nurse had greeted him in such a friendly, almost supportive tone. Maybe she had noticed his worried face, his distant gaze. It was the first time he realized that, on top of it all, she was a very attractive woman.

Then, Alejandro secretly insulted her. Darkly, he knew that a woman could handle other people's emotions even if she was a detestable stranger. But that day, he couldn't stop thinking about her. He completely forgot that he had once told himself that thinking about an affair was like getting drunk: it served to forget one problem by creating another. But that revelation, like almost everything, was forgotten by both of them.

El Pepe seemed sad

Little summer of July 2011

When Carlitos II finished his second glass, he made the typical gesture halfway between satisfaction and the burn of alcohol, as if he had completed his routine, and as he shifted his gaze from the void, he saw Pepe Mujica leaning on the table next to him, breathing in the steam of his freshly served coffee with his pointy nose. Willian always said that no one could even guess if Pepe was worried about his lame dog or about what he was going to say to Barack Obama at the next summit.

He wasn't surprised. He had been looking for him for days in the darkest corners of the bar on Misiones Street. He never knew exactly what he was going to say. He knew he wanted to see him again. He was going to tell him that the little revolution of his Tupamaros in the 60s had ruined everything. At least, they had destroyed his thread and button business, which he had worked so hard to build, through sheer imagination and effort. And he was going to tell him that because of all that, he had always been on the opposite side of the Frente, the Blanco Party, which happened to be the only one that still respected family, property, and those who never asked for anything. And that despite it all, he held no grudge, because in the end they had both ended up the same, though through different means, each living in a shack on the outskirts of Montevideo, ruminating over memories with only the company of bad wine or undrinkable grappa in a Galician bar, heading back to the den every evening, as Quique Lacalle called it, heading to an unmade bed, with their backs hunched and swaying like penguins. He also thought about asking him when he was going to meet with Obama because he, Carlitos, had an important message to send him.

But now that he had him within reach, perhaps meditating on the brevity of human life or bitter about how poorly the unions had treated him since he became the country's president, he couldn't muster enough inspiration to get up and repeat that first phrase he had memorized: "Excuse me, Mr. President... or Pepe, if the title bothers you..." Who knows if Pepe wasn't actually at that limit where it's impossible to tell if an old man stays silent out of wisdom or just because he's old. That's why he didn't get up to ask him about Obama. He felt relieved to free himself from an obligation imposed by pride or the opportunism he had cultivated so much in his best years as a client hunter. Pride was gone, and opportunities to do something important were even scarcer.

Besides, what's the point, Carlitos thought, if it was most likely that Pepe was having one of those bad days and would tell him to go fry asparagus. It was better to keep the good image of Pepe, who every now and then seemed about to murmur something but then kept quiet. What did it matter, since at any moment Willian would arrive, having promised to clarify the matter that troubled him so much.

"Don't be a fool, son," he imagined Pepe saying. "Don't you realize the poor bloke is too busy with the problems of the Empire? He scheduled me for next year, he did," just as Willian was pushing open the door of the old bar on the corner.

Seeing him, Carlos clearly relived a summer day in 1944. The same sun, the same time, and not much else. Back then, Willian was less skinny, taller, and obviously dressed much better. He didn't have more money than now, but he dressed like a millionaire dandy. When he got married in 1956, Carlos wanted to do him a favor and at the wedding congratulated the father-in-law, assuring him that Willian had a bright future, but the mother-in-law chose that moment to have her clearest moment of lucidity in all her years of living up to that point and replied that she was very glad, since for the moment that was all he had—a future. But it wasn't all. Only Carlos knew all the dreams that had kept them alive into their eighties. "We were truly rich," Willian once told him in the late nineties. Not even Bill Gates, at that time, would have had so many illusions about what to do with so many millions in his pockets. They had founded several tiny branches for thread and buttons, fabrics, and cushions. Willian insisted that in the late fifties they had also opened a lingerie section in La Aguada, which lasted three months because, according to the greengrocer across the street, Carlos had hired an old, overweight saleswoman to run such a business. But Carlos denied it, vehemently at first and almost skeptically by the end. In any case, all these commercial ventures had flown shorter than a chicken's flight, to put it in Pepe's words. The nicest part had been inaugurating them and hiring some girls to run them, their illusions also bigger than the salaries they could receive.

In the half-light, the shabbiness of Willian's clothing was well concealed. Despite everything, there was something that transported Carlos to that afternoon in 1944 at El Águila, as if beyond appearances the spirit of a person persisted, announcing itself to everyone it somehow knew.

It must have been February, because it was Carnival. Carlos had sat at a table with an impossibly white tablecloth, decorated with champagne glasses, red napkins with gold trim, and silverware. He had taken off his jacket but not the memory of the provocative gaze of a dancer who was something like a Swedish goddess with nearly white blonde hair, sky-blue eyes, and Brazilian—or rather, African—accessories covering her small breasts. Carlos hated Carnival, but he had gone to the restaurant El Águila, the famous restaurant next to the Solís Theatre that filled up with opera lovers between shows.

The door of El Águila, which must have cost as much as the entire bar on Misiones Street, still resembled the very same door of the bar on Misiones Street. There were no more smokers, but the windows were stained from lack of cleaning.

Besides Willian, who had entered through that door of El Águila one February evening in 1944 and had bumped into the first person he encountered at the annual meeting of salesmen from the London Paris and other shops, he didn't remember anyone else. God knows why. Willian looked like a Hollywood actor back then. He had rented the finest suit, but still smelled of poverty, like Felicia's father who at his daughter's quinceañera smelled of fish, even though he had scrubbed his hands with soap and kerosene for hours beforehand. The rich say it's style, but they also sniff each other out, just as dogs sniff each other's butts to recognize one another.

"Something similar happens to us poor folks," he thought. In truth, Carlos disliked gatherings with lots of people. They didn't make him nervous, because he had outgrown that nonsense when he turned twenty-two, almost without realizing it, like someone losing their wallet. He disliked rich people's parties, which he attended frequently, but only because they took him away from an evening in his thread and button shop, from his whiskey over the evening paper *El Día* at six in the afternoon, from Elena's complaints at eight, when she had finished listening to her radio soap opera and dinner was starting to get cold. But he never missed one of those gatherings because, as he proudly said of his sacrifice and his cleverness, that's where his clients were. "You have to socialize," he used to tell his late wife, who never understood this sacrifice of having a good time.

In part, Carlitos was right. From the forties until the death of General Oscar Gestido just before Christmas in 1967, he had achieved meteoric prosperity in his thread and button business. Retailers fell by the wayside after curiously glancing at the shop windows he had in his favorite store on Ejido Street and in the larger one on Constituyente Street, filled with photos of London, Paris, and New York, of Marilyn Monroe, always smiling, always happy thanks to the quality of Don Carlitos's threads and buttons, always complicit in his success even after death. But the serious business was done with the wholesalers he met at those social gatherings, like the ones at El Águila.

Attending every party, invited or uninvited, hurt his pockets. He was stingy and knew it, but not a bad investor. While he was young and fanciful, while he knew how to dress up as a rich man, he bet and won more times than he lost, and thus amassed considerable capital for how poor he was when he had to leave home at seventeen. Until the dictatorship, more or less. Of course, at first he supported the military coup, fearing the communists would end his brilliant business career. But things started to decline anyway. With the collapse of the infamous *tablita* and the dollar's spike in 1982, one of those economic inventions that occasionally inspired the military, who believed things could be fixed by talking loudly and decreeing that rivers should flow backward, the decline of his fabric and button business began, and with it the decline of a man who had invented himself. Fabrics and buttons, opulent parties, new employees and new openings, were much more than a business, something poets and shepherds would never understand. It was an entire life. Or several lives.

He inhaled the scent of the wine. They always say you have friends when things are going well and lose them when things go wrong, and in part, it's true, he thought, in a fraction of a second. But the progressive decline into which Carlitos fell in the eighties and, definitively, in the nineties, left him with only two or three true friends. And though you might think it's the devil's work, one of those loyal friends, Willian, he met at one of those dinners he attended purely for economic interest. "*Bisnes*," they both said. Yes, purely for economic reasons, he met his most loyal and least self-interested friend.

ON THE FOURTH DAY OF THE TENTH MOON, *he discovered the engine room's storage. After a long apprenticeship, he managed to recognize that blind space of 00λ. Little by little, he confirmed that his suspicions were logical. There was, at least, a large section beneath the third level, adjacent to the engine room. This he deduced by looking from above the belly of 00λ. For a long time, this region was an obsession. He knew that any leak from that section would mean the end of 00λ, because he wouldn't be able to gather the information in time nor have any chance to successfully repair even the smallest crack in the hull, a natural result of the oxidation that progressively attacked the ship. For some reason, he imagined there was a critical point where a crack becomes a jet, and then an explosion.*

After several excursions to that lightless region, he managed to find something resembling a door, and a few days later, he opened it. For several days, he rummaged through a museum of indecipherable objects that smelled like a storm. For hours, he wandered and retraced the labyrinth that led to the center of the storage and back to the dim light of the main cabin on the first level. Thus, little by little, he rescued useless but interesting things. A painting of a woman with a child. A deck of cards. A box of paints. A green device with glass buttons. A large glass vessel with wires inside. A black plastic square basin. A reel of transparent photographs...

At first, he didn't pay attention to the film. The colorful images that repeated themselves against the sun amused him. Only many days later did he discover that the images, when put together, told a story, the story of a man and a woman and some children and some cars.

For a long time, he dedicated himself to deciphering the story of the man and the woman. He almost forgot about the drainage tasks and almost forgot about Ann.

May the global *guormi* end it all

Indian summer of 2011

Willian had entered through that door of El Águila, that evening in 1944 with the same intentions as him—to do business, to seize the opportunity and gain an advantage by rubbing shoulders with the rich, because that's how the guys who knew their stuff did it in the movies at the Rex. By accident, he found a friend, who, when he fell into disgrace and was imprisoned as a moneylender in the seventies, was always there to help him. If not with money, at least with moral support, he said, and it was true.

And there was poor crazy Carlitos, Willian thought, sitting at the same shabby little table in the bar on Misiones Street where he had gone almost every Saturday for the last twenty years without knowing its real name, because he had never bothered to look up and read the sign at the entrance, now without lights, that said *El Asturiano*.

Willian had taken a while to spot him, even though they always chose a little table against the wall facing Misiones Street. It was already too dark inside or there was still too much light outside.

"Hey, Willian," Carlitos said to him, without greeting him, "what would you ask Obama?"

"Are you crazy? What's gotten into you?"

"A flea in the sack. Are you going to answer me or not? What would you ask the president of the United States?"

"How the hell should I know what I'd ask…"

"I mean, something important."

"Like Michelle, for example."

"You're always the same, obsessed. You've got a bee in your bonnet."

"For conversation, I mean," he said.

"Like you've ever learned a single word of English in your damn life."

"Ah, but I've always managed just fine."

"See what I mean? At least you're not a liar… But I'm talking about something important."

"But you already know what I'd like."

"But Obama can't make it rain."

"Of course he can."

"Why would you want more rain? We've already got more than enough."

"I'm not talking about this miserable drizzle, this crappy rain. I'm talking about something serious, a storm that would flip everything upside down. You know that's what I'd like to see before I die."

"If I didn't die that day."

"He could send a hurricane or something like they do over there."

"Look," Carlitos said, pointing at Pepe with his eyes.

"Did he come back to the bar?"

"Can't you see him?"

"And?"

"What do you mean, *and*? Pepe's going to meet with Obama next year. You could go and ask him..."

"No, I'd rather leave it alone. I'd prefer a natural storm. I don't want to feel guilty afterward..."

"Did you see it's going to rain?"

"Exactly."

"I don't know why, but I'd love one of those storms that wipe everything out, one of those Katrinas that turn everything upside down."

"And why's that, huh?"

"I don't know."

"Me too, to be honest. Something that sends it all to hell."

The major makes a decision

December 2011

Unanimously, Don Xico's family was in favor of the operation, so the patient could no longer find excuses, though he delayed the date of the intervention for as long as he could.

One cold morning, he felt ill and was taken to the emergency hospital. He arrived with a pre-heart attack. Santiago attended to him until he recovered. Once again, events had proven the young doctor right. By then, his fame had spread throughout the sanatorium and beyond among his colleagues and new patients. Lourdes Vitabar from Radio Uruguay had interviewed him a few times about the latest surgical techniques.

Daniel Castro from Channel 4 had tried to reach him without success to discuss a certain issue the anesthesiologists had with President Mujica. Abusing unnecessary excuses, Santiago had avoided any political matters. One of his colleagues commented that he acted like he was the technician of the Uruguayan national team or the composer of the national anthem, which was why he insisted on hiding that he was a staunch supporter of the most hardcore right wing of Pocitos, so as not to gain the antipathy of some of his admirers. Carmencita, Don Xico's wife, had invited him several times for tea at her house in Carrasco, so he could meet her daughter, who was only two subjects away from graduating as a pediatrician. Carmencita wasn't so old-fashioned as to find a good husband for her daughter; she was modern enough to seek friendships that could secure her good jobs. But Santiago had repeatedly used the excuse of his profession, claiming it had no set hours or rest.

Carmencita had waged a psychological campaign to get her husband to agree to the surgery and had promised him a vacation in Miami.

"Have you ever been to Miami?" she asked Santiago.

"Yes, many times."

"We've never been to the United States," Carmencita complained. "Can you believe it? A career military man like my husband, who always fought for the values of democracy during the era of the rebels, never wanted to go to the United States. When President Bush was in Uruguay, hugging that unmentionable colleague of his who was then president of this blessed country (and who didn't improve anything with the change, quite the opposite, as you can imagine), I joined that letter that the families of the military personnel imprisoned by the regime sent to the American president, asking him to remember all we had endured here during the years of the Tupamaros and to lend a hand to those who had once extended theirs to them. I was one of those who signed, though I didn't use my real name in case it didn't work out. We're still waiting for a response. Actually, we're not even waiting anymore, at least as long as that socialist Black man is president of the United States. Socialist or Muslim, who knows what that hybrid called Mubarak Hussein Osama really is. My husband says he won't go to the United States because he can't stand how communist they've become. But I remember he always said he doesn't go because he doesn't speak a word of English, and to me, it seems like just an excuse. Don't you think?"

"You don't need to know English to visit the United States," Santiago said. "Besides, in Miami most people speak Spanish. Same in Los Angeles."

"Of course. Imagine, there are all the exiles from Castro's regime. My husband would have plenty to discuss with any of them. Did you hear that, Bebe? What the doctor said? In Miami, almost everyone speaks Spanish."

Xico made a face. Carmencita continued with her usual routine:

"We're not going to die without seeing Miami. Los Angeles is also an option. But San Francisco isn't even worth dreaming about. A friend who lives there told me that in San Francisco, they're all communists or close to it. And honestly, I'm not up for that. When I take a vacation, I want a real vacation. We've already been to Europe. Miami is the one thing left on my list. Or New York, why not? Once you've had the surgery, we'll go. And no more arguments, as you like to say. No more excuses about the language. Do you hear me, old man?"

"I'll have the surgery," muttered Don Xico, as if chewing his words, "but I'm not going to the United States. Just the thought of having to go through all those investigations to get a damn visa makes my blood boil. The Yankees think they're the cream of the crop, but they're nothing but traitors. They use you and then throw you away like a dog. They treat dogs better. They have no consistency, because while some defend freedom, others with their professor airs hide behind that farce of a 'nation of laws' to throw even Rambo in jail. But they forget all the laws when Rambo is doing what he's supposed to do. No, no, sir. I'd rather enjoy my last days among my people, here, in our little country, which I've earned after a lifetime of service to the homeland."

"Hallelujah! At least you're going to have the surgery, old man. That's already a lot for a stubborn grump like you…"

The surgery was scheduled for Friday, May 20th, but the major canceled it at the last minute. He said he had "a very important match" that day, which left everyone puzzled. But no one dared to inquire directly, not even Carmencita, who chose to accept an invitation from her friends to a concert at the Teatro Solís, and everyone preferred to speculate about the major's professional activities, which were still very important and secret despite his retirement. At the Rambla Perú restaurant, it was said that the colonel belonged to the Lodge of the Lieutenants of Artigas and that no one could stop the former subversives now in power from calling for early elections. Others, more moderate, commented that it was precisely the Lodge of the Lieutenants of Artigas that had so far prevented the country from becoming a communist regime like Cuba's. That's why the news wasn't that something surprising would soon happen, but rather that, thank God, the worst hadn't come to pass.

The major also liked to maintain an air of mystery around himself. Only Carlos, one of his nephews studying architecture, joked that, for a moment in his life, the major showed signs of weakness. Someone told him this, but he just laughed it off, as was his habit when he knew the answer but preferred not to respond; or perhaps he simply didn't know.

"A man," he declared solemnly, "is master of what he says and a slave to what he keeps silent."

Obviously, he was right. But Don Xico had taken the art of silence to another level, using it to his advantage.

Carlos said that when Uncle Xico didn't do something because of a simple indigestion, the rest of the family assumed doing it would have put everyone's safety at risk.

Carlos II and Willian take care of Quique

Montevideo, December 24, 2011
At 6:15 PM, just before Christmas Eve, Quique passed by the corner of the *Misiones* bar at the worst possible moment.

"Poor guy, huh. Is that Alejandro's half-brother?" Carlitos asked.

"Yeah, that's him, no doubt about it," Willian said. "They say Quique likes to stir up trouble. Since no one dares to lay a hand on him because he's blind, he takes advantage of his condition to annoy both God and the Devil. But you know what? The few times I've dealt with him, he struck me as very wise and balanced."

"They say the blind can see what the rest of us can't."

"Yeah, maybe. Maybe he can see beyond, and that's why he's the least crazy, the least nervous, the least lunatic of all of us. I mean, it's not like he was born with that condition."

"Blindness?"

"Blindness and that calmness you see in him. He's only calmer when he's dead."

"Hey, did the old man finally give up on making him lose his virginity with a prostitute?"

"I don't know. Probably not."

"That's the downside of not having uncles around. An uncle took me. I remember she was a huge Black woman, really big. I had always imagined I'd lose it to a blonde like Madonna, and when I heard someone say 'another one' and my uncle Felipe got up and tapped me on the shoulder to follow him, I was so shocked when I saw the woman. Not only was she not Madonna, but she was enormous, like Michelle but ugly, all lumpy like that. I almost backed out of fear, but my uncle put his hand on my back, giving me the little push I needed. I couldn't duck

241

out of it, it felt like hell. In the end, you go there to prove your manhood, not to chicken out at the first woman, right?"

"And?"

"And nothing. I toughened up and stepped into that messy little dark room, with a smell I can't describe, but it was strong and I've never forgotten it. A total mess. I've always gone for the authentic, you know?"

"And?"

"And nothing, I told you. What had to happen happened. At first, I was so scared, I couldn't get it up. It was pitiful. I was as soft as a turkey's wattle. And on top of that, mine's small, you know…?"

"No, no. I didn't see anything."

"It's just a way of talking, man. We're all men here, right?"

"Come on, finish the story. I'm losing interest."

"So I tried to think about Madonna, but the Black woman looked tired, she had laid back with her legs open and her privates were shining under the TV light. She expected me to do all the work. You know how it is, you pay and still have to do all the work, right? 'What's wrong, honey?' she said. 'Nothing,' I said, 'it's just that I had to wake up early and I'm tired.'"

"How nice. I have a cousin who said the same thing, even though he had spent the whole day waiting to get into the stadium."

"Okay, don't call me out. I know, I was foolish and unoriginal, but what did you expect from a virgin teenager, jerking off out of necessity and scared out of his mind at seventeen, already too old for that kind of thing?"

"At least say something nice."

"Like what?"

"'Darling.'"

"Go fuck yourself…"

"Did you finish, or did you run away like some people?"

"I finished, I finished, as God commands. After that, you know how I felt? Like Schiaffino. Young people always give things more importance than they should. That's why they can faint over a singer who doesn't even know how to wipe his own ass. Honestly, I say it out of envy. More envy than resentment. If I could sigh over some stupid actress or a singer of the same type, I'd probably be happier." Stupidly happier, but happy, in the end.

"At least you finished…"

"I finished, yeah… Actually, the Black woman finished me. Since I couldn't get it up, she sucked it with * that mouth that looked like a cow giving birth to a toothpick. And when it finally started working, she had already finished me. After all, the Black woman was pretty, if you looked at her from behind. It was fear that made her seem so big, but she wasn't that old. Her ass was like two Brazilian cantaloupes, but her tits were still small. In comparison to the rest. Now that I think about it, she hadn't even been a mother by that time. God knows where my first woman is now."

"Maybe the condom broke and you knocked her up."

"No, knocked up my ass. I'm telling you, the Black woman finished me with her mouth. You didn't get it."

"Look…"

"She must've had her pussy tired from so many workers with their freshly paid wages, and she put extra effort into sucking that rookie. Poor hooker, after all. Who knows if she's even dead. With that kind of life, she probably didn't make it to sixty. When I think about her, I wonder if I'm not some kind of widower who'll never find out he's a widower."

"So that wasn't your first time."

"Yeah… Or I don't know. You're right, maybe that wasn't my first time. It was the weekend after. Since I already had some familiarity with the Black Maria…"

In the street, several firecrackers went off, forcing Carlitos to hold his breath.

"Don't tell me her name was Maria."

"What's wrong with that?"

"No, nothing. So? Did you really do it the second time?"

"Yeah, the second time I was like a bull and even made her scream."

"Don't fuck with me. You're such an idiot."

"Well, that's what I thought back then."

"And you kept believing that story for twenty years…"

"What do I know?"

"You don't know anything, man. You don't even know that hookers lie."

"Alright, hookers may lie. But I'm sure they don't lie more than your wife when she screams and doesn't say your name…"

"If you're looking for trouble, just say so."

"Come on, I'm stupid and ignorant, but I'm not clueless. You know a man keeps quiet about everything he discovers about his wife out of dignity. Right?"

"What do you know if you've never had a wife?"

"Not as stable as you, no."

"I never believed Lorena when she said she was a virgin. It wouldn't have bothered me if she'd just told me upfront: 'Look, I'm not a virgin; I had a boyfriend who popped me first...' I would've accepted that. But no, Lorena insisted from day one that she was a virgin, that the lack of blood on our honeymoon didn't mean anything, that she didn't remember the exact date when we did it at Parque Rodó, either..."

"And you stayed quiet..."

"What was I supposed to do? I loved her."

"What, you don't love her anymore?"

"I didn't say that. But it's not the same anymore. I kept accumulating evidence that she'd slept with some boyfriend before me..."

"And what bothers you?"

"The lie. That's what bothers me. Because I told her about all the women I'd slept with, and I deserved the same honesty. Over time, I lost trust in her and couldn't fix it."

"But you're still together, right?"

"Yeah, together, with that thorn in the middle."

"And if she did it once, she probably did it other times..."

"Did what?"

"Lie, I mean."

"If I hadn't thought it myself long before, I'd have punched you in the face right now."

"Come on, tell me how that Quique guy solved it."

"Solved what?"

"The thing with the Colombian hooker. If he couldn't do it the time his father took him, I imagine he wasn't going to settle for defeat for long."

"That's right. You're as dumb as a farm boot, but it seems life's taught you something, at least."

"Another beer with olives," Carlitos shouted to the waiter passing by. "Come on, tell the story."

An unfinished matter

Costa de Oro, June 1989

The following Saturday, he decided to put an end to all the plans and speculations that had been tormenting him all week and asked his old man for the car.

"You're in luck," Sosa said, "because I'm wiped out and not going out tonight."

When he handed over the keys to the old Beetle, he warned him:

"Drive carefully. And be careful with what you bring into the car. You know, like watermelons, it has to be just about to burst." Always check if the girl has an Adam's apple; it's like the lack of hips or a deep voice…

"I'm going to the beach with the boys, Dad."

"Yeah, I used to say the same thing back in Rivera."

Quique returned to the Colombian's brothel. But as he parked, he saw a group of workers entering, joking around, and thought his Plan A was either madness or simply beyond his capabilities. He was going to make a fool of himself once again, and he knew that afterward, he wouldn't be able to recover from another defeat.

So he went for his Plan B. He raced along the coastal boulevard at a speed that ignored every speed limit sign, took Avenida Giannattasio, and veered toward Costa de Oro. In one of the darkest areas of Atlántida, close to eleven at night, he arrived at an address he'd found in the classified ads from the previous Sunday. The ad promised respect and professional discretion from all the girls at Casa Amarilla.

He tucked the map into the glove compartment and pulled out a plastic gun, which he hid in his jacket. The night and the silence amplified the salty smell of the sea. That feeling of unreality dulled any sense of calculation and carried him like a wave toward his destination.

Plan B turned out to be simpler than expected, as soon as he crossed the threshold of the door. It was indeed a brothel. The house was organized like the homes of the last century: a central courtyard surrounded by arches that during the day provided shade for the hallway and at that hour cast black shadows over the doors where "women of the night" waited, as his father called them.

ESPECIALLY IN THE LAST TWO WEEKS, the waters had shown a troubling change. They'd grown colder, dirtier, sadder, and more interesting. Almost daily, he spotted some piece of plastic on the horizon, as if it had belonged to some other 00λ like his. He couldn't imagine another sailor throwing pieces of their ship overboard, because he knew how valuable these materials were, like teeth, irreplaceable; each loss brought them closer to the fate of the fish that end up in their guts or in the guts of other fish. Every day, he discovered some new evidence of the death of a fellow human and threw himself into the water to retrieve it.

The new trash always had some use. Sometimes it filled a need of many days, like a piece of wood that replaced a small pillar that held up the green tarp under which he slept during siestas and communicated with the gods or with other versions of himself. Other times, it ended up in the semi-flooded hold, waiting for some purpose.

Another significant change that followed the increase in trash was the birds. White birds with black beaks that flew much higher than the shiny fish of the early days. Those fish were harmless, like the dolphins and the clear waters, but these flying creatures seemed almost as menacing as the sharks that once followed him day and night, waiting for the final shipwreck.

He knew there was no salvation. If he sank, the sharks would tear his body apart; if he died on the ship, the black-beaked birds would do the same under the sun's light before the 00λ sank.

For days this thought haunted him as he adjusted the sail to speed up his journey. Incredibly, in the last week he'd managed to double his speed—or so it seemed at one point—thanks to the new shape he'd given the sail, a kind of triangle hanging from one of the antennas that ran from the bow to what had once been a pool. Every time he looked at that triangle inflated by the wind, made up of patches of canvas, he felt like a minor storm god.

A perfume of green eyes

January 2012

It must have been a coincidence. At night, the nurse returned shortly before Alejandro. When he saw her putting the key in the main door of the building, he pretended he'd forgotten something. He turned around and checked his pockets. He went back to the car. He searched for a receipt from the last pasta delivery he'd made that afternoon. He didn't read it. It was a mechanical gesture.

When he headed back toward the entrance, she was still there, checking her mailbox. Predictably, she didn't greet him when she saw him come in. Alejandro felt relief and disappointment. On a surface level, he thought, almost as if talking to himself, that the usual snob had returned to her usual self. On a deeper, darker level, he knew she'd been stalling for time. No objective indication revealed this dark certainty. But it was a certainty, as if at that very moment a silent dialogue was taking place between the two of them.

In the elevator, two floors up, their eyes met. Alejandro felt hatred for this woman who looked down on him, for who knew what reason, while he discovered that her eyes were green, not blue as he had always thought. She held his gaze for a second, just long enough to stir something in him without saying a word.

Alejandro looked at the panel. Someone had scratched it with a sharp object. They had managed to carve a poorly drawn P and A. Alejandro thought, almost with the coldness of a biologist working in a lab, that it would be enough to lock two people who hated each other in an elevator for them to eventually desire and love each other like dogs. He thought of Santiago manipulating mice in the United States. He thought about the blackout last month. Perhaps he had surprised two people in that same elevator. Two proper people, and nothing had happened. Nothing had happened because the confinement time had not reached the critical point.

The beep sounded at each floor.

The nurse's purse was white with a tiny red cross. Her perfume grew stronger as she left without saying goodbye. She left without saying goodbye, but Alejandro knew she had been watching him the entire time he was thinking about Santiago's mice in the United States and reading *P... A* on the panel.

Quique's first time

Costa de Oro, June 3, 1989

On a hot winter Saturday, with Quique having no inkling that his life was about to change forever (not because of an act of madness but, as one might say, because of the fulfillment of the duty that then fell upon any eighteen-year-old boy), he headed to Casa Amarilla, this time with more confidence and determination.

The moonlight fell on the face of a girl, too young, with a smile more like crying than the sweet words (supposedly sweet) she was saying. By then, Quique had no clear idea of where he was going, so he kept walking a little further as if he knew what he was doing. The smell of honeysuckle was a sign that something important was about to happen without him realizing it. It was hot, but not just any heat. It was that unsettling heat that sometimes arrives unexpectedly and settles with its silence and immobile things, as if waiting for the moment to break; or as if it knew that at that moment, at that instant, everything had already happened and what remained was to know how it had happened.

He decided on the second face that smiled at him under a curved shadow. It wasn't as beautiful or belonged to a woman in her forties, maybe fifties, but it inspired more confidence in him. Beauty terrified him to the point of paralysis. He placed a hand on her cheek, and the woman took his arm. She smiled and said to him, "Good evening, welcome, I was waiting for you."

Without looking at him, with movements that Quique guessed were routine in her profession, the woman headed to the bathroom while asking him, "Where have you been all this time, dear?"

Quique didn't answer. It was obvious that this was another stock phrase, part of the trade. He saw her buttocks, quite firm for her age, her breasts somewhat sagging after being freed from her bra. He thought about his sex, which hadn't yet responded to the situation as it should.

The woman had to work hard to get the client to ease into the usual fifteen minutes. A television illuminated her face in red and blue, advising him to trade in his *old car for the new Ford*. Marcelo Tinelli was laughing uproariously, and at times, the woman attending to him glanced at the television and smiled.

Almost at the end, Quique managed to focus. He convinced himself that this scene was real or resembled reality, and in that way, he fulfilled his duty as a man. He saw the woman's breasts, large, agitated but flabby, her eyes open toward the ceiling, as if she were suffering while repeating that he was doing very well, that it was almost over, that it was already happening. Finally, she shouted without much feeling. She was a bad actress, he knew it, he didn't care. He knew that she was faking badly, that her movements and words were mechanical, but at some point, he could also pretend to believe her.

She gave him five extra minutes. Quique wanted to know something about the woman who had been his first, the one who had made him a man. He learned she was from Colonia, that she had lived in El General for five years before being enlightened by a man who convinced her to move to Cerro, in Montevideo; that life in the capital had not been as easy as she had imagined. That long before that mistake, one of those inevitable mistakes that cost a life, she had been queen of the Vendimia, had a boyfriend at the experimental station in La Estanzuela who almost took her to Russia, but her mother didn't let her get involved with the wandering engineer. The owner of a winery, a Swiss man from one of the best families in Colonia Valdense, had told her that with her beauty she would first become queen of Montevideo and later of Buenos Aires. That's why she dared to participate in the national selection for Miss Uruguay, but a foolish jury failed to appreciate her pride for having arrived in the capital with broken shoes to show the world what it means to be a true queen, a condition that isn't inherited but carried in the blood, and they accused her of arrogance, so she could never fulfill her true destiny. After that blow, she couldn't recover. She tried all the known methods of the time, according to the experts, but none worked before shame and misery caught up with her. One day she woke up to reality, and from then on, she never dreamed again.

"Because there's a time, an age for dreaming," she told him. "Once you lose that ability, it's like losing your virginity. You can never get it back, even if doctors now say otherwise. I'm not poorer now. I haven't gone hungry for years, and I buy what I want. But I can't dream like I did when I was a girl back in Colonia. That's over. It's over. Over…"

Quique, who had introduced himself as Ignacio from the start, was about to ask her how she had ended up there, but he understood that Laira must have heard the same question a thousand times and that she would have always repeated the same lie as an answer. He also thought the story of being Queen of the Vendimia in Colonia was fake. He had met many other outsiders exaggerating their merits, and they had even convinced themselves of their own fantasies.

But Laira seemed sincere, unnecessarily sincere, despite her condition, he thought.

ACCIDENTALLY, AS WITH EVERYTHING, *he discovered the Roman method for making fish liquor. The fermentation of fish in a container forgotten under the sun for days produced the miracle. A period of scarcity or bad luck in fishing completed the rest. The blasero ate and drank the Roman liquor and hallucinated for three straight days.*

This accident, however, wasn't useless. Neither were the hallucinations. As noted in his notebooks, in week fifty-three, he saw Ana at least five times. The first time was in Ann's room. The second, at the end of a side hallway on the second level. But this time, Ana was desperately fleeing. He also saw a group of men and women like those in magazines, celebrating and swimming in the pool of 00λ. At first, all those noisy people caused him an inexplicable panic, so he chose to flee and hide. Later, when he managed to master the fear and other minor emotions, he approached the same people sunbathing. But when they saw him, they jumped into the pool and disappeared.

He saw Ana twice more. The last time, he almost reached out to touch her, but instead of grabbing her arm, he let her fall into the water. She seemed to defend herself, and he hallucinated indifferently. But it wasn't indifference, it was hatred, a feeling he had never known since he could remember. And after Ana fell into the abyss, he ran in search of other ghosts still wandering the hallways or hiding desperately in their cabins. But the blasero had an irresistible force in his right hand, and the doors exploded with a single blow. The beautiful eyes of a young woman stared at him in terror before closing on the floor, before that madness intoxicated him and threw the girl into the void where Ana had fallen, along with a man in uniform, another in a swimsuit, and three more young girls.

Quique's New Attempt

Costa de Oro, July 1989

The following Saturday, Quique returned to Casa Amarilla. He never saw the yellow color of its walls, despite the moon's strong intensity, perhaps, he thought, because that color is one of the first victims of darkness.

He looked for Laira. No one knew her. He thought it was a made-up name, that maybe she invented a different name every night, so her companions couldn't identify her. To a woman with a huge smile, who invited him in, he explained that he was looking for Laira, the woman with a mole on her cheek, near her left eye.

"The house has many girls, and many have moles in better places. And if they don't have them, they put them on." You can get all kinds of stuff here. You can't complain, sweetie, you've got plenty to choose from.

"The girl I'm looking for has blonde hair and is older than you…"

"Look, chickie, I think she's not here, and she's not really blonde either, just dyed, like the rest of us."

"What's her name?"

"Oh no, we don't give out personal details here. Take what's on offer or keep looking around."

The girl was what you'd commonly call beautiful or very beautiful. She looked a lot like Salma Hayek from *El Callejón de los Milagros*, but more real. The moment she stopped talking and looked into his eyes, it was as if the vulgar dress she was wearing had fallen away. She had a dark, deep gaze. She was probably the same age as him, but with a much longer life behind her. But she'd been born female, and she'd never questioned it. In silence, she seemed like a different person, younger, less aggressive, more open to any kind of feelings. Her act had faltered for thirty seconds, and she hadn't fully recovered when Quique thanked her and left.

A week earlier, the story would've been different. But now Quique only thought about Laira.

He spent many days unconscious, lying on the edge under the intense rays of the tropical sun. He nearly perished, scorched by the heat and the salt that thickened the crystalline air, just as it thickens and clarifies the waters near the uninhabitable islets. But a storm of water and fire saved him.

He often had nightmares about the inevitable sinking; he'd wake up trying to breathe underwater, drowning like the stormy night he was born. Some of those nightmares involved the monster sleeping in the depths of 00λ. Sometimes, 00λ would sink under the weight of the monster. Other times, the monster would become a ball of fire.

In other nightmares, no less incomprehensible, it wasn't him sinking into the abyss but a woman stretching out her hand in vain. Or two men raising their hands to the sky only to fall backward into the water. Or another man wrestling him, trying to stab him in the face without succeeding.

Sometimes sea monsters would rise from the deep waters with their dragon heads and crush 00λ like a paper boat.

"Why clean the basement?" the Russian always said

Manhattan, August 2011

Old Glinka died on Friday night or Saturday morning. Defying his doctor, he had been working until the very last moment on the translation of Polzin's final letter. On the table were some scribbles in Russian and English. None of them, Miguel thought, had anything to do with Aleksandra and Grandfather Mijail. They were other names of men and women, other cities in Ukraine. None started with A, M, or П.

"Too many abbreviations," said his wife, "impossible to know what they mean."

It was as if the old man had feared someone else might understand them.

In truth, even the old man himself hadn't understood them. He'd been trying to understand himself and probably hadn't had enough time.

Miguel apologized and left the old store. He knew he was running away from something that now surrounded the widow. The widow would have to shoulder all that sorrow for the coming hours, for the years ahead.

It's not my business, thought Miguel, walking down Hudson Street. Soon he'd pass that street and see a new store, renovated, brighter. Maybe an Apple or Microsoft store. It would be good for the block, which had been a bit dull.

He walked to the *South Cove Park* esplanade. It was getting dark. At that hour, almost all the benches facing the river were empty. He sat on one, near a girl who seemed to be holding back laughter. She was reading something on a phone, black leather boots accentuating the elegance of her long, young legs. A moment later, he noticed the girl was crying inconsolably.

He almost went over to offer her help. But he understood how ridiculous the scene would be and left in time. He knew that if he didn't rest well on Sundays, he couldn't perform during the week. And that put him in a very bad mood.

MARKED DAY. The hell of a torturer

Montevideo, April 5, 2012

The operation took place on a cold Thursday in April. The waiting room filled with family and friends in uniform, and the patient showed everyone, amid jokes and laughter, that he wasn't afraid of the operation or death.

As soon as the anesthesiologist had adjusted the dosage that started to drip, Dr. Santiago Zabala asked the anesthesiologist and the assistants to leave him alone with the patient to confirm his psychological state before the procedure. The assistants didn't understand what he meant but obeyed the request, more motivated by the cardiologist's prestige than by the regularity of the process.

Don Xico tilted his head and asked if everything was okay. Santiago confirmed:

"Everything is very good. In a few hours, you'll be even better."

"I'm in your hands, doctor. I trust in your science."

"You're doing the right thing. How do you feel?"

"Very good, a bit more relaxed. It's like I just had a little whiskey. One feels really good, little by little. The day I die, I'd like it to be like this, relaxed and optimistic."

"I thought a man of arms like you would prefer to die on the battlefield."

"Nonsense, doctor. That's all well and good in movies and when you're a teenager with a lot of imagination, trying to decide between a career in the military or architecture. But who likes to die bleeding out with no one around to even deliver the coup de grâce? No, doctor, I prefer something like this, in a soft bed like this one and with the euphoria of anesthesia, which is much better than the best whiskey, doctor…"

"Yes, it's something like that. Back in the day, before anesthesia, they'd amputate legs with plenty of whiskey. Anesthesia not only relaxes but also helps the memory release the oldest memories, did you know?"

"Of course! In the military, one doesn't only learn to hit the target."

"Do you remember anything from your childhood?"

"Yes, yes… many things."

"Like what?"

"I don't know… now that you mention it, I clearly remember a horse the old man gave me for a birthday, back in Rivera. I can see it. I can even smell it, that smell of horse and saddle blanket… Actually, it was almost a pony, but to me, it was huge… The stiff mane, a white star on one eye. The field is carpeted with macachines. There's the scent of pitanga…"

"Did you ever fall off the horse?"

"I fell and landed face-first in the macachines."

"Is that where that scar on your trapezius muscle comes from?"

"Trapezius muscle?"

"The one shaped like a Z."

"Ah, yes… this one, here by the neck…"

"Yes, that one."

"No, that one I got trying to climb over a barbed wire fence during training. A damn rusty barb… it hooked into my skin like a fishing hook, and it wouldn't come loose. And I, from the pain, pulled the wire to free myself and ended up cutting my skin and flesh in a terrible gash that later was hard to heal. Because of the infection, you know? The worst part was that I passed out from the pain… It was my first year in the army, and the veterans made fun of me for a year. I had to wait for the new batch of rookies to arrive to earn any respect… I had a rough time back then, but now I remember all that, and it seems fantastic. Can you believe it? How even the ugliest things can seem fantastic, doctor?"

"It's the anesthesia. It makes you feel good even about the worst memories."

"That's right, doctor…"

"I remember that scar too. With another one like it, you'd have a perfect swastika tattoo."

ON THE SECOND LEVEL, *the most extensive and diverse of the three, in the room marked with a 23, lived Ann. On the 11th day of the 11th moon, Ann "according to her diary, on the folio marked with a number equivalent to 56" spent the entire afternoon pensive, with her antennae upright and her mandibles closed.*

It's very hard to know "she wrote" what Ann might have been thinking when she closed her mandibles, and even harder to predict what she would do in the blink of an eye. Ann had spent an entire month walking along the edge of the table. There was plenty of space, almost no competition to cross the table diagonally, going back and forth without any obstacle. She ran from one corner to the opposite one and halfway got distracted by some bread crumb that had been lying there forever, or something else he himself provided so she wouldn't starve, or to keep her from getting bored during those long summer days when the sunlight from the window took forever to shift and make room for the most desired shade. According to his observations, Ann could cross the table from side to side a hundred times a day, but she usually preferred the shortest path of distractions. Probably Ann was afraid of continuing with the momentum and falling off all at once, which perhaps would have been for the best since she landed on the table from Ana's shoulder, who, as he remembered, hated all insects in general and ants in particular, especially when they climbed onto her shoulders during lunch. Ana "the blonde woman with dark glasses he had discovered in a photograph hidden in a book" would have swatted at her, and the poor ant, the one that ended up hitting the beer glass, now empty and dry on the table. The ant almost drowned under a drop of sweat rolling down the glass,

*still with a bit of foam. But she survived the drop after a heroic strug-
gle to free herself and since then had remained inhabiting every mil-
limeter of that table. That had been her small triumph, her little van-
ity: having survived Ana's swat, the noisy fall onto the table, and the
sweating drop from the glass. Perhaps Ann had withered in some part
of her body, but that was impossible to know. Ants don't scream, they
don't complain, and even half-squashed they keep walking and carrying loads like beasts.*

*But it was evident that Ann had suffered the impact. After sur-
viving the triple accident, so to speak, she spent her time walking
along the edge of the table, as if watching something, as if attempting
something she didn't dare to, pointing at distant objects, alternating
moments of euphoria that led her to run diagonally across the table
and moments of immobility where she blended in with a dead insect.*

*Either she practiced, pretended, or suffered from all sorts of dis-
turbances, he wrote accurately. Like a mysterious habit of not walking along the edge on moonless nights, as if ants relied on their eyes
and not their antennae. On the third days of each new moon, Ann
retreated to the space between the breadbasket and the beer glass. It
had nothing to do with the shadow cast by the breadbasket or the
abundant dry bread inside it. The sun doesn't distinguish between
days of the week, and therefore the shadows don't either. But Ann
did, or at least that's what it seemed to him, with very rare exceptions.
Exceptionally, on a third day of the new moon, she approached the
edge of the table. Ann seemed determined to keep going. But she
stopped, turned around several times along the edge of the table, and
returned to the shadow of the breadbasket. It was possible " he
thought, with somewhat obscure signs, like incipient forms of abstract*

thought " that in her behavior were sketched the signs of a transcendent message or that it was simply an ant and nothing more. Something that cannot be categorically asserted no matter how many observations are made of her. On the contrary, the possibility of concluding that Ann was something more, that Ann wasn't just an ant, increased with the observation time. The moments she remained still, with her mandibles closed, her antennae either down or up, meant something, but the very fact of not being deciphered transformed her into an insignificant insect.

What went on in Ann's head was a mystery " he wrote " a mystery that perhaps she would never reveal, even though the fate of λ011 could depend on this revelation. Yes, it could be observed that she had a fondness for hard pieces of bread and slightly less fascination for soft chunks, when the cloudy sky filled the air with hot steam. But little more, and this made him terribly nervous.

The truth turned out worse than the lie, the drunk said

Costa de Oro, August 1989

Quique left but came back on Monday and the following Tuesday until he started catching the attention of the women in the house.

Almost a month later, on a Friday, after three hours of patient waiting in his car, he saw her arrive. She came walking, so he deduced she had taken the bus. He waited half an hour and went in. Laira, or whatever her name was, was in her usual spot. Quique smiled at her:

"Hi, Laira. How are you?"

Laira didn't respond. Her face showed surprise and terror. She stepped back and said she wasn't available. She tried to close the door, but Quique put his hand in the way. The door squeezed his fingers, and Laira begged him to please remove his hand or he would get hurt. Almost murmuring, Quique told her:

"You're hurting me, Laira. You're breaking my fingers."

"Go, please, leave. That's enough. I'm telling you I'm not working today."

"Why are you lying to me, Laira?"

"My name isn't Laira, and just leave me alone or I'll call the police."

"What's wrong, Laira? Didn't you like it last time? Am I that worthless to you? Do you want me to pay you more? I have money. Why are you crying? You're breaking my fingers."

Laira gave in, and Quique, with a push, managed to get inside. He threw her onto the bed and undid his pants.

"I'll scream, and the other girls will come. Please, don't be stupid," said Laira.

Quique threw himself on top of Laira, and Laira started to scream.

In an instant, one of the women from the house came in and lunged at Quique, throwing him to the floor. But Quique got up and slapped her. The woman responded by grabbing his hair. Hysterical, she screamed, "abuser, abuser!"

Until she caught her breath and, without taking her eyes off him, slowly collapsed, sliding down Quique's body.

Quique had pulled out a knife that pierced the Argentine woman's abdomen, and when he realized what he had done, he was paralyzed with horror. The Argentine woman was already dead when Laira took Quique's arm and told him:

"Get out of here, Ernesto, get out now, before the police come."

Quique looked at her in shock. For a second, he was about to ask her how she knew his name.

Finally, he fled. On the beach, the Beetle crashed into a wave and flipped several times. Quique lost his sight and his sense of smell. Thanks to precise surgical intervention, he managed to recover some glimpses of twilight, but he could never again smell the salty sea air.

Laira confirmed in her statement that Quique was a little drunk, that he had wanted to have sex with her, and that she had refused because she knew Quique was the son she had given up almost twenty years ago to the good Sosa, who believed the story of his paternity and never dared, or didn't want to, confirm it. Laira started screaming, and Raquel, the Argentine woman, had come to her aid. But during the struggle, Liliana, whom Quique knew as Laira, had accidentally hurt Raquel with the knife she always kept on her bedside table, more to scare off violent men than for anything else.

Santiago's Bet

Montevideo, April 5, 2012

Don Xico tilted his head and looked at the doctor with drunken eyes that still revealed astonishment. He thought about the effects of the anesthesia, about the possible unreality of the moment. He thought about screaming, but his mouth was dry, and he couldn't catch his breath.

"I never forgot that scar," continued Santiago, adding some invented details. "My parents had a farm in the North, and I always played with a little truck without wheels in the dirt yard. One day, two *jeeps* from the army arrived, and my mother ran to the kitchen. I have fragmented memories. Shattered, like a broken mirror. Kid stuff. Then I remember the soldiers grabbed my father by the arms and tied a very thick rope around his chest. My mother tried to intervene, but one of them dragged her back into the house. One of them looped the rope around my father's chest and dragged him with a horse, as if he were a plow. My hero, who was actually a skinny guy, held tightly onto the rope. It didn't matter how the rocks and thorns slowly tore him apart. If he let go of the rope, he'd die from suffocation. Did you know Jesus died of suffocation? That was the death of those crucified in the days of the ancient Roman Empire. The muscles in the arms would tire, and as they relaxed, the body would hang, preventing the condemned from breathing. Ironies of history. A while ago, I did some brief *research* and concluded that Che Guevara, the other rebel killed by the empire of that time, also died of suffocation, no doubt drowning in his own blood…"

Santiago moved closer to Don Xico's face, who was trying not to look at him.

"Look at me," said Santiago, grabbing his chin. "Suddenly, you have nothing more to say? The screams of my mother still echo in my memory. I was in the shed, in a very high fruit crate where the hens laid eggs. From there, I could see how they first took my father and then my mother. They put her in a *jeep*, almost naked. Finally, the two remaining soldiers searched everything, the house and the shed, until they found me hiding there. I don't remember ever crying." My father never cried either. Or did he? No, of course not. I'm sure my father didn't die in a soft bed like this, and he wasn't tortured with anesthesia. My father never cried, at least not over those things. Neither did I, you know? If I cried, I couldn't see what I needed to see. Like when one of those soldiers from the fatherland grabbed me by the arm and took me in the remaining *jeep*. He held me tightly by the nape of my neck's hair, while I tried to tear open that Z-shaped scar. And the scar wouldn't open. My nails slipped over the sweaty skin, and the scar wouldn't come undone… Now, colonel, tell me where they are…"

"I don't know what you're talking about…"

"Colonel, you don't have much time left. The anesthesia is taking effect. You remember that moment perfectly. You handed me over to the Zabala Arbiza family. I love my adoptive parents, but I want to know where my real parents are. I want to know my name, my first name. Was I maybe called Karl or

Santiago? What was my name before I was called Santiago Zabala?"

"I don't know what you're talking about."

"Look at me closely. You have only a few minutes left to
make the most important decision of your life."

"Are you threatening me...?"

"Yes."

The major looked the doctor in the eyes. The light from the
operating room blinded him.

*FOR A LONG TIME, Ann had no name. There were many possibilities,
and none of them seemed right. Finally, he called her Ann, because
it reminded him of the woman named Ana or Hanna, the woman
who slapped him to make Ann let go of his shoulder, which was a
form of being born.*

*In the ninth moon, when some insects appeared on the second
level of 00λ—mostly flies and ants that lived off the waste and stench
of fish—and after noticing a sluggish behavior on her part, the man
got her an ant very similar to her. There was a stage of mutual recognition. Ann's companion seemed more stable: no inexplicable races
around the edge of the table, no languid diagonal crossings, no
thoughtful waits in a corner or in the center, under the shadow of the
bread basket. Ann's companion explored the table, the beer glass, the
bread basket with its three loaves, the wine glass, the plate with the
remaining bits of cheese ravioli, the crumpled napkin that so often
served as a mountain range for Ann.*

*The two ants crossed paths a few times, felt each other with their
antennae, deliberated around a bread crumb, traveled across the*

newspaper, from the column *"Boomers shook up culture"* with the photo of Elvis Presley to the main headline *"The year we stopped talking,"* back and forth. But Ann's companion couldn't handle the table for long and took the predictable path to the edge first and then to a leg until she disappeared. It was expected that Ann would follow, and she did, to the edge, but didn't dare go further. Obviously, saying she *"didn't dare to continue"* was quite a judgment.

"We're always making judgments—Ana had said". Just speak, and you're making a judgment..."

Only Ann knew if she stopped at the edge because she didn't dare or for some other reason. Maybe she didn't even know. Maybe she thinks she knows but doesn't, like when he himself was playing with a hammer as if it were a riveting machine, and Ann went straight ahead to pass underneath. If he hadn't stopped the mechanical and predictable movement of the hammer, it would have crushed her. Didn't she know she was going to be crushed to death in the worst imaginable way? Who knows what Ann thought, but the truth is she wasn't aware of that fate from which he saved her at the last second. Of course, animals probably aren't conscious of what they do, they're not rational beings, but generally, they're not suicidal either. They kill themselves unintentionally and save themselves by instinct, although Ann's instinct failed her, and the man had to prevent the disaster.

Something had gone wrong

Montevideo, April 5, 2012

"Alright…" said Don Xico. "Alright. Don't get upset. I'll tell you everything. Anyway, the…"

"Anyway, the law protects you. Don't worry."

"I handed over the boy… I mean, I handed you over to the Zabalas. The Zabalas were a good family. One of the best in Buenos Aires. They were on a waiting list, but they were close friends of General Máximo Monzalvo… Among their preferences, they had marked 'blonde,' because they were smarter and the adoption would raise fewer suspicions, and…"

"The previous family. What was their last name? The last name…"

"Fuentes. I think it was Fuentes."

"What happened to the Fuentes?"

"Everyone knew the Fuentes had a communist daughter… Product of the bad influence of a man she met in medical school… An anarchist used to the good life of the capital… Also, we needed more leads on three escaped Tupamaros who… were trying to cross the border… Can I have some water?"

"Continue."

"I took the young couple to the Rivera barracks and then to the Regiment and interrogated them myself. Two kids in their early twenties… 27 and 26, respectively. He had shaved off his mustache. Without it, he looked like a tired boy with dark circles under his eyes."

"Which one?"

"Which what…?"

"Which regiment did you take them to?"

"…To the ninth. The 9th Mechanized Cavalry Regiment…"

"What happened after that?"

"I don't remember…"

"Yes, you do. You remember perfectly."

"I left them there…"

"No, no, sir. Don't test my patience. Just by the movement of your eyes, I can tell when you're lying to me. You have no chance of playing games with me, so I advise you, for your own good, not to force me to make mistakes I wouldn't want to make."

"Shit…"

"And what else?"

"I used the usual methods from up north. Cattlemen's land, they said. The methods of branding. For the wild steer, breaking it in. For the calf, the stick, the prod, the lasso… castration, vaccination… and branding with fire. But all with measure. In the capital, it was different. There was a soldier who didn't know how to control the force of his blows… When the boy was left without parents, I felt sorry for him, and I offered to take him to Buenos Aires myself. That trip in '74 was torture… But we made it, and I had to hide from the Zabalas that the boy suffered from asthma… The Zabalas, an excellent family… I was just following orders… What are those flies, doctor? Are they wasps? They're wasps, doctor. Get me out of here… Please, get me out of here."

"ANN STOPPED AT THE EDGE and stayed there, watching, observing, or simply sniffing as the other ant descended the leg of the table and disappeared into the shine of the floor. Shortly after, Ann returned to the shadow of the bread basket. One could speculate endlessly about the advantages of living at the foot of the bread basket, with three pieces of bread that seem endless or will undoubtedly outlast her short life. But any speculation would be futile. The fact is that Ann does not leave the table and persists even when I proceed to increase my harassment, whether through the action of the hammer or the music of my fists striking, which sometimes make the table boards vibrate. Perhaps one day I should remove the pieces of bread, though it doesn't seem like a wholly legitimate decision to me. Of course, if I crush her with the hammer or with a finger, Ann will cease her obsessive, inexplicable behavior. But that's not the point. At least I think it isn't. It's about understanding the incomprehensible behavior of an ant without losing my calm. It's not about an ant understanding a man, but the other way around."

Was so much cruelty necessary?

Montevideo, April 22, 1983

Later, the lieutenant learned that María had allowed herself to be violated because she knew her son was hiding somewhere in the shed. Once, on a summer night, soaked in sweat on an unbearable pillow, he woke up with another of his absurd ideas: María Fuentes de Ocampo had died pregnant with his child. For two or three consecutive days, he woke up in the early hours with the same thought. Then he would step out onto the balcony to get some fresh air, and everything would return to normal. Until the next night.

"Was so much cruelty necessary?" an older Don Xico once asked at the gun club.

The TV had started playing *Heidi*, but no one could bring themselves to get up and change the channel.

"Of course it was," replied Colonel Rago in his familiar hoarse Italian-New Yorker voice, half ironic and half surprised by such a question, like a believer doubting their minister's sermon". We were at war. Or have you forgotten what Che Guevara did when he won in Cuba? He executed a few from the previous regime. That's what they would've done to us."

Tell me, grandpa,

what the wind sings in its song

"Yes, that's what they would've done," someone confirmed from the back.

Silence fell in the dark club room. Twilight was setting in, and no one could bring themselves to get up and turn on the lights.

Tell me, grandpa,

why it rained, why it snowed.

"And why didn't we execute them too?" said Major Almeida y Laprida. "We would've saved ourselves all the rest..."

"We needed information. That's why," someone said from the back.

Tell me why every white is
Tell me why I am so happy
Grandpa, I'll never stray from you.

Santiago's Mistake

Montevideo, March 15, 2012

"Were you just following orders too when you squeezed my father's testicles and made him crawl across the field before tossing him like a dying animal onto the *jeep*, huh? My father was tied up, and you had other armed men by your side. Was that what you learned in the army about how to be a real *man*? Were you just following orders when you groped my mother and said to save her for the captain…? But back then, you were probably just a fourth-rate lieutenant, and you had your fun with her a bit before handing her over to your superior, right? Because you were already libidinous, but your sense of pimping was stronger. Forgive me if I'm being unfair; back then, I was only about three years old, give or take. So this last part I infer from a single image, the image of a woman—more specifically, my mother—being dragged toward the *jeep* with her breasts exposed, amidst a crowd of men like you. And since the law still protects you and will continue to protect you until the day you die (or do you think I didn't notice how worried you were about the parliamentary vote on May 20?), because there's always a discount for wholesale criminals, all I have left is to keep speculating about fragmented memories I hold like shards of glass in my chest. Now tell me, Colonel, what did you do afterward?

Was all that humiliation not enough, that you also had to blow them up and throw them in some pit, to leave no trace, huh? Tell me, tell me, you son of a bitch... Don't fall asleep now. You've still got a few minutes left...

Santiago slapped his face several times, but the patient seemed unresponsive. In his eyes, wasps fluttered. It was the first time he acted without calculation, and he made the biggest mistake of his life. He shouldn't have wasted those crucial seconds unleashing his anger. Don Xico was on the verge of revealing where they had buried his parents—or at least that's what it seemed like.

He couldn't have been faking it. The anesthesia had sent him into a deep sleep. Perhaps back to that moment when the lieutenant, in his early thirties and at the peak of his physical condition, had subdued María Ocampo in the kitchen—Santiago would never know that her last name was Ocampo and that his mother's name was María—partly by force and partly by promising mercy for her husband.

The First Letter

On Friday, May 3, Juaquín Fuentes, the father of María Fuentes de Ocampo, received two letters. It wasn't a remarkable day; it was simply a day that would never be erased from his memory, if anything can ever be completely erased from human memory.

He opened the first one, which bore a government seal and was from the Regimiento General Fructuoso Rivera in

Montevideo. Someone signing as Dr. A. S. Núñez informed him of his daughter's disappearance in the Seccional Quinta de Rivera, recently reported by a neighbor in the area. Below, a phone number and an address in the capital of the department were provided, where he could go to give a statement. The notice urged Mr. Fuentes to take charge of his daughter's and son-in-law's belongings, as well as the rural property she had inherited from her father and which was still under her name.

He was about to open the second letter when his wife appeared.

"Any news?" María asked.

"…No, nothing."

"Sorry if I startled you…"

"No, no problem."

"But you've turned pale… Are you sure nothing's wrong?"

"Of course," said the engineer, putting the letters in his coat pocket. "It's just that you appeared behind me like that, silently, as if you were a ghost. You could at least make some noise with your feet…"

"Yes, dear, don't worry. Next time I'll honk the horn."

The engineer found an excuse to be away that weekend. As always, due to his work in the general inspection of UTE[1], it wasn't difficult for him.

Mrs. María Fuentes didn't have trouble either. On Friday and Saturday afternoons, she could be seen strolling through

---

[1] UTE: Transmissions Electrical. State-owned electrical energy company of Uruguay.

the galleries in the center. In *Kotorro*, one of the finest lingerie boutiques in Montevideo, a man named Norman had been replaced by a new salesman, and Mrs. Fuentes had set herself the serious goal of doing with the new one what she had done with the previous one over the past two years. Inquire about the quality and prices of the latest products (a stage she had already surpassed by far), look the young man in the eyes every time he tried to convince her of the advantages of the most expensive item, walk past the display windows to see how much attention she had garnered, and finally, in some way, brush her hands or arms against his while examining the quality of the microfiber of the items in question. The young man's nerves were the greater part of the trophy. A probable erection from his victim was the grand prize, but things could not go beyond that, since Mrs. Fuentes was terrified of sex, which was never as safe as the masturbation that followed this careful and lengthy act of seduction, which she often repeated in the shopping centers of Pocitos, with the risky variation of being close to her home.

With fury and relief, she had discovered that perhaps her husband had had an affair during one of those inspection trips, not only because the idea provided her with some fantasy during her boring marital sex sessions but also because, obviously, it freed her from the feelings of guilt that overwhelmed her on Sunday mornings when the excess of the previous night's Martini took its toll on her liver and her entire mood.

The second letter

Montevideo, May 10, 1974

In the early hours of Friday, while waiting for the departure of an ONDA bus to Rivera, he sat on one of the benches in Plaza Cagancha and, after smoking several cigarettes without pause (he had switched from the usual blond Nevadas to black La Paz), he opened the second envelope and read his daughter's letter. The sender must have been fake, and, judging by the postmark, the letter had been sent from Tacuarembó.

With an ambiguity that forced him to read and reread between the lines, Marita informed him that she was two months pregnant, and that if she was writing, it was not for herself and certainly not for her husband, who was not even aware of the letter, but for her unborn child and for the one she had met at the Sarandí jetty last winter... She didn't need money, as she planned to give birth at her grandfather's farm, where both he and Aunt Raquel had been born. She only asked that, for at least a few years, he would not tell "Uncle Botitas" where she was living, or with whom. They were no longer involved in politics. They had been expelled from the newspaper for straying from certain editorial guidelines, which had led them to decide to dedicate themselves entirely to the countryside for a prudent period, until things improved.

"Uncle Botitas" must refer to her sister Raquel's husband, who was not a soldier nor had ever set foot in a military barracks, but in family conversations, jokingly, he had often been alluded to for his work in the intelligence service and in the

Triple A, something he never denied, perhaps because it was true or because it gave him all the prestige he always needed in a family of engineers and journalists, as he himself used to say during Christmases. María had been one of his most unconditional defenders. She had never believed those stories nor did she appreciate the jokes about poor Uncle Rodolfo, the only one who had taken her, along with two friends, camping to Punta del Diablo in the summer of 1964, perhaps the best summer of her life.

Uncle Botitas' role had been rather ambiguous, and no one knew, not even Raquelita, whether he had ever contacted the communists, the Tupamaros, the fascists of the JUP, the military, or all of them. At the newspaper, Carlos had combined the list of Tupamaros and alleged informants for the police, the army, and the American embassy, and had created a new and more sinister list of names that appeared in at least two. It seemed that having been part of some subversive group in the 60s, when everything seemed to suggest that the triumph of the revolution and the New Man was inevitable, had become valuable capital by the early 70s, when the supposed utopia had hit a stone wall and was desperately searching for a hole to disappear into. In the age of information, knowledge of something had a price that was paid in dollars and settled with one's life.

But in none of these lists did the name of Rodolfo Ballesteros appear, Uncle Rodolfo, the good uncle, the fighting husband of Aunt Raquel. In the 1990s, a medical student and member of the FEUU[2] came across this list of 13 names that, for a time, was confused with a list of creditors of the notoriously infamous newspaper 69.

The letter was deliberately obscure, but it made clear that for some reason María had changed her opinion of Uncle Rodolfo. It wasn't unusual for María, her father thought, always a victim of her changing moods that took her from love to distrust, from rejection to affection. It was because of this emotional instability that she had abandoned her own family and her Catholic convictions to blindly devote herself to an irresponsible young man in every sense. He, Joaquín, might have been able to accept the young man, despite his radical ideas, if only he had shown even a shred of responsibility. He could have lived with his childish theories about imperialism, the Latin American bourgeoisie, and the tyranny of foreign capital, if at the very least he had been capable of finishing his medical degree or had dedicated himself to some sustainable business to support his family. He had told María that if her passion was journalism and not medicine, he could help. He knew many people at the newspaper *El Día* and at *El País*. But María had only smiled in response. This smug smile didn't sit well with Joaquín, as if he were the childish one and not those young men who drifted aimlessly from place to place, unable to feed themselves on their own. Joaquín considered himself far more open and tolerant than the young man and his comrades, always

---

[2] Federation of University Students of Uruguay

brimming with ideological rage, always seeing everything through the lens of class struggle. The proof (thought Joaquín, watching two pigeons fight over a tiny piece of some dead animal), was that he hadn't hesitated to lend them the house and the land in Rivera, even though from the start it had seemed like yet another of those naive ideas of young men poisoned by books. Or perhaps because of that very reason. Because deep down he knew that neither that hermit-like life nor the marriage itself would last long under those conditions. The worse, the better. Someday, very soon, they would come to their senses, and he would have her back home.

One of the pigeons won and swallowed the piece of meat with fur. For a moment, it seemed to choke.

Joaquín thought it would die, but the pigeon managed to gulp down the carrion and then turned to the others to mark its territory with pecks.

He thought of Rodolfo. Since his daughter's estrangement, he had grown much closer to him. Rodolfo had gone through the same thing with his son Alberto when he hooked up with a girl of questionable reputation. The solution, Rodolfo said, was to forgive. If God can forgive everything, how could we, imperfect and sinful beings, not do the same?

Suddenly, Joaquín Fuentes remembered all the times Uncle Rodolfo had shown up at his house, with the finest Chilean wine, with his leisurely conversation, with almost the same disdain he had for his daughter's husband, who probably wasn't even named José but Joseph (he had said), first as the secretary-general of the medical students' union and later as an honorary writer and cartoonist for anarchist pamphlets. A disdain that fluctuated between hatred and the wise advice to learn to forgive.

At some point, Rodolfo had told him about the case of a student activist from the MLN who had been found floating in the Santa Lucía, executed by her own comrades who feared she would denounce them. A well-known case, since there were many others where subversive members simply disappeared. They disappeared into the Río de la Plata or were sent to the Montoneros' bases in Argentina, where they were dealt with.

He reread the letter. The cigarette smoke and the lingering darkness in the square forced him to bring his face closer to María's rounded handwriting, with the same *m* she had written since she was a child, which looked like *w*. He had never been able to correct those *m*. Maybe because she didn't want to. She hadn't even changed the shape of that letter when she was trying not to be identified, which proved her naivety, her immaturity.

The writers of those pamphlets didn't even have a typewriter or had run out of ink ribbon, thought Joaquín as he said "no, thanks" to a garrapiñada seller. Then, noticing the seller's hole-filled pants, he thought he would have preferred his daughter to have fallen in love with that young man who carried his entire business on his back, or with that other one who, barefoot, shouted the latest news from the newspaper *El País* (a terrible earthquake had buried over ten thousand people in China), rather than with a useless idealist. The poverty of a garrapiñada seller wasn't so hard to fix, he thought. But the idiots who can't sort out their own lives want to fix the life of an entire country, if not the world.

Among so many visits, so many banal conversations, he couldn't recall if he had ever mentioned to Uncle Botitas that he had ultimately been unable to sell the land in Rivera. Somehow (had he mentioned it himself?), he knew that Raquel wanted to visit her parents' house before Joaquín sold it. But why, if she had always hated that house without electricity? At least that's what she had confessed when she sold her half to buy the apartment in Pocitos. Was she the one interested, or was it him? More out of family shame than anything else, Joaquín had told Rodolfo that the house was vacant, that it was a ruin already almost sold to a Brazilian agronomist. He didn't remember, then, saying anything about his daughter and much less about his grandson, whom he had never met until a few months ago, when he turned or was about to turn two years old.

A soldier approached him but continued walking slowly, leaning on his carbine. Joaquín put away the letter and lit another cigarette. The soldier turned around and looked at him for a moment. As he walked away, Joaquín tried to count on his hands the days that had passed since his daughter's letter and the one from Dr. Núñez. It hadn't been that many. It hadn't taken the Regiment many days to conclude that María had disappeared, nor did it take their army of bureaucrats long to find out where her father lived. Two days.

The National Being, According to Carlitos

Saturday, March 31, 2012

"It's in the infancy of this country," said Carlitos, looking toward a table where two other men were commenting on the expulsion of a coworker from the Central Bank. "All Uruguayans carry within them that sacred idea of the defeat of the spiritual and ideological founder, General Artigas, self-exiled and dying in poverty in a distant country, as Paraguay was back then, being served mate by the black Ansina…"

"Lower your voice," complained Willian. "That word's forbidden these days."

"The dark-skinned one, however you prefer it. The poor enslaved dark-skinned man that the general ended up freeing, but who knows how and at what price… I mean, who knows if those two lonely men weren't a couple."

"Oh, come on!" said Willian, lowering his head and looking around. "Shut up, don't be an idiot. How can you even think of such nonsense?"

"And why couldn't a hero be gay? With those blue eyes and such blond hair…"

"Don't be a jerk. Not General Artigas. Pick on anyone except the father of the nation."

"Don't get all sentimental on me. We're old now."

"And don't you go acting all gay when you're far too old for that stuff. And if you keep up with that joke, I'm getting up and leaving. Let's not have them confuse us too."

"Alright, stop messing around. Leave whenever you want. Besides, that wasn't the point…"

"Then what was?"

"A while ago, I read an article in the newspaper that said the General had been a defeated man. I'm saying that between the sacred defeat of Artigas and the radical modesty of Pepe Mujica, 'the poorest president in the world,' as the BBC called him, good or bad, the president who plants flowers and lives in a little house that would have scared even Diogenes himself—it's all a line of continuity, as they say now. All of which isn't bad at all, if you consider the excesses of the colonial oligarchy, the old-time caudillos, and today's consumerism."

"Damn, you've gone all intellectual on me."

"Does it bother you?"

"No… I don't know. But what got into you? Because I know you better than yesterday. You're triggered by what happened to the bald guy next door. The idiot bank teller got fired for graduating as an economist. That's it, isn't it? Well, he shouldn't have said he'd graduated as an idiot. That's it, right?"

"Yes and no."

"Yes and no, but what do Artigas and Pepe have to do with it?"

"What really gets under my skin is something else. You remember the anonymous notes I used to get at the store when things were going well?"

"Things of the past…"

"There are things from the past that never pass. After I went bankrupt in '83, no one ever slipped a note under my door. Not a rumor about the supposed ill-gotten money to put the neon lights above the door, or to renovate the window display with the best brands... No, sir. After I went bankrupt, everyone pitied me, which is what they do best..."

"Who?"

"Us. Uruguayans. Uruguayans aren't just sad and modest. In a hundred ways, they're admirable: being so few and so small that every time someone coughs in Maldonado, someone tells them to be quiet in Salto or Rivera, being so envious of others' success, it's more or less a miracle that so many important figures have come from here. Because the practice and visceral need of this little corner of the world, a kind of wedge between two continents with two national egos competing in size, is to stone anyone who dares to raise their head above the rest." Hence, the famous humility of Uruguayans might be nothing more than resentment and the demand for general mediocrity. Hence, whenever someone dares to do something different, long before it begins to take shape, the national and democratic passion for envy leads an entire people, almost as a gut reaction, to the practice of tearing out each other's eyes. Hence, it's not uncommon for individuals to suffer more from others' success than from their own triumphs and, therefore, dedicate their entire lives to slandering, despising, and reducing to mediocrity anyone who might have something in common. Hence, there are so many people without their own lives, living parasitic lives, enjoying the little or much harm they can cause to their neighbor, not just any neighbor but their fellow countryman. Deep down (and since it's deep down, they'll never admit it but rather the opposite, they're likely to burst into an improvised patriotic speech), the average Uruguayan needs to criticize Argentinians, Brazilians, and Americans to mask the existential and inherent fact that those they truly hate are Uruguayans themselves.

WITH A MAGNIFYING GLASS, ONE COULD OBSERVE their reactions more clearly, though it's likely that, if objectivity existed, it wouldn't matter much. The first time he was under that gigantic glass dome, he saw the world in a different way. It's impossible to know what he might have thought then, but it's clear that the new object didn't go unnoticed. He spent a long time looking upwards. On Ann's chronological scale, it might have been something like five or six hours. Five or six hours looking upwards, with his antennas raised, waving slowly, observing the magnifying glass or the distorted reality coming down through the large glass. Then he retreated to the darkest corner of the table, the corner closest to the wall of the cabin.

It was clear that Ann was caught in an indecipherable drama.

It was clear that if Ann had been without emotions, she would have been happier. But she didn't know it and spent all day and night suffering, pointlessly.

Ann went over each line of the letter that was half-covered by the newspaper.

"...before someone labels me with that and we waste days discussing me, I'm going to admit to being a cynic. In truth, I don't think I deserve that kind of praise. We already know that cynicism is an advanced state of maturity. Having said that, I don't think there's any reason to waste time discussing me, or why I live one way while

criticizing what I do, while criticizing the world I'm complicit in, innocent or indifferent, to cite just one example. Like anyone, one has to survive in a real world where not everything is teddy bears. There are stones, thorns, hunger, cold, heat, desires, grievances... Having said that, I think we can discuss what really matters. Not me, but reality. If I say this world is unjust and I partake in all that injustice, it doesn't mean the truth that comes out of my mouth ceases to be true..."

Ann walked over these little black shapes on the paper, from the d *to the* d *and back "...ceases to be truth hturt be ot sesaec..." Perhaps she pitied them as much as a man pities a path of ants. Anything but the truth. And Ann, with her tweezers, gripped the paper by one edge and could barely make a faint mark. She had to hold the magnifying glass close to see those tiny and useless marks that might have been important to Ann.*

For some reason, as soon as she reached adulthood, she heard it.

Rivera, April 1974

The macho of María Ocampo had broken before they had calculated, they had told him. Don Xico had heard the curses of Colonel Máximo Monzalvo, who was shouting that those damn soldiers hadn't learned anything at the Academy, that for severe coercion there were doctors who controlled how much a detainee could take before they broke.

"One day these damn soldiers are going to make me snap," shouted the colonel.

Lieutenant Laprida remained at attention, trying to suppress the nausea caused by his stomach fighting to expel the fried milanesas with old oil he had eaten at a bar in Bella Italia. He could see Colonel Montalvo pacing nervously back and forth, passing through the half-open door, always preceded or followed by a long shadow that occasionally escaped into the hallway, cursing the laziness of an entire generation of recruits who weren't worth a quarter of the previous generation.

"And do you know why, Captain? Do you know why?"

"No, Colonel."

Don Xico couldn't remember the captain's name, that man with thin, almost translucent lips, flaccid, which he tried to mask with a yellow mustache. Before hearing the two men in the same room, the lieutenant had held some admiration for the captain, whom his soldiers nicknamed The German despite his Irish surname.

"Of course you don't know, Captain, because you're part of the same damn generation of cadets who can't take a stick up the ass without screaming like queers. And do you know why, Captain?"

"No, Colonel."

"Of course you don't know."

Colonel Montalvo cursed the lack of taste in the national army. If they were more macho (he had said, or at least that's what Lieutenant Laprida thought he heard while clenching his mouth and all his guts), they would know how to handle a classy woman, a fine bitch with a bag of information... You should understand that a woman isn't a communist or a patriot, because that can change as quickly as the man who sleeps with her. A woman is a woman, damn it. Is that so hard to understand? Tell me, Captain, is it so hard, damn it? A woman either has class or she doesn't. She's the genetic heritage of a nation or she's some Indian inedible, one of those Bolivians who don't reproduce but are handed over to the troops…

The colonel slammed the desk with something metallic.

"As if that wasn't enough," he shouted "you also went too far with the skinny one. What did we get out of the whole process, Captain? Not saying anything? What new information was worth all this work and sacrifice? Don't even bother answering. Besides, we're not criminals. What we do, we do with a clear objective. Do you realize, Captain, the waste of time and resources in this unit? To hell with you and your damn soldiers!"

Lieutenant Laprida was about to faint when, finally, between the colonel's shouts and his blows on the table, the violent sound of vomiting was heard.

The officers arguing in the room fell into an alert silence. It sounded like a punch to the stomach. As he tried to recover, Laprida saw a shadow several meters long that turned out to belong to Colonel Monzalvo, who, after a brief silence, said:

"Captain, come see how the girls in your battalion behave."

After the captain's apologies, the colonel ended the conversation:

"Save your breath. I don't even want to know your name. Just take this waste out of here and bring me something strong to drink."

An inconsolable cry illuminated the Zabala household

Buenos Aires, April 22, 1974

So both the woman and her husband broke in the hands of amateurs, revealing nothing, not even one of those fake names detainees invent to escape the electric prod. The female (a waste, as the colonel put it, with those blue eyes and those breasts in full bloom, screaming for her child instead of loosening up and cooperating) died of a heart attack. At least that's what they told Lieutenant Almeida and Laprida before assigning him a minor mission.

As punishment, he had to take charge of the child and the trip to Buenos Aires. For Don Xico, it was like a consolation prize. Though nothing depended on his decision, he at least wanted to make sure the child arrived in good condition and that the family he ended up with weren't starving wretches.

Carmencita didn't know it, but two of her retired friends guarded the secret like two tombs.

The day Pedro Zabala awoke

Buenos Aires, March 1987

In truth, Don Xico knew many secrets of the Zabala family, partly because of his profession and partly because Don Zabala had unwittingly revealed details, perhaps thinking they were ir-relevant to anyone. They weren't irrelevant to Don Xico.

When Santiago was still a child, Don Zabala had an accident that left him in a coma for seven years. When he opened his eyes, the first thing he saw was María's face in the darkness. It was a coincidence that many interpreted as a miracle. Don Xico said it was a coincidence because Mrs. Zabala almost never showed up at the hospital, according to the patient's closest friends. It was as if he had been waiting for her to wake up. Or perhaps somewhere in the depths of his unconscious, navigating who knows what seas, he heard María' peak"and woke up.

But on the afternoon of March 15, 1987, when the last sun through the window began to cool behind the blinds, Don Zabala did not see María but a ghost. He uttered her name in confusion and fear:

"Marta?" he asked.

"It's me…"

"Marta…?" he repeated.

"No, Pedro," said María. "Mom died a long time ago. It's me, María."

Don Zabala made a great effort to recognize María Arbiza in that face. But the ghost of Marta lingered in María as she said, "Pedro, finally, Pedro…"

Don Zabala was still drunk, without understanding. He barely remembered the events of the day before March 23, 1980. The argument in the kitchen. María climbing the stairs to the bedroom and him following behind. He was reproaching her about something Lucía didn't want to hear. What was he trying to say? He didn't remember.

"Pedro, finally, Pedro…" said María, who had uttered those words when she saw him wake up.

According to the lieutenant (María had never denied it, and Santiago knew the same version of events from his mother and his grandmother Marta), Don Zabala had fallen down the stairs one drunken night, with such bad luck that he ended up on the first step with a nasty blow to the head. According to what Zabala himself had told him in the hotel lobby, without going into much detail, that unfortunate night he had stormed up the stairs with a fury that wasn't common for him. At least not as common as his habit of having a whiskey after work. One or two, depending on the day's events, he joked to downplay one of the most important moments of his life.

One might speculate that he had had too much to drink that day, because no matter how hard he tried, he couldn't reach the top step. Don Zabala had placed a particular emotional emphasis on that last sentence. Don Xico wanted to say it seemed to him that Don Zabala had paused when recalling this memory, stressing the fact and the vagueness of that moment: "no matter how hard he tried, he couldn't reach the last steps," as if he were searching his foggy memory for a clue that at some fleeting moment seemed to surface.

Perhaps it was his military bent, thought the major, but to him it was as if some force had prevented him from reaching the last step. He wasn't clear on that moment. He did remember, in vivid detail, the vertigo, the ceiling lights, and the taste of blood that must have come much later. For a while, the major had secretly speculated about that melancholy and

293

mysterious tone in Don Zabala's voice and the last step that led
him to a seven-year sleep, until at some point he decided it was
a waste of time.

Don Zabala was a rather secretive man, the major recalled.
He never knew if he was telling the truth or making things up
to protect his privacy. He had never wanted to talk about his
son, of whom he said he had many problems. For seven years,
Santiago had avoided the living tomb of his father, and when
his father had returned to the world of the waking, communication hadn't been great, which was why he didn't even know
if his drug problems had led him to an incurable illness or some
sexual practice condemned by the Church.

Still, Don Zabala was looking for someone to talk to, and
whenever he crossed the River Plate, he stayed at Don Xico's
hotel. In the evenings, Don Xico would invite him for a whiskey
with chestnuts. Their conversations invariably began with the
economy, moved on to politics, and ended with family. From
his former profession, Don Xico had gained intuition, if not a
clear idea, that conversations always start with what matters
least; so one could think that family was a subject of particular
concern for Don Zabala. After the third or fourth whiskey,
when the laughter and witty remarks about the national situation and the hips of Uruguayan women had given way to resigned grimaces, Don Zabala would always ask about the major's daughter and the life in the countryside he had abandoned
long ago. At this point, the tone of the conversation would become more somber, as if Don Zabala were suffering from a deep

nostalgia for his Peregrino, a provincial town he invariably described as a village of mediocrities and slackers.

After seven years, which for him might have been minutes, if that, María had become the living portrait of her mother, he said. Occasionally, in fleeting moments, Don Zabala could still see in that face certain details that distinguished her from her mother (the occasionally affectionate gaze, the posture of her full lips), those signs of the tender and passionate love of the early years, the years that had lasted so briefly and explained—or perhaps justified—the rest of it, a life of misunderstandings, jealousy, and constant arguments.

When he awoke, the world and his family had changed, as always, in ways he hadn't foreseen. María had not only aged seven years—far more for someone who hadn't witnessed the process—in the blink of an eye. The little boy he had seen the day before, a child distinguished by his grades and good manners, had just been expelled from school for marijuana use. The cheerful and restless boy now had thick, darker hair, a distant gaze, and incoherent conversation. The worst part: his son couldn't muster any emotion, good or bad, toward the people around him. His most frequent responses were "yes" and "no," which to the convalescent Don Zabala sounded like "I don't know, I have no idea" or, worse, "I don't care." The only things he cared about were dissecting frogs and collecting butterflies, which had led his mother to futilely encourage him to take his biology studies more seriously. Santiago frequently took refuge, like clutching a lifebuoy, in anything except one of the many businesses his father still owned, thanks to María's commendable administration.

At first, Don Zabala had to make an even greater effort than with María to recognize in that tall, thin young man—in that adult—his son. By the magic of a single blow, the father had lost not only a part of his son's childhood and adolescence, his past, but also his future. The boy, whom the father referred to by his second name, Ulises, in front of Don Xico, had been condemned to an existence of delusions and lies, the father said. But Don Zabala never confessed what he meant—whether the boy had contracted an incurable illness or had lost himself in vice. Don Xico, out of tact, he said, also hadn't wanted to press too much.

THE 6TH DAY OF THE SAME MOON, Ann suffered the worst earthquake of her life. The blasero moved through the dim, sweltering hours of dawn and bumped into the edge of the table. The cereal boxes and spoons on top came crashing down with a clatter. Immediately, he began searching for Ann, fearing the worst. But Ann was on the edge of the table, running back and forth in what seemed like a panic attack. At times, the blasero thought Ann might finally jump, taking advantage of the darkness of the void.

But no. Instead, she headed toward where the cereal boxes were. Perhaps Ann would never know that she had lived on top of two rich cereal boxes. Her antennae are blind to the images advertised on each side of the box. Or perhaps her antennae are so powerful that they perceive something of the scent that lingers beyond the cardboard and the plastic bag sealed for eternity. Perhaps she senses that treasure, and perhaps that's why she hasn't abandoned the table until now. She didn't know what she was waiting for. For an earthquake to open them? Is that why she had run toward the boxes when the tremor occurred?

By herself, she would never manage to open the box. The companion the blasero had provided for her long ago hadn't collaborated in her greatest obsession either. Probably, Ann hoped the blasero would take pity on her and open the box. It was hard to guess what might be going through an ant's mind, he thought. Though the truth was, even the blasero didn't know if he would end up opening the cereal box for her before the final collapse. Would Ann know better than the blasero what he was going to do in a few days?

The blasero wondered if Ann could see him. In reality, yes, she could see him, but only on occasions when the blasero got within five centimeters of her almost nonexistent form. In those moments, Ann would stop and raise her antennae. Perhaps she didn't see him, but only sensed him through one of her many senses. She couldn't see him when he simply observed her, because he was outside her perception.

But to see the blasero, she first had to understand what she was seeing, the blasero thought. When she stumbles across a crumb of bread, she knows what it is, recognizes it at least, because she carries it off and somewhere eats it. But when the blasero got close enough to stop her normal pace, did Ann know what she was seeing? Yes, it was a threat sometimes, something else at other times, because Ann would wait expectantly. That threat could open the cereal box, crush her with a finger, or release her in an anthill in the engine room, or doom her to the torment of the wrong anthill.

Without a clear purpose, the blasero had tried to figure out which anthill Ann came from. In the hold, there were at least two. To find out Ann's origin, the blasero had placed a pair of ants from each anthill on the table. It was chaos. The ants from the same anthill clashed with those from the other. Ann didn't intervene. She watched them without acting. The blasero tried to bring the five ants together at the same time and in separate sessions following a complicated combination. The only thing clear is that Ann was not appreciated by any of the members of the known anthills. If she were taken to any of them, she would be torn apart immediately.

Ann belonged to some other anthill or to none at all. It's possible she was a cursed ant. Since her arrival, even the weather had worsened. That unbearable heat, even on moonlit nights when not a single ripple disturbed the grim mirror of the sea.

He should crush her with a finger or let the other ants take care of dispensing justice, ant justice, incomprehensible to a man.

"They seized symbols of crimes against humanity"

ARGENTINA'S JUSTICE SYSTEM seized 43 Ford Falcon cars from a naval base in the province of Buenos Aires, the vehicle preferred by the last dictatorship (1976-1983) for kidnapping political opponents, judicial sources reported today.

The vehicles were found in a shed at the Puerto Belgrano naval base, about 700 kilometers south of the country's capital, as part of an investigation into crimes against humanity committed by the military regime, led by federal judge Eduardo Tentoni.

Starting in 1976, when a bloody dictatorship began, leaving 30,000 people disappeared, the Ford Falcon, usually green, became the car of choice for "task forces" to kidnap political opponents.

By late 1977, due to the almost daily use of these vehicles for such illegal operations, the then Minister of the Interior, General Albano Harguindeguy, ordered the purchase of 90 "unidentifiable" Falcons to equip provincial police forces.

The secret file detailing the specifications and objectives of such a purchase survived the destruction of incriminating documents ordered by the dictatorship and is currently stored in the National Archives.

El Espectador, EFE. March 27, 2012

For a peaceful change

Montevideo, December 22, 1986

When María Ocampo's mother learned of her daughter's disappearance, allegedly at the hands of the Tupamaros first and then Argentina's ERP, she turned to alcohol and died three years later, on February 3, 1977. The night before, as if she knew she was going to die, or as if she hoped for divine relief, she confessed to her husband that she had been unfaithful, a reason for which God had punished her with the worst punishment a mother could receive. Joaquín asked her with whom. With many, she said.

"With how many? With how many did you sleep?" he insisted, surprised.

"With none," she said, trying to ease a sharp pain in the left side of her abdomen. "With none…"

"Then? I don't understand," he said.

"All my life I've been a flirt…" she said. "More than that. I've gone through this world provoking men… It's what our daughter would have defined as a vice of the idle bourgeoisie."

"But darling…"

"No, Joaquín. I know what I'm saying. These weren't the actions of a teenage girl, of young women who one day discover they're attractive and desired and don't quite know what to do with it. I wasted my time provoking boys, like an old pervert."

"Don't talk nonsense," said Joaquín, running his hand over her forehead. "If that's the case, we're all sinners. We've all fantasized many times… What do you want? Do you want me to forgive you? I forgive you. You're not guilty of anything…"

"No, Joaquín. I don't expect you to forgive me. I only hope that God will forgive me… What I ask of God is that He keeps our daughter by His side and forgives me, forgives me so I can see her once more. I want to see her once more, at least once more. That would be enough for me to ask forgiveness for so many things. So many things…"

"Come on, darling, this conversation makes no sense. Rest."

"Yes… that's what the doctor always says… Rest… As if that were possible."

Engineer Joaquín Fuentes had been dismissed from his position at the state agency a few months earlier, in December 1976. At the time, professional negligence was cited first, followed by dereliction of duty.

Until his wife's death, Joaquín Fuentes defended the theory that his daughter had been taken by the subversives, though deep down he never fully believed the explanations given at the Rivera police station, where he met with the police chief and the lieutenant colonel in charge of the Cavalry Regiment. He eventually came to know, at least by sight and by the feel of a cold, flaccid hand, Dr. Núñez, an extremely gaunt official, almost hidden beneath a brown jacket one or two sizes too large for his diminished frame. From it emerged, like a turtle, his spotted baldness and wrinkled features, more resembling someone who had gone hungry for a long time than a supposed university professional. Dr. Núñez, hunched over an old Underwood typewriter, nearly blind despite thick myopic glasses, searched for each letter with a nervousness that struck the engineer as excessively servile. He chased every word that he, the police chief, and the lieutenant colonel spoke in deliberate disorder. The Underwood clattered as if firing each letter. To Joaquín, despite his profession as an engineer, the fact that the typewriter factory had also manufactured carbines during the Second World War always seemed mysterious. That old and deadly association he had once read about, with unease, concerning weapons and letters, now held a more painful meaning for him than if he were having a hand amputated at that very moment. Everything in books was real, but it belonged to a reality already lived by others or yet to be experienced by oneself.

In August 1976, he became certain that his daughter, son-in-law, and grandson had disappeared in a Montevideo regiment, shortly after the letter in which she had warned about Uncle

Boots had been sent. He was also certain that both his daughter and son-in-law had been murdered. From the very day he met with the police chief in Rivera, he began a search at all levels, which, he understood years later, led him to lose his job and his relatively powerful position, not only in the government but also among acquaintances of all kinds.

In the summer of 1978, an anonymous note left on his car's windshield, darker than his daughter's last letter, urged him to abandon the search. According to the note, the child had died in an accident on the same day as his parents. Other allusions in the note were utterly incomprehensible to him. The fish, the swallows of Bécquer, the founder of Montevideo—none of it made sense. The anonymous note was allegedly signed by four River Plate players: Leopoldo Luque, Ubaldo Fillol, Daniel Passarella, and Norberto Alonso. These names caused him to lose nearly a month of searching, leading him to think their purpose was, rather, distraction.

Far from accepting the note's claims, the engineer understood that the government or someone involved in the process was following him. The letter was typewritten. The keystrokes did not match the typewriter Rodolfo had at home or any other known machine. However, only a few, including himself, could have known he was searching for a child who by then would have been six or seven years old. His daughter's own letter had warned him against disclosing details that could be fatal or irreversible. The police chief in Rivera had never mentioned the child, a detail that had obsessed him for years. He had mentioned it to his lawyer, who had unsuccessfully sent his secretary to search for a birth certificate that was never found. It was possible his daughter had not registered the child with the civil registry. Both she and her husband had lived for some time in an ideological cloud, Joaquín thought, where a new man and a new society would soon emerge, one that would have no need for money or bureaucratic processes, which, according to them, were designed to control the individual on behalf of the state. Even he, Joaquín, might have joined this movement if he had possessed even a shred of that hope, which he labeled radical childishness. It was also possible that the birth certificate had been confiscated by the military. If they were capable of making people disappear, how could they not do the same with simple poorly written papers from some insignificant justice of the peace in a small town?

The Archbishop of Buenos Aires

Buenos Aires, June 16, 1980

A known official who had ties to the former Minister of Social Welfare, López Raga, and the former Minister of Economy, Martínez de Hoz, suggested he speak with the archbishop. After several attempts, he managed to schedule an appointment for a Monday in June. For some reason, he never wrote down the name of the clergyman who had attended him. Perhaps because he himself had proceeded with a fabricated and probably false piece of information, claiming that a Uruguayan military officer had informed him his grandson had been smuggled to Buenos Aires. Based on the mentioned date—between April 22 and 28,

1974—the child would have been around nine years old. The archbishop lamented his situation and, after quoting a passage from the Gospels that Joaquín could not recall, mentioned that the Episcopal Assembly had turned heaven and earth to find even a single victim of forced disappearances but had found none to date. Although the Church's mission was not to involve itself in politics, all its members were sensitive to the situation many of their parishioners were enduring. The archbishop did not want to raise false hopes, but the best advice he could offer at that moment was not to lose hope.

According to what the altar boy who accompanied them would recount years later, Joaquín had knelt on a pew before the altar. Perhaps more due to the weight of events than the foreseeable gesture of someone who prays because they have definitively lost all hope.

"Do you believe in God?" the archbishop then asked him.

"I don't know, Father," said Joaquín, visibly demoralized. "God has never appeared when I've needed Him. Still, I'm not too harsh on Him. At least not as harsh as He has been with me."

"My son, I understand your frustration. I have often felt what you're feeling now."

"Don't be so sure, Father."

"The best thing is to keep praying. Many people underestimate the power of prayer. As if the power of the Creator of the Universe were just a minor detail. Think. What would you ask of God?"

"To exist, Father. That's all I'd ask of God. To exist."

Engineer Joaquín Fuentes died on December 22, 1986, in Montevideo, in absolute poverty and in a state of neglect that clearly revealed his mental incapacity, just days before being evicted from his home on the waterfront due to unpaid debts. The engineer had taken out bank loans for large sums of money, which he squandered on all sorts of travels and bribes between Montevideo and Buenos Aires. He had attended five consecutive River Plate matches. The last one against Independiente. In a note still preserved between the pages of a book from the old *i Margall* bookstore, the engineer had written: "May God grant me understanding amidst this stand that screams desperately for a goal by Daniel Passarella. The world is this, and I don't believe there's any science that can solve the enigma."

"María was a saint," he told her

Buenos Aires, May 1991
María Arbiza de Zabala was also reluctant to engage in dialogue, though she said that was only a very subjective judgment of Don Zabala and, naturally, was due to his physical and emotional state. A person who has spent seven years in a coma does not recover overnight. Not only had his muscles suffered from inactivity, but the world had become something unrecognizable to someone who had not witnessed all its dramatic changes.

When he awoke in 1987 (she joked that this was the year of her true rebirth), Don Zabala felt nostalgia for the day before. The first hours had been confusing but joyful for the nurses who called him San Martín because of his long sideburns, perhaps the result of years of being shaved by a stranger with growing haste and apathy.

Likely, the doctor had called María because he had detected changes in his condition. Her face was the second face he saw before understanding what had happened. But as the days passed, things began to change. For Santiago, the man who had awakened was no longer his father. For María, he had ceased to be her husband.

Over time, the desire for Don Zabala to awaken had turned into resentment. Mother and son had barely survived. They had learned to live without him. They had even learned to live with a father who was neither alive nor dead, which was worse than being alive or dead.

Perhaps he had to listen, with remorse (as Don Xico said), to every detail of how his son had spent years dedicated to basement music and marijuana due to bad influences; or how he could also contract AIDS at any moment because of some botched tattoo. All while he was asleep. Because that's how it all happens (Don Zabala had said), without one even noticing, while asleep, literally asleep or as if one were.

Santiago had been a brilliant student in elementary school and rather mediocre and careless in high school, but his hell had begun with tattoos and addiction—not just to marijuana but to an unlimited number of things and activities, like programming his computer or practicing *skateboarding* until he fractured his elbows and ankles.

María had managed to carry on with her life and that of her son, who insisted on blaming her for all his misfortunes, including those regarding his father, with the moral and financial support of a man with whom, a few days earlier, she had decided to live with permanently. She couldn't sell the house, nor could she live with him there. So she planned to leave it to Santiago, who saw this change as the beginning of his illusory liberation. The father's return complicated things as much as his absence had.

Everything (Don Zabala finally confessed one night at the hotel bar), because of one drink too many. To Don Xico, it sounded like a cliché, but not a lie. What reason would that man have to go around inventing stories?

Pedro Zabala kept things hidden but didn't lie. He told the truth. It's just that the truth was mistaken.

STARTING FROM THE 10TH MOON and up to the 11th, 00λ it was no longer the same. The first unsettling change occurred one night when the steward went up to Ann's room to take the usual notes. His calculations, based on the observations of the past few months, predicted that Ann would finally leave the table. The table had stopped reeking of dried fish, perhaps due to the ravaging tropical climate that had consumed any traces of organic remains, but they hadn't yet managed to persuade Ann to abandon the rectangle.

It was a crescent moon, and the steward knew that with this moon Ann grew restless. But that night, he couldn't find Ann in her usual corner of the table. A woman was leaning there, writing on the paper that usually served as Ann's entertainment. The woman wasn't alarmed by the steward's presence. She lifted her gaze from the sheet on which she was writing and looked at him. Her eyes were very moist, like a fish's, but they were sweet.

The steward fled as best he could, bumping into the door on his way out, and took refuge on the first level, in the engine room. He didn't move from there until he guessed daylight had come and proceeded with caution.

A few hours later, under the mild sun of an unexpected sort of winter, everything that had happened during the night seemed impossible to him, like when he thought he could see the port on the horizon or when he pulled a fantastical, marvelously fantastical creature from the sea, only for it to turn out to be a large fish.

"Everyone takes some secret to the grave," said Don Xico

Costa de Oro, March 1991

Five years later, in 1992, one evening in the kitchen of the summer house the Zabalas owned on the Uruguayan coast, more precisely in Atlántida, at his own insistence, María clarified some details about his accident and the circumstances that had caused it. One summer, Don Zabala had developed the habit of drinking too much and would get irritated over anything. Why? He didn't know; business was going well, things weren't that bad between them.

One night, María reproached him for the bad example he was setting for their son. They argued, and she took refuge in the upstairs bedroom. He went up the stairs, and before reaching the top step, he fell backward.

Pedro Zabala remembered this last part, the difficulty of reaching the last step, of grabbing the handrail. Then that vertigo of falling from a very tall building, a dream he had frequently as a child and which he had started dreaming about again after the coma, persistently, over the last four years.

María stared at him as if studying his face.

"Do you remember nothing else?" she asked.

"No," Don Zabala replied. "I don't remember anything after that."

"And before?"

"Nothing either. Should I remember something important?"

"No," María answered. "I just want you to recover."

Pedro Zabala felt tired but recalled many things simultaneously, like a person who has woken from a night of deep rest. One day he told María he had some fragmented memories. He lied that he was starting to remember the argument that had led him to the stairs.

"We were arguing about someone, someone driving a white or gray car..." said Don Zabala, pensive.

"No," María quickly replied. "Don't form false memories. We were arguing because our relationship had deteriorated greatly, and you had invented that story about another man. There was never another man until..."

"Until when?"

"Until long after you fell into a coma."

For a moment, neither of them said anything more. Zabala stared at certain details on the table, absorbed, as if he didn't care about what María had just confessed, more compelled by a linguistic slip, he thought, by one extra word, than by any of her plans.

"The life insurance ran out in less than a year," María continued, "and with my job at the Ministry, I could barely pay the bills…"

"So… it was out of necessity."

"No… If it had been out of necessity, I would've found another man much sooner."

"Well, at least you fell seriously in love once."

"See?" María complained. "You haven't changed at all. Of course, seven years haven't passed for you. You're still the same. If you want an idea of who you were, just take a good look at who you are now, and that's it. Though if you were never capable of that kind of self-reflection, incapable of any self-criticism, I don't see why you'd do it now, with little more experience and a few extra gaps in your memory. Anyway, yes, I fell in love, but not for the first time. The first time was in Rosario. I was sixteen. A nearly platonic love, if you don't count the kisses in a little square in Carlos Paz. It wasn't what it is now. The second time I fell seriously in love. I don't know if you knew. It was at university."

"But that love died," said Don Zabala, with sadness, as if asking. "Maybe when Santiago came along, or a little before, who knows, right?"

"Yeah, who knows. But I know that love didn't die, we killed it little by little," she said.

"I have the impression we had this exact conversation once before," he said.

"It's not just an impression. We had this same conversation many times, and we always ended up arguing."

"Maybe that love didn't die; it turned into a horrible monster..."

"It's getting late," she said, and picked up her purse.

Zabala gave up trying to retrace these paths. He still cared for that woman (he almost told her so), now gaunt and filled with sadness, but he couldn't tell if he still loved her as he had the first time. Maybe that was the central issue, he thought: insisting that things remain the same despite the passage of time, without learning to recognize and appreciate those very changes, the different forms love took to renew itself, to stay alive.

Certainly, she didn't suffer from these complexities. She once told him he was the feminine side of the house, and she the masculine (or had her mother said it to him that night she lay dying in the hospital, as if it were more of a warning than a comfort?): she was passionate, simple, and practical; he was complicated and sentimental, obsessed with romantic love, which, by definition, is the bloom of only a few days.

While he recovered, she visited him in the afternoons and always left promptly at seven. Once she told him that the other man (Don Zabala didn't know his name; he didn't need to, because Santiago had decided to go live with him and María hadn't put up much resistance), contrary to what he believed, wasn't sad about his coming out of the coma but quite the opposite. Now she could free herself from his ghost once and for all. She could also divorce and live a normal life.

It was then that Zabala remembered that it had been precisely this, the divorce, the other subject of argument that had led to the accident. She had asked him for a divorce more than once, and he had evaded answering, saying he needed time to think about it.

"Think about what?" she had challenged. "Do you still need to think about whether you love me? Or do you still need to think if your ego is big enough not to let me live my life the way I want?"

One night, Zabala asked her if they already had a wedding date, and she replied that it wasn't his problem. The only thing he had to do was sign the divorce papers. He didn't answer, which she interpreted as a threat. She managed to break the silence with an argument that grew increasingly heated.

"You've been drinking again!" she shouted at him.

"No more than you. Are you not feeling well? Yeah? Because I'm still very lucid…"

"You're the same cynic as always," she said, and left the kitchen.

She went up the stairs to the bedroom. Zabala followed her. She stood on the last step. He remembered those eyes, hard as marble, waiting for him on the last step. And he remembered that while they struggled, he intoxicated by alcohol and jealousy, he wanted to tell her that he loved her, that he loved her like an adolescent and almost like a child. He hadn't known how to love her either, or he loved her like a madman. Both of them were sick, or that passionate, romantic love Zabala had invented had made them sick.

But he was caught off guard by her hand, pushing him on the shoulder. He tried to resist, like in one of his old childhood nightmares he had never been able to forget. At that moment, he knew that the pain he felt was for her. For her, he had forgotten the same hand that seven years earlier had prevented him from reaching the last step first and the banister afterward.

Then Don Zabala did not advance. He was still weak and became breathless at the slightest effort. However, this time he was able to stop midway and think for a moment. Then he went back down to the kitchen and sat down again next to the glass of wine. Later, he saw her hurry past and rush out the front door.

The next day, Santiago said, the forensic doctor confirmed that his father had died from the injuries sustained from falling down the stairs. A very high level of alcohol was found in his blood. Perhaps he had been drinking in the kitchen and when he tried to go up to his bedroom, he couldn't reach the last step. On the kitchen table, he left a note that somewhat resembled the ones he used to leave in the early years of his marriage. Almost the same words, but in a different order:

María, I would have preferred not to know.

I would have preferred not to have loved you like that.

And with a less neat handwriting, much further down on the little yellow paper:

It's raining, María, it's raining. Keep warm.

Everyone was of the opinion that alcohol had destroyed that family, and it was a miracle that poor María had finally managed to move forward. Her second husband, the journalist from La Nación, Alberto Anchorena, had helped Santiago with his studies, practically paying the entire rent for the apartment in Montevideo during the first three or four years. It was never clear whose idea it had been to study medicine in Montevideo and not in Buenos Aires—whether it was Santiago's or Mr. Anchorena's, or both. What Santiago did know was that he wanted to be as faraway as possible from Mr. Anchorena, his new stepfather, and from Beatrice, the girlfriend, almost wife, of Miguel Polzin. *La Nación* Alberto Anchorena, had helped Santiago with his studies paying almost the entire rent for the apartment in Montevideo during the first three or four years. It was never known whose idea it was to study medicine in Montevideo and not in Buenos Aires, whether it was Santiago's or Mr. Anchorena's, or both. What Santiago knew was that he wanted to be as far away as possible from Mr. Anchorena, his new stepfather, and from Beatrice, the girlfriend, almost wife, of Miguel Polzin.

The Refuge

Montevideo, January 22, 2012

Perhaps he had been wrong. But how (thought Alejandro, looking out the window over the edge of the sheet covering his nose), how is it possible to hold so many convictions for years, decades, for an entire lifetime without even considering for a moment whether those convictions are based on even the slightest hint of reality. Until something comes along to shake one out of the comfort of believing they know how things work in this world, and what once seemed as solid as a medieval castle turns out to be nothing more than a little sandcastle, freshly built by the childish hands of two children and threatened by the gentle waves of the evening tide.

That's what Santiago would have said, he thought, that as a young boy he always rambled on about complicated things he read in his father's encyclopedias before going to bed. He said that everything that seems to be ultimately isn't, because what truly is, that is, what is yet to be, is almost never seen with the eyes. No one could have foreseen the Second World War by looking at a photograph of Paris in 1938. That's what he had learned from the ancient Greeks, he said, curled up in stall number 81, the stall in Villa del Parque in Buenos Aires. As a young boy, Santiago visited him almost every Saturday. He was a fanatic of that stall. He didn't call it The Castle, like Alejandro did, but The Refuge. A castle could also be a refuge in times of danger, Alejandro had argued, but Santiago said no, that he didn't like castles. "You don't like castles because you live in one," Alejandro had said, with a sneer, which had left Santiago even more pensive. "No, it's not that…" Santiago stammered. Castles were too visible. So? So a refuge was something else. It was a small place, he said, a place where one disappeared from the world. From there, one could see the modest house of Alejandro's parents and part of the street. From there, one could see the danger of the world. What danger? The danger of the world. The world is full of dangers, that's why one needs a refuge, a hideout. He always dreamed that he was running across a field like the pampa until he found a place impossible to find. And there he would stay, watching his pursuers. home? And part of the street? From there, one could see the danger of the world. What danger? The danger of the world. The world is full of dangers, that's why one needs a refuge, a hideout. He always dreamed that he was running across a field like the pampa until he found a place impossible to find. And there he would stay, watching his pursuers.

Santiago remembered Alejandro's Refuge on the following March 23, in the funeral home, while he waited for the night to pass and for the morning hours to arrive to finally put an end to that painful story. He remembered it again on April 6, while he was cutting open the chest of Major Almeida and Laprida.

In dreams, there is no death

Montevideo, February 4, 2012

He realized he was in a halfway house, on an island off the coast of Mozambique. The heat of the sea had settled in every corner of the old room, in every moment of that quiet afternoon where only the fluttering of palm trees and the distant murmur of the ocean could be heard. From time to time, a breeze stirred the fabric curtains. The curtains had African patterns and colors. Yellow, red, green, black, blue. The walls were white, exaggeratedly white even in the shadows.

He had just realized it. La Negra—who wasn't black but mulatto, his grandmother had said—had adopted that difference as the center of her existence. Now he understood those colors. Only now. And he understood that heat, and that air coming through the window, and that scent of dry savanna grass, and he, and the air and the window were on an island in the Indian Ocean, near the coast of Mozambique, in 1979…

He yanked the sheet away from his nose with a quick motion. No, he had been dozing. In reality, he was in Montevideo, in 2011. In January of 2012, he corrected himself. He couldn't recall the day. It must have been Saturday, because he remembered leaving work earlier than usual the day before. La Negra had gone to the Punta Carretas Shopping Center. It seemed to him she was in a bad mood. When she was in a bad mood, La Negra would go to the mall to look at shoes, so she wouldn't forget she was a woman, she'd say with a ton of irony.

The magic of the island in the Indian Ocean had lasted only a moment. As if life were playing a riddle with its elements. He'd destroyed it himself with his right hand when he struck the sheet, as if he were drowning in time or couldn't bear the weight of a revelation so simple, as simple as the pleasure of being alive and feeling the things around us, the things that are or the even more mysterious things that belong to the infinite set of what once was or could have been.

Then, he thought again about the ephemeral, about his life, about his illness. He only felt uneasy, but there was no pain. Please let it stay like this until the end, he whispered to himself.

He then remembered that many times, until not long ago, he had thought that the best way to change was to hit rock bottom. For some reason, he hadn't seen or didn't want to see that in life there is no bottom, that the only bottom is death. At best. Now he knew it, or believed he did. Just when it no longer mattered.

Would this be the year he would reunite with his parents, back at the farm in Cerro Largo?

"Mami… Papi…" he said softly, under the sheet, remembering a morning when his parents had woken him.

Alejandro had had a rough night, with fever and snakes floating in the air. His parents hadn't slept, fearing the worst.

At two-thirty in the morning, he had a fever of 40 degrees.

At three, and after the *aspirin tablets* every four hours that the doctor had prescribed as a last resort, Alejandrito was still at 39 degrees.

The only thing you can do for measles—the doctor had said—is to keep the temperature below 38, at the very least. There's no cure for it, and almost all children have to go through it, sooner or later. When they do.

Papi said the temperature was going down, that the medicine was working, as if his words alone could secure Mami's peace and the whole of reality.

At four, the temperature hadn't dropped, and Papi took him out of the crib and brought him to get fresh air in the backyard, like desperately pulling someone drowning out of a river.

"Chichi, chichi," Alejandrito said, almost without strength. Neither Mami nor Papi understood that he was referring to the snakes floating in the air. Several times they'd put something bittersweet in his mouth, changed the damp cloth that sometimes dripped from his forehead, small drops that burned his face before running down his neck.

His little eyes closed, the fever rising moment by moment.

"He's out of it…" Mami said, squeezing her desperation into the silence of the night. She thought that any bad thing she might say could have a negative effect. But she couldn't fake the forced optimism of Papi either.

"At dawn, we'll go to the town," Papi finally said, kissing Alejandro on the forehead, which burned like an ember.

But, as usual, the fever subsided at dawn. Alejandro's fragile little body had withstood the relentless attacks of measles.

"Thanks to God and the Virgin," Mami said.

He remembered their two faces smiling at him like gods from the sky. For some reason, he remembered them with a clarity that frightened him.

Later, when Papi fell ill, Alejandro couldn't say the same. It's true, Papi was already old, but not that old. He still had black hairs on his forehead, and his cheek looked the same as always. 74 years old.

He couldn't say, "Thanks to God and the Virgin," because Papi died after three days of agony in the Clinicas hospital, with needles in his arms and hands and tubes in his mouth.

"I'm here," Alejandro told him, "I've come, it's me… Alejandro."

He never knew if Papi heard him. It had been two years since they'd seen each other because of a silly argument over the use of the car. Alejandro thought the old man had been right, in the end, but pride had been stronger than his intelligence.

He had thought that simply saying he was finally there, by his side, that he had come to be with him again, would be enough to wake him up. Papi didn't wake up. Or he couldn't. His breathing quickened, he squeezed his hand, or at least that's what Alejandro thought he felt. But he didn't recover, and Alejandro couldn't say, "Thanks to God and the Virgin."

The next day, he saw the attending doctor coming down the hallway with his "I've done this before" face, and he told Alejandro and Mami that the patient in room 523 had unfortunately died of cardiac arrest.

The doctor left respectfully, and while Mami wept, Alejandro watched him walk away in his green scrubs, realizing that the most important things he had to say to his father could never be said. Because he only realized he needed to say them when it was already too late, as it always is, on a fall day in 1991.

Later, the old woman, who wasn't that old. Just 69, having turned that age on June 19, 1993. A damn taxi, one of those always in a hurry. It didn't stop at the crosswalk, and Mami, who since she'd been alone had been distracted at all times—burning the food, forgetting the keys, not looking at the traffic lights—just kept walking. It wasn't her fault but the taxi driver's, though it no longer mattered.

In less than two years, he had lost them both. But there was something that caught his attention for a while, especially when he woke up agitated and reflected for a moment under the shower: Mami and Papi hadn't died in his dreams. He could never dream them dead. That was another fundamental truth he hadn't noticed until January 2012, since he was always too busy: loved ones never die in dreams. His parents always came back, with their smiles, with their worries. There they were, exactly as they were and would always be: Papi with his commanding voice and his friendly advice; Mami with her caress, her sponge cake, and her comforting words…

He wanted to understand, but it was already too late

Montevideo, February 4, 2012

Alejandro pulled back the sheet and looked out the window as if he had discovered the law of universal gravitation. But no, he hadn't discovered anything important, he thought. Then he thought of Papi again, of la Negra. He definitely hadn't been right about almost anything, except for what he had desired for so long. In his own way, he had been successful in his field. He had dedicated himself body and soul and had become what he wanted to be. But now the medieval castle revealed itself for what it was: a little sandcastle threatened by the rising waves.

And he, Alejandro, always treating la Negra's little paintings with respect, yes, but with obvious condescension. A few little paintings, a color here and a line there, weren't going to save humanity. They weren't even going to create jobs for a country always anguished by the lack of work. No, of course, those little paintings weren't going to save humanity or make money, but maybe they could save someone. If not la Negra's paintings, maybe Cortázar's stories, which fascinated him so much. After all, he thought, we've advanced so much in technology and little or nothing in mastering emotions and the relationships between a handful of people. No one would say the Egyptians or the Chinese were more advanced in technology than us. We have the Internet, virtual networks, cell phones, GPS... Likewise, no one would say we are more advanced than those Egyptians who fished in the Nile, or those other Chinese and those other Arabs from Aladdin. No one could claim we are happier than a mad Buddha or a Japanese man drinking tea amid a silence that would take away the little patience we have left. No one could say we are geniuses or have learned to control our emotions, to live with our frustrations, to let go of the pride that keeps us away from the people we love most. We haven't learned anything in that sense. Each of us, for thousands of years, improvises as if every generation had to reinvent gunpowder and writing. Everyone starts from scratch—because there are no sages, only geniuses of science and technology—and by the time we finish building our first pyramid, by the time we've just discovered the printing press and the telegraph, it's already time to leave this life full of predictable and avoidable anguish and frustrations.

Alejandro imagined El Torito, replying to him, as was his habit. And he answered back: True, history records moments of slavery, of machismo... But in our time too, children die in bombings, and not always in distant, backward countries but as a consequence of our own advancements. But this isn't about the progress of history. I'm talking about human emotions. If we compare ancient Egypt in times of peace, which were most of the time, with our times of peace, as ours should be now, there's no indication to think we are happier or wiser in mastering our emotions. Pride, love, jealousy, the fear of death—they're always the same but handled differently. Why? Because we've spent almost all our time figuring out how to invent things and we don't know what to do with our anger, our frustrations, our stupid pride, our stupidity, in a word...

It was already late

Montevideo, March 15, 2012

After almost a month of barely speaking to her, of sleeping on the sofa in the living room, he realized he had miscalculated. "Miscalculated." He had repeated this tiny, goddamn phrase, he told himself, about a thousand one hundred and thirty-five times in the last six years.

In the end, he hadn't achieved la Negra's disdain or anything like it but something entirely the opposite. Now, like a child who's just grasped something so simple, he felt there had never been a need to torture that woman to save her from the inevitable.

The night before, he was woken up several times by the heat, the discomfort of the sofa, and the movement of the curtains.

At quarter to three, he got up and went to the bedroom, slipping into his bed. Not his bed. Their bed. She didn't wake up until he hugged her from behind. A moment later, he heard her breathing and a moan that was like a stifled laugh. He ran a hand over her face and her eyes.

His hand saw that her eyes were crying.

THE WOMAN NAMED ANA had been sitting at the bar talking to a tall man with three stripes on his uniform. He was a warrior, she thought. He had bombed the last known island until it disappeared. She remembered these impossible images from that war: two large ships like 00λ fighting over a piece of the seafloor that jutted above the surface. It must have been an island, one of the specialists deduced. The ships exchanged fire from sunset until deep into the night. Finally, one of them disappeared. The island too.

When they saw him approach, she looked down and drank from her glass. He nodded and left. This movement reminded her of Ann, the ant, because she had quickly changed her pace and direction.

The man was the same one who appeared in a portrait hanging on a wall. He had a white hat and a flag in the background. He must have been the captain.

Something had gone wrong

Montevideo, March 23, 2012

La Negra Laurie took out Alejandro's cellphone, which she had kept in her purse, and placed it under his right hand, against his chest.

The funeral home employees exchanged glances and, after a few seconds, closed the casket.

That night, she dialed his number. It rang a couple of times, three times, and she hung up. She called again at midnight. She didn't wait too long and hung up again. At 3:35 in the morning, she called one last time.

Alejandro's voice answered for him:

"Hello, I can't take your call right now. Please leave a message and I'll call you back as soon as possible. Thank you..."

Pray for us and lead us not into temptation

Montevideo, March 23, 2012

Back from the cemetery, Santiago had remained silent. Hermetic, Paula had said. He claimed he handled grief better alone, that he preferred to walk, but Paula had insisted on accompanying him. After wandering through a few blocks, Paula decided to head back.

Paula began to complain about the moral decay society had fallen into. The loss of values and all that. Santiago thought it was a way of defending himself against sadness.

A boy, or rather, a twelve-year-old child—one of those they called *juvenile delinquents* to refer to criminals who had lost their innocence but not yet their childhood—had approached the people waiting for the bus and, after repeatedly failing to get a coin, had let out some obscene word.

Someone had told Santiago that a friend of Paulina's had mentioned something about a mysterious friend she had seen him with at a restaurant on 18 and Minas. Paulina hadn't wanted to bring it up directly. She hadn't even asked any questions. She had simply let him believe that she knew something. Deep down, she preferred not to lose him, even at the cost of giving him several chances. For his part, Santiago had also re-sorted to a similar tactic. He was beginning to realize how little he could stand Paulina, but he didn't have the courage to tell her.

Paulina had quietly commented on the incident with the juvenile delinquent, returning to her talk about the loss of values. A year ago, Santiago would have agreed with her diagnosis.

"The devil has taken the reins of this country," said Paulina.

"The devil... To hell with the devil," said Santiago.

"I know you don't believe in God."

"It's not that I don't believe in God, just like that. But I'd believe in God more if between him and me there weren't so many fanatics blocking my view, so many chosen ones claiming Paradise, good morals, and good manners while practicing moral terrorism, clutching a book they think they understand just because they've read it day and night and underwater."

"It's not enough to believe in God. You have to believe Him."

"Nice phrase from Luis Guerra. And what if the Creator, for a moment, didn't agree? Neither with all the books written in His name nor with all the professional sermons? What if God disagreed with His ministers and the many spokesmen who have proliferated throughout history and continue to terrorize us today? What would happen if, for a moment, we let Him speak for Himself?"

"I suppose in your worldview there's no room for the purity of the soul," said Paulina. "Otherwise, they'd run out of orgies, the kind leftists and liberals like you boast about. I don't want to think your time in the U.S. changed your mind so much, and especially not in that direction. Unless some bad company brainwashed you."

"If it's about washing, bring it on. Especially if it's the brain, that dump always so full of garbage they later call 'values and good manners.' But look, I don't boast about my orgies. First of all, because I haven't had the chance. They don't keep me up at night, and I don't dedicate so much energy to them, like those who go around legislating other people's sexuality. Nor will I give a sermon or a speech about sexual purity, like many holy rollers I know, half-dazed from the night before or after abusing some minor."

"Hail Mary, most pure!"

"As for purity, it depends on your definition of purity. To me, there's nothing pure about locking yourself in a convent and remaining a virgin until death, mistaking orgasms for mystical ecstasies, praying day and night while the sinful people work to maintain that whole hive of drones. To me, a truly pure man or woman are those unfortunate souls who do good without thinking it will get them to Paradise. Who knows if God also considers the true goodness of these unbelievers and rewards them with what you think belongs to you. Haven't you ever considered that maybe Paradise is reserved for the filthy, not for you, most pure and immaculate souls?"

"You're an idiot. May God forgive you."

"He's already forgiven me. Look, that's the 121."

When he was alone again, Santiago couldn't stop thinking about la Negra Laurie, devastated behind her dark glasses and uncombed hair. She had told him about her life over the past few months, as if revealing a secret, one of those domestic misunderstandings that never leave the house out of shame, pride, or because the solutions aren't outside: Alejandro's reproachable and sometimes incomprehensible behavior, which (she had only now realized) was due to his illness, she said. She could have helped him, had she known.

Santiago also understood Alejandro's absurd behavior, but in a different way. It wasn't due to his illness but to a mistake, he thought, as he boarded the next 121. And he could have lessened that pain if he had told the truth to la Negra. He could have. Maybe. He couldn't even see it clearly now, now that he knew the end and the consequences.

The India Pacha

Buenos Aires, Saturday, March 31, 2012

Yes, I worked for two years at the Zabala household, let's see… between '78 and '80. No, I wasn't there anymore when the señor had the accident. They fired me a little before, about three or four months earlier. I don't know why. Or yes… The señora started complaining about every little thing. It wasn't fair. By that time, I already knew how to do my job. I had learned with the Ortegas at their estate in Pergamino first, and then with the Ocampos at their big house in San Isidro, before the coup. By then, I knew what I was doing and what a proper cleaning looked like. The Zabalas had a Doberman, I can't even remember her name… Sofía, I think… Yes, her name was Sofía.

Can you believe that name for a dog? The poor animal lived locked between the patio and the living room, and when she spent too much time in the patio, she'd lick all the glass on the French doors in the living room. I'd come by and clean it, and when the señora passed by, the glass was all dirty with drool again. Sofía would howl like a dog every time the gossip passed by on the other side of the wall, singing *"In a forest in China, a soldier got lost, may they all get lost, the mother who birthed them..."* Imagine ending up being responsible for what the señores' dog did, no matter if her name was Sofía. So, that's why I didn't believe them at all when they fired me. Well, what can I say, that's already in the past, but I think they got rid of me for something else. Something else. No, it's not that I'm not sure. I'm sure it was for something else, but I feel a bit icky. I don't know if it's right to talk about things concerning someone who's passed, may he rest in peace. The thing is, señor Zabala was sterile. It's nothing shameful nowadays, but not too long ago, especially among certain kinds of people, it was seen as a punishment from God, or even cast doubt on the manliness of the man in question. Yes, it seemed to me that it weighed on don Zabala. More than that, I'm sure of it. And that's why I told you they fired me. No, it's not what you're thinking, I never had anything to do with the patrón. In that, I kept myself clean, even though back then I had everything in the right place, and both fathers and sons from every house I scrubbed would eye me and more than once tried their luck. And me, because I needed the job... you can imagine, but I kept myself as clean as I could. None of them went past the hands. Anyway, the point is that don Zabala had frequent arguments with the señora. Every so often, they'd say things to each other, none of them nice, reproaches over this and that. How do you expect me to remember what they were saying? That was over thirty years ago. It's easy to say now. No, he wasn't the kind of man to shout, much less a violent one. He was a delicate man. Quite refined. No, no. He would insult quietly and with style. He had his way, believe me. What happened was that the señora told him that if he had let her live her own life, she'd at least have had a child of her own. You know those modern women who get pregnant with someone else and then the cuckolded husband takes care of the rest? Well, it seems like he wasn't that kind of man. A delicate man. I mean, delicate in his manner. At least that's what I know. If there was something else beyond that, I don't know and I'm not interested… So yeah, as I was saying, because of that unfortunate eavesdropping, I lost my job and found out that little Santiaguito was adopted, even though he looked a lot like his father. If there's one thing I never forgot, it's the names of the kids in the house. Don't ask me about numbers, but I remember all their names. Maybe I'd cross paths with them on the street and not recognize any of them, but their names? Yes, to me, they're like my own kids, or like grandchildren who are way back there, lost in time… No, no, what happened is that the señora caught me. Me, being so foolish, I stood there dumbstruck when I heard that she had wanted to get pregnant by anyone else but get pregnant, because she wanted a child of her own blood, and the señora must have realized there was someone on the other side of the main archway leading to the living room, and she caught me right there, listening to what I shouldn't have been listening to. That's why now that I'm old, I don't want to have a maid myself, because maids hear everything they shouldn't. Yes, exactly. After that, I must have lasted a couple more weeks there. That's why I said it wasn't because of poor work, but for something else. Do you work for the government? Ah, and are they still going on about the disappearances? Stop going in circles with that. I always say, what happened, happened. What do the Zabalas have to do with any of this? Are you with the prosecution? Prosecutor of... Sounds very distinguished. You can tell by the way you speak. But you told me earlier you were a doctor. Yes, I know... Not a lawyer. Cardiologist. I thought you said cardiologist. Yes, I see. Well, yes... Anyway, young man, I've already answered a few questions for you, but the truth is, I don't want any trouble, so it's best if you leave through the same door you came in. Don't you think I'm old enough to live peacefully for what little time I have left? Alright, goodbye, thank you... Pocha? Were you going to say Pocha? How do you know my nickname? Really? I just found out that all the María Jesús are nicknamed Pocha. Always learning, even at death's door...

Vigilante Justice

Montevideo, April 6, 2012

At a quarter to six, Dr. Santiago Zabala appeared in the waiting room and announced that the surgery had been a success. The first to hug him was Carmencita. Then his three children and his comrades in arms, the younger ones in uniform.

"Doctor," said Carmencita, tears in her eyes, "you are a hero, you deserve a monument. May God bless you, my child."

Exhausted after several hours of intense concentration, Santiago (or rather, that other person who still didn't know his real name) went for a walk along the coastal boulevard. He knew he would never meet the major walking there, but at least now he knew that what had been an absurd, whimsical nightmare throughout his life was actually his childhood memory resisting. He had almost no new information; just confirmations. Fuentes was a fairly common surname in Montevideo. Besides (he thought, as he approached a granite bench), his mother must have used her husband's surname, as was customary at the time. About him, he didn't even have that, a surname, a name. Now he knew the neighborhood where it had all happened, but in Rivera there must have been hundreds of fields with a giant tree at the entrance (which maybe wasn't even giant to a forty-year-old man) and another in the backyard, maybe an ombú, maybe an old oak tree. Maybe the ombú or the old oak doesn't even exist anymore. But, somehow, some of the truth had managed to break through the collective madness and, surely, it would die mute with him and with the major.

A strange complicity with his parents' murderer had been established since then, amidst the labyrinth of people ("of voters, of judges," he thought) who came and went, unnoticed, along the boulevard.

The Little Doctor Didn't Love Her

Montevideo, April 7, 2012

Lucía had distanced herself from the boy, thought Don Jordi. Something strange had happened. He no longer showed up at the bookstore looking for books he wasn't interested in. She no longer smiled while watching TV or heating up Gold of the Rhine pasta. She no longer arrived two hours late. She no longer greeted cheerfully when she entered. The silences, which had once worked so well for communicating with his daughter, no longer served to understand what was wrong with her.

From that friendship so akin to love and the certainty of a future as small, almost happy, happier than he had been himself, Lucía and the little doctor transitioned to a darker, more distant tone. Lucía had become a fragile girl again, that teenager who vainly tried to be indifferent to the people around her, which showed she wasn't as independent nor beyond the heart's clichés, of romantic loves, almost straight out of magazines.

"They Investigate Dozens of Allegations of Suspicious Adoptions"

THE FOLLOW-UP SECRETARIAT *of the Commission for Peace (Comipaz) is discreetly investigating dozens of cases of individuals residing in Uruguay who suspect their origins, as a way to certify whether they are children of detained-disappeared citizens.*

The agency, part of the Presidency of the Republic, has been working for years on the search and systematization of information about events from the 70s and 80s, including the recovery of identity for children born in captivity and illegally taken by agents of the dictatorship.

In this sense, the Follow-Up Secretariat is studying "dozens of cases" of adopted individuals who suspect their origins, as a way to certify if they are children of detained-disappeared citizens, explained Eduardo Pirotto, a member of the agency, to La República.

The reported cases mainly refer to citizens between 30 and 40 years old, residing in Uruguay who suspect their origins, either due to the lack of response from their adoptive families or the absence of reliable information to clarify their personal history. The complaints are filed with the Follow-Up Secretariat and human rights organizations, such as Mothers and Relatives of Detained-Disappeared Persons.

The presentation of the case marks the beginning of a process of information gathering, and the young individuals are explained the situation "with the greatest possible precision." "The idea is to provide them with guidance so they can, to the extent possible, uncover their origins," Pirotto explained.

In this regard, the Secretariat coordinates with state institutions, such as the Institute for Adoptions and Legitimizations of INAU and bodies in the Argentine Republic, to certify potential familial ties of these individuals with detained-disappeared citizens. The existence of such ties leads to the initiation of judicial actions for DNA testing, Pirotto stated.

The work of social organizations in Uruguay and Argentina has allowed for the recovery of identity for dozens of young people, born in captivity and taken from their mothers' arms in both countries.

The children of Uruguayan citizens were primarily recovered in the Argentine Republic.

Meanwhile, the appearance of Macarena Gelman, the daughter of Argentine parents, opens the possibility of more cases of children born in captivity living in Uruguay. "We suspect there may be more cases," Pirotto said. In this context, the main hypothesis revolves around the possibility that these are children of Argentine citizens, taken as part of the Systematic Plan of Child Appropriation developed in the Argentine Republic, and given to Uruguayan families, he emphasized.

The investigation is being conducted "under strict confidentiality," given the extreme sensitivity of the matter, Pirotto explained. "It is very important to reach the truth, but how we reach the truth is even more important," which is why constant counseling and support tasks are carried out for the young individuals, Pirotto said.

Diary *La República*, March 26, 2012.

MARKED DAY. The white peseta always returned

Barcelona, February 9, 1939

They searched the entire house with growing frustration. When one of them approached him, he asked what he was hiding in his hand. Jordi did not respond. Then one of them stepped forward and forcibly opened his hand until the white peseta fell to the ground.

"My God," said another. "What are we going to do with so much money?"

Jordi rushed to pick it up, but one of them was quicker and placed his foot on the coin.

"What's your name?"

Jordi did not respond; he kept his eyes fixed on the dark boot that pressed all the weight of the uniformed man onto his white coin.

"Has the cat got your tongue? Well, if you don't answer me, you won't get your coin back."

He remembered screaming in desperation as someone grabbed him by the shoulders like a pair of pincers.

"Again. What's your name?"

"Jordi…" he said.

"Well, what a lovely name. And your father?"

There was no answer.

"If you don't tell me your father's name, I won't give you the peseta back," said the uniformed man, grinding the coin under his foot as if extinguishing a cigarette.

"Jordi, too."

"Well, what a lovely name. Jordi… And where is Mr. Jordi the First?"

"I don't know."

"But how? How can a son not know where his father is? Doesn't your father love you?"

"Yes."

"Then, where is your daddy?"

No answer.

"Very well. We'll have to take the coin."

"No!" Jordi repeated, unable to hold back his tears anymore" "No..."

"Do you want your white peseta? Then, tell us where your daddy is. We need to pay him for a job. If he gets paid, he won't have to keep working..."

"In the truck."

"In his truck?"

"Yes..."

"But the truck isn't here... Where did Daddy Jordi go with the truck?"

"To the border..."

He remembered his mother's muffled cry saying *no*, that it wasn't true, that the boy didn't know, that her husband had gone to Sierra, to Sierra del Rio.

"To the border, Mom," Jordi had to clarify" "Dad told me he was going to the border."

And his mother screamed louder *no*, that he had gone to Sierra del Rio, as always.

Jordi remembered that at first his mother's *no*'s were sharp, short, and by the end they dragged the vowel, a long *o* that faded into helpless silence.

"Good boy," said one of them, picking up the coin from the floor" "Here's your white one."

Jordi grabbed the white peseta and clenched it tightly.

"That's how the sons of those who believe in nothing turn out," said one, leaving Jordi's room" "Real Judases."

"He'll be good for business," said another.

Foundational lies last forever

Montevideo, April 7, 2012

He had spent his whole life repeating it with pride (thought Jordi), trying to convince poor devils, his employees, his daughter, any innocent within reach, that the only thing that mattered was the future. But for a moment he understood that this conviction was much more than a valuable fanaticism. It was the way he had found, at some point, to annihilate his past. The strategy had worked so well that it had lasted for sixty years. Sixty years were enough to prove the true value of a lie. But for some reason, the truth sometimes returns like a shadow freed from the object that cast it.

The future had been his religion. Perhaps not only his. The future is the modern religion of an entire civilization, beyond cultures and traditional religions. Even though we cannot see it, even though we move toward it blindly or it comes at us from behind, by surprise, we are almost obliged to praise it, for social or personal reasons, he thought.

Even now, immersed in nostalgia, he wanted to repeat the usual mantra, that what matters is the future, because that's where we're headed. A foundational myth that demonstrates the immature character of our civilization.

But the truth was different. One starts this life and, as soon as one becomes aware of the world, almost everything is future. Then we have to endure the present as best we can. Everything is full of urgencies and "I have to's." Until we grow old and, one way or another, end up living in the past. Yes, he would have liked to repeat the usual, that what matters is the future, that everything is heading toward tomorrow. But the only truth is that our future is the past. That's where we're going, inexorably. Until the light goes out, that mysterious light.

ONE MORNING THE MIRACLE HAPPENED. *The bottom of the sea rising above the horizon was there. Upon waking, as every morning, he looked to the East and saw it, between the cloudy sky and the shine of the sea. He rejoiced. He almost raised his arms in triumph. But his heart began to pound violently. Not even in the worst storms had he experienced such uncontrollable beating.*

He managed to control himself, though the excitement of the discovery lingered in the blinking of his eyes and the useless movements of his hands. He reflected, or rather, he froze for a long time over the discovery until he decided to trust his survival instinct. He had understood just in time the terrible mistake he had made and sustained his entire life.

Then, just in time, he turned and set course for the warmer region, where the fish fly and the water is transparent. He headed toward where he had been born, thirteen moons ago. It had taken him his whole life to understand the correct meaning and direction.

A week later he realized he was being pursued. This time it wasn't the monsters of the sea. Nor was it the sea. It was another boat, like 00λ. They were other men, like him, like the inhabitants of his dreams and nightmares. Or rather, they were the inhabitants of his dreams and nightmares who did know why he was running.

The worst that could happen to the major

Montevideo, April 7, 2012

Don Xico had a normal recovery. However (his wife would say later), from then on he would never be the same. He had lost his taste for exercise and almost never walked along the ramp, except at inappropriate hours. Dr. Santiago would tell him it was normal for many heart surgery patients, a certain depression easily controllable with the medication he had given him. The major's daughter, who was about to graduate as a pediatrician, would confirm it. The important thing, the doctor would say, was that his life expectancy had now been extended by at least ten years. Carmencita would think it wasn't much, but since cowardice and optimism are limitless and always blend together at the most necessary moment, she would think it was just an average that her husband was going to surpass.

It was exactly what the doctor told Don Xico as soon as he opened his eyes and asked why he was still alive. Santiago told him not to imagine that the surgery had been a success because the doctor was a good man. On the contrary, he was certain that the major would never tell him where his parents' bones were, and that there would be no justice, no national referendum, no twisted parliamentary vote to force him to confess. And since there was no confession, there could be no repentance, and thus no forgiveness.

"Justice delayed is justice denied," the doctor said, handing him the TV remote.

Don Xico watched every move of the doctor, trying to understand. Santiago finished filling out a form, signed it, and hung it on a hook at the foot of the bed.

"From now on, you have ten more years, Colonel," Santiago said. "Ten more years. God willing, eleven. Precious time. Not to regret anything. To think. To remember, Colonel."

When he was left alone, the major realized that Santiago Zabala had decided to do his best work so that he would live, so that he would live a long time. Because, unlike Don Xico and his wife Carmencita, the doctor didn't believe in hell, nor did he believe in justice anymore.

So this was the worst that could happen to the major: to live, to live a long life, remembering what he would never confess, cursing that son of a bitch for every new day of life God gave him.

Carlitos and Willian Were the Last

Montevideo, April 7, 2012

It was late, and the bartender wanted to close.

"I'm closing in five minutes," he warned them.

"Yeah, yeah, I know!" Carlitos complained. "Quit busting my balls."

Willian didn't seem to notice. With his elbows on the worn marble table, hunched over a small glass of grappa that he twirled as if unscrewing his thoughts, he kept mulling over his words:

"Back in the sixties, we were still people. The money we made didn't have a name. But at some point, everything started to change. I don't know if it was the country or us or all three. I got tired of hearing that 'money comes and goes,' and I never paid it any attention until I realized that the saying was missing a part, something so obvious that for some reason it had been left out: 'Money comes and goes, but when we go, we don't come back.' One day it hit me. I don't know when, but somehow I realized it. From then on, I stopped being a stingy old man. I didn't get poorer because of it, but I stopped caring so much about my kid's expenses and, most of all, my wife's... That dear woman who put up with me for so many years, and here I was, always measuring out her little expenses in the store here, some there, clothes she didn't really need, but it was also true that it was money I wasn't going to use for anything better. So what... So I learned to enjoy her silly little things, those adorable little whims she had, which I don't have anymore and can't afford..."

"Let's go," said Carlitos. "It's already late. Another day you can tell me that story about Claudia."

"What for? It's not even worth it. Just a silly little fling. I didn't even end up sleeping with her. Just another admirer of *El Águila*, like so many others who are probably dead now, with their little bones piled up in some forgotten urn in the Buceo Cemetery. Who knows. Just in case, it's better to let her rest in peace."

"You're right, man. She's probably already gone, the poor thing. I wouldn't want drunks to talk about me the day I die.

They'd say I was young and rich. Well, not rich, but successful. And that I ended up like almost everyone else, badly, drinking too much in a dive bar and waiting for the poor Galician to kick us out with some curse."

"That's how it is, man," said Willian. "We were born in a certain time. We learned something. We grew. We suffered for no reason. We loved the way we should. We hurt our hearts beyond repair. We broke a few others. Maybe we made someone happy. We saw our children born. And we saw them leave the nest. We knew it would happen. That we weren't forever. We had to watch our parents die. We saw ourselves losing our youth in our hair and our bellies. We knew we didn't have much time left. That it wasn't as far off as it seemed before.—That's life. You have to enjoy it while you can. And when you can't, you have to endure it with dignity. That's all. The rest is a mystery. Period."

"I'm not waiting for you, damn it!" the bartender yelled at them, lowering the blinds. "If you want to philosophize, go to the university, for Christ's sake."

"Screw you!" Carlitos shouted back, ducking to slip under the halfway-closed metal blind.

"Forget it, man," Willian cut him off. "Next time, we'll go to the bar across the street. At least the Galician woman cooks, and then we can stop drinking so much and thinking about stupid things…"

Don Xico

Montevideo, early morning of April 7, 2012

Don Xico's insomnia had worsened, so his anonymous comments at the bottom of opinion articles in the newspapers had increased considerably. The colonel was DonX in *El País*, Fenix73 in *La República* and Rafa007 in *Clarín* from Argentina. His contributions and his abundant insults, filled with adjectives and backed by copious data he copied from Wikipedia, were at least notorious. They kept him occupied for several hours a day and kept a collection of other distracted commenters busy, as they considered him a serious dialectical adversary. Between one comment and the predictable reactions, Don Xico edited various sections on Wikipedia related to the seventies in Argentina and Uruguay, where he was known and respected as Wilfredo1811.

That day had been productive, and he had managed to overcome his insomnia almost at dawn. He closed several pages Google had brought up while he searched for data or inspiration to respond to Wilfredo1811. The last one was an article from *El País* in Madrid, dated May 24 (he couldn't remember how or why he had ended up there):

"Ghost fishing boat from Japan tsunami arrives in Canada."

He didn't read the rest:

A ghost fishing boat, swept from the coast of Japan over a year ago by the tsunami, has been spotted off the coast of Canada, according to local authorities. "It seems fairly intact and has rust from being out there for a year," Marc Proulx, maritime coordinator for the

*Victoria Rescue Coordination Center, told CNN. The fishing boat
was sighted about 120 miles (220 kilometers) off the Queen Charlotte
Islands. It was located by a Canadian Army air patrol, which believes
there is no one on board and that it was carried there by the tides.*"

He didn't read it. He turned off the computer.

MARKED DAY. It was still there, somewhere

Montevideo, early morning of April 7, 2012

The coin had disappeared. Jordi tried to imagine where it
might be locked away, buried, abandoned. Surely, at that moment, he was the only person in the world thinking about a
white peseta. One among millions of other coins that very few,
if any, remembered.

"To the border, Mom. Dad told me he was going to the border."

"Good kid. Here's your white one," said the man in the green
uniform and dark boots, *smiling.*

Jordi grabbed the white peseta and squeezed it tight. He remembered the pain of the coin in his hand, clenched in desperation. He remembered the ship that brought him to Uruguay
and the profile of Spain sinking into the sea. He remembered a
boy at the Houston airport, whose mother tried to comfort him
by saying he was American, that he could return someday. "If
my country doesn't want my mother, I don't want my country,"
the boy had said with such profound conviction that it felt to
Don Jordi like hatred or resentment. But he knew it wasn't exactly either of those things, or perhaps it was all of them

together, mixed like a poisonous potion in the stomach of a child who repeatedly dreams of falling from a very high tower.

Seventy-three years later, he remembered that unforgivable moment. Then, with fearful clarity, he remembered his father's smile, the waning moon that silently accompanied him after his father told him, for the last time, that he would return "next week."

It was a sad smile that hurt like a knife. But it was as if he had finally recovered his father.

For a moment, he felt that indescribable sound that emerges from the deepest silence. Before dawn, the darkness had grown so dense that red curves and yellow rectangles easily emerged from it. For a moment, he felt dazed, a bit dizzy, but soon he caught his breath and could see a still-dark window, dimly lit by a weak moon that slowly faded behind the clouds.

It was then that he saw them both. His mother, in her thirties with all her black hair, tiny, pressed against his father's body, and he with his left arm wrapped around her. Both of them were looking at him and smiling. Then she had rested her head on his shoulder. For a moment, he saw him barely move his head and close his eyes, as if approving something (he had always told him, "don't worry, son"), and when he opened them again, they both began to smile and disappear once more. It was then that he realized it might all have been just a hallucination.

"But no," he told himself shortly afterward"; "I know it wasn't a hallucination. Only I know…"

A day of no importance

Montevideo, April 7, 2012

Around the time the sun began to rise from beneath the sea, Santiago returned from his *jogging* along Pocitos Beach. That day, he calculated he would finish a few minutes early. He felt tired. He climbed up to the rambla and leaned against one of the light posts. He noticed he was short of breath but attributed it to stress.

A woman who was running stopped, first hesitant and then surprised, and greeted him. Santiago pretended to recognize her while trying to recall a patient with that face and that voice speaking to him so familiarly. She mentioned the faculty, and he thought he saw the face of Rosario's mother, a study and party companion back in the nineties. Finally, he guessed it was another classmate, whose name he couldn't remember, when she mentioned the practical they had done at the Clínicas Hospital. She had also graduated in 2001. He imagined himself in her eyes, older or changed, at best. He noticed she paused her gaze for a second on his cheekbones, perhaps on some graying hairs already becoming evident. But he couldn't recall the name; he barely remembered the woman's face. So much time abroad had developed in him a special ability to remember, to reconstruct the past, but, as a consequence, the habit of always being surrounded by new strangers had left him with a certain incapacity or, perhaps, on the contrary, a rare skill for not recognizing faces.

He walked with some difficulty to the nearest bench and sat down. Someone had forgotten *La República* or had decided to share the newspaper, already old at that hour of the morning, with some stranger.

He glanced disinterestedly at the first pages. The same old urgencies: a dispute between politicians, a conflict, the same conflict in the East and Middle East, the crisis in Europe... The country would never find out about what happened at the British Hospital, about the kidnapping of that boy who later became Santiago Zabala Arbiza. He would never know that he had once been called Jaime Ocampo and that his parents were María Fuentes and José Ocampo.

Then he remembered when his father, the father he knew and loved, was dying in the hospital. Now he understood that he had always sensed something beyond that kind face, and it wasn't an unfounded unease. But now he also knew (or had a better idea) of the immensity of all he would never get to know. It wasn't like the research at Emory, where armed with a lot of patience and a bit of inspiration, one could solve the posed mystery.

The face of the father he had known had been the denial of the father who had disappeared. The unconditional affection he had felt for that man barely mitigated the pain of the lie.

He looked at the horizon beginning to form between the sky and the sea. The most important things are indecipherable. They can only be felt, he thought. That man, that face that had accompanied almost all of his childhood, was like the sea at midnight, full of mysteries, forgotten secrets, indecipherable reasons, irretrievable, forever sunk in the deepest part of the ocean.

Suddenly, he remembered all the times he would go to sit by his side while he read the newspaper or watched the news on ATC. Ten or a hundred times he had almost sat down beside him and said, Dad, what's new in the world? Dad, how did Racing do? Dad, do you really think Carlos Saúl Menem is that necessary man for the nation, like Gerardo Sofovich says? A Jew campaigning for a Syrian president, that's this country for you, Dad. Could it be that you think that way because you didn't live through Raúl Alfonsín's government? They were heroic years, according to my math teacher. Yeah, okay, I was bad at math, but I have good memories of that long-haired old guy who rode his bike to school and insulted us saying he was happy. Crazy Guido. Once he invited me for a beer at the corner bar. For the kids of that time, it was like Fito Páez inviting you for a coffee. I liked Raúl Alfonsín more, with his kind face and that heroic trial of the military. Heroic, according to Crazy Guido, who was a Peronist but preferred the Radical Party, which is essentially Argentina's conservative party. Only in this country would a conservative party be called Radical.

The old man loved reading and listening to the news. He was obsessed. They say it's a man's affliction.

Ten or a hundred times he had been on the verge of sitting down next to him and saying, Dad, what's new in the world... But no. Ten or a hundred times he preferred to keep walking in silence, to his room, to lock himself in and listen to music. Many times he was close, but no...

One day, suddenly, without warning, his father was in intensive care, with a plastic tube in his mouth helping him breathe. Santiago knew this time he wouldn't recover. He tried to offer comfort and whispered in his ear, "Dad, don't worry, stay calm; I promise we'll go out for a walk later."

He touched his hand. He recognized that hand as if seeing his face. He recognized the kind hand that had always rescued him from a tree branch, from a bad fall. He even thought it would be better if he died soon and stopped suffering. At times it seemed he could hear him. Every time he told him to stay calm, that they'd soon go out for a walk, his breathing would quicken.

The walk was the path that led them to niche 126, where his father would rest, on a sunny, cold summer day in 1991. An employee of the funeral company gave the final push, and the casket slid a few centimeters to where it would remain for years. Another threw the wreath sent by a supposed Masonic brotherhood. Then the flowers from his wife, and finally Santiago's. Someone had thought to buy flowers in his name, as if they knew he'd never have thought of that detail at that moment.

As he walked back toward the entrance, surrounded by a crowd he couldn't see, he realized Alejandro and Miguel were walking beside him. They walked in silence, as if they understood perfectly that Santiago didn't want words. But their steps spoke. Then he felt two hands on his back before they disappeared for a long time.

A cyclist interrupted him, stopping to ask for the time.

"Ten to six," he said.

Almost absentmindedly, he glanced at the second-to-last page of the newspaper. In a small section, he read about a Japanese ship that had been sunk by the U.S. Navy.

The Japanese ghost ship that had appeared two weeks ago off the coast of Canada was sunk by the North American Coast Guard.

The Japanese fishing vessel had been adrift since the tsunami on March 11, 2011, and was found a year later on these shores. For safety reasons, North American maritime authorities decided to sink it, "for the safety of sailors, sinking the ship was the fastest way to adequately address the danger posed by this uncontrolled vessel," stated Daniel Travers of the Coast Guard.

The operation was carried out by the coast guard vessel "Anacapa," which fired 25-millimeter cannons at the fishing boat. In an operation that lasted about five hours, the ship was sunk to a depth of 1,850 meters.

He read carefully, though that news too held no real importance for him. It was just another distraction among the countless distractions we're exposed to every day, he thought.

He stared for a moment at the horizon of the widenessy where the sky was starting to brighten. Then he thought of Lucía. He thought he had been unfairly harsh with her, walking away without even a vaguely clear explanation.

He left the newspaper to one side and continued running.